Licking Our Wounds

by

Elise D'Haene

THE PERMANENT PRESS
SAG HARBOR, NY 11963

Library of Congress Cataloguing-in-Publication Data

D'Haene, Elise.
Licking our wounds/Elise D'Haene.
p. cm.
ISBN 1-877946-81-8
I. Title.
PS3554.H25L53   1997
813',.54--dc20   96-19008
                                                              CIP

First edition, 2400 copies, March 1997

THE PERMANENT PRESS
Noyac Road
Sag Harbor, NY 11963

ACKNOWLEDGMENTS

Abiding love to Celeste Gainey, who has taught me, in the most profound way, how to return love, over and over and over. Without her, I honestly don't know where I'd be.

Eternal gratitude to Terry Wolverton, a woman of huge talent, huge love, and unending inspiration.

To all of those who believed in this novel: My agent, Debra Rodman; my publishers and editors, Martin and Judith Shepard; Peter Cooper, and my male twin, the greatest guy on the planet, Steve Machado, for seeing me through from page one.

To all those loving, broken, human circles that have surrounded me. My mom and dad, my seven sisters and three brothers, and their families. Especially, Maria and Bob for sharing my home and supporting my efforts. And my sister Peggy, for her unflagging enthusiam. To my brother in spirit and love, Gary Brice. To my dear sweet friends who have sustained me, especially Lynn Becker, Sharon Morrill, Wanda von Kleist, Marsha Langford, Amanda Pope, Nancy Leff and Leslie Robbins, my Thursday night writing group, my Uncle Bob and Aunt Carol. Finally, to all my clients and colleagues who taught me more than they'll ever know.

dedication

To all the men who graced my life for far too short a time. Especially, Barry D'Haene, James Harning, my brother, Pat, my dad, and my Mt. Washington family -- Rick, Ara, Rodney, Michael, and Ray.

Part I

One

I just had a pitiful orgasm. It doesn't even qualify as full-fledged. Let's just call it an *org*. It was fast, less than a minute to cum, and before the first beat of the clitoral tom-tom sounded, tears were pouring down my cheeks. Emotional cumming. The ache was loss and as soon as I conjured up a picture of your sweet sweet face and those moony eyes, well, all was lost. My vagina misses you too, like my heart, and both of us spilled forth, gushed tears and wet cum like two blubbering babies hungry for a nipple. What's that song say? I'm a whimpering simpering child, romance finis, and all that shit.

I had to try again, and since necessity *is* the mother of invention, I pulled out the electric toothbrush (you took the vibrator) to shudder speedily across my clitoris; not the bristles, but the smooth blue side of the toothbrush.

Nothing happened. My vagina packed up and left no forwarding address.

"I just can't stand the pain no longer," she said, as she boarded the bus and headed nowhere in particular.

Cup, I tried all my best material. You sucking me, engaged in serious mouth-to-clit resuscitation as your fingers skitter and slide all over and I beg you to enter me and wear me like a glove. Didn't even get wet. Dry as chalk and sore like slamming your palm on hot cement trying to break a fall from a bike that's too big. Shouldn't have been riding it in the first place.

Now, Cup, I'm lying here—alone. My DKNY black skirt is pushed up around my waist, my DKNY black tights scrunched at my ankles, an electric toothbrush dangling like a sorry limp cock between my legs, and I'm screaming in my head, "Mona! Come back little Mona, please come back."

I remember the first time I told you that I named my vagina Mona, because it sounded like sorrow, like the word melancholy, and you laughed and then asked me to come up with a name for yours, and without missing a beat, I said, "How about Lizzie, as in Borden?"

After you squeezed my inner thigh until I apologized, you said, "Amelia, I'll call her Amelia."

Sure enough, you and Amelia have flown away and disappeared and my Mona's taken flight too, and I'm lying in a wrinkled heap, in my funeral outfit, fresh from another memorial service and I don't know where to turn.

The only thing I want is your head buried between my legs. I call Christie and tell her there is no way I can show up tonight to pass out meals to dying people. She made that noise I so cherished when we were lovers: Fuck you meets I'm disappointed meets you're so pathetic. Of course, she's secretly thrilled that you're gone, Cup, and thinks I deserve every excruciating moment of anguish that's coming to me.

After she discharged that noise, she says, "It's important to keep commitments, Maria, at least it's important to *some* people."

(Fuck you.) "I wish I had your strength, Christie," I say. "I gotta go now, the dogs are threatening to eat me unless I take them for a walk. Bye."

Molly and Sadie are sleeping peacefully on either side of me, unaware that I've used them, shamelessly, to get away from Christie Madigan, whom I've come to refer to simply as "the Vatican." She has that awful effect on me, that quavering air of superiority. Her spiritual plane is soaring; mine hasn't even left the runway.

Christie was my first real relationship. Two years of dried flowers, lazy cats, antique quilts, oatmeal, and homemade bread. We lived in a wood cottage in Silverlake. It was cozy. We shared hushed quiet orgasms, tender and loving. We cuddled a lot.

After a year, I started having fantasies of squatting on the antique quilt and taking a shit. The only music I would listen to was Billie Holiday and Janis Joplin. I worshiped Sylvia Plath and I wanted my life to be a loaded gun, not a loaf of rosemary bread. I hated myself for hating it. I felt there was something bad inside of me for wanting to escape lazy cats, pots of dried flowers, and fruit tea. This was B.C., before you, Cup. Before death too.

I strip off my funeral gear and put a T-shirt on sans underwear. Theoretically, one wears undergarments to protect one's private areas. My privates have gone public, so what's the use?

At the memorial service today, I was thinking how insensitive you are Cup, for not being there to pay your respects. It occurred to me, though, that you probably don't know that Eduardo is dead, and I can't call you because I don't know where you are. Then I realized that Eduardo belonged to Christie's circle, and that you hardly know him, and I hadn't even seen him for over a year, and then it all came crashing down. The only reason I wanted you there today was for me, not him, just so I could hold your hand, and after the service we could come home and go to bed, and forget, for at least those moments, forget that friends are dying, one by one.

Your departure, Cup, is one thing. As for Mona's leave of absence, I don't know what I'll do. I feel as if I've lost a vital organ, and there's no one around with a donor card, offering me a transplant.

I reach over to the bedside table and grab a book from a pile of yard sale paperbacks I bought. Wouldn't you know it, *Portnoy's Complaint*, the book that began this long whine:

I'm twelve years old and poring through the pages of the latest paperback I've swiped from my older brother Joseph. Technically, I steal them, if mom finds out, but actually, Joseph puts the books he's done reading in a pile for me at the back of his closet. We have an agreement.

Today I'm reading *Portnoy's Complaint*. I'm halfway through it, and I still don't know what the complaint is. I don't really understand half of the books Joseph reads, I just stuff the words into my brain.

I'm lying in bed in the middle of a sunny Saturday afternoon. It's hard to find peace and quiet in the house. Noise is constant. Outside, in the backyard, I can hear the high-pitched ting of the ball as it's kicked into the air by my little sister Beth. She squeals and Paul is yelling at her, "Run the bases stupid." They have a regular weekend game of combat kickball with our neighbors, the O'Brien's. They have ten kids in their family, we have seven. Mr. O'Brien and my dad work at the same auto plant.

So, I'm reading away: *"While here is a honey of a girl, with the softest, pinkest, most touching nipples I have ever drawn between my lips, only she won't go down on me."* I stop. Contemplate the words. *Go down on me.* Suddenly I find I'm staring at my bedpost. The sleek, shiny wood ball. I put the book down and climb on top, just like getting up on my brother's bike. I bounce a little and swivel and pretend I'm Annette Funicello on the *Mickey Mouse Club* riding her horse.

I gyrate and wriggle and feel the most joyous pleasure imaginable. I'm stunned and wonder, does everybody know about bedposts?

When I climb down, I put my hand between my legs, and I have a big wet spot on my white painter's pants. Did I pee without knowing? I unzip to investigate and scoop up with my fingers a substance that's gooey and sticky and in my twelve-year-old mind I figure this was where Elmer's glue comes from.

I go back to the page: *"...it is her pleasure while being boffed to have one or the other of my forefingers lodged snugly up her anus."* I stop, again, and dreamily gaze at the bedpost. Boffed? I'll have to ask Joseph what that means.

My mother flings open my bedroom door. I slam my legs shut and my face heats up red. She has a basket of laundry in her arms which she drops to the floor. "Maria, fold these clothes for me."

"Sure, Mom," I grunt, as I carefully cover up the book with my hands, and tightly squeeze my legs.

"What's that you're reading?" She grabs it from my lap. "Joseph!" she screams.

"He's not home, Mom, I stole it from his room."

She glares at me. "I've told you a hundred times, Maria, you are not allowed to read grown-up books." She swats my leg. "Now fold those, and then go outside and play with your brothers and sisters. Go have fun!"

"Okay," I mumble, knowing I have just discovered the most fun thing ever.

She begins to leave, and then turns suddenly. "I'm doing a load of whites, take those off so I can wash them, they're filthy." She's pointing at my pants.

I panic. The wet spot! The Camel nonfilter hidden in my pocket that I also stole from Joseph! "No mom!" I bark, "I just washed 'em!"

She eyes me suspiciously. There's a tense pause. "You kids," she whines, and then leaves.

I love my white painter's pants. They have these little loops on the side where I rest my thumb and pretend to be a cowboy. All these pockets and secret side compartments where I slip my stolen cigarettes and matches. I never get caught. I'm a bookworm, not a brat. I don't get into much trouble, except for stealing Joseph's books. Mostly, I do what I'm told.

I begin taking a lot of baths. All objects, including the bed-post, come to life. Umbrella handles. Shampoo bottles. My lit-tle brother's plastic football with the ridges. I am a bookworm, who takes a lot of baths, and does what I'm told.

When I was a child, I played like a child, I thought like a child. Then there came a day when I left behind my childish ways. This developmental hurdle was ushered in by Helen Gurley Brown and *Cosmopolitan* magazine.

I'm fourteen and in my parent's bathroom and I'm rum-maging through my mom's toiletries. It's become a peculiar habit of mine. I'm a scavenger of all her scents and smells. The sweet aroma of the White Satin perfume my dad gives her every Christmas. The pink bars of Dove soap she buys only for her-self. (We kids get plain old Ivory or whatever is on sale.) The box of Calgon blue bath beads, called Midnight Luxury. And, my favorite, Pond's cold cream. My mom's nighttime smell. She used to leave slight traces of it on my cheek or forehead when she'd come into my bedroom, bend over me, and whisper, "Night punkin." I'm too old for that now.

I unscrew the lid, and inhale deeply, dip my finger into the white oily goop and spread it on my cheek, just like her, then wipe it off carefully with a tissue.

I reach way way back in their bathroom cupboard, the top one where my mother puts her stuff to keep it away from us kids. I reach past my mom's makeup bag and her Estee Lauder's gala collection of ten different colored lipsticks, past a basket filled with rose-shaped soaps. Then I push aside the pile of musty old towels we got after grandma died. That's where I found the magazine, hidden where a kid's arm shouldn't be able to reach, unless that kid is me and I've already learned how to balance myself, one leg on the bathtub and one leg on the toilet, in order to snoop.

One of the magazine subscription cards is sticking out like a bookmark. Page forty-six. *Sexual Advice for the Seventies Woman*, by Dr. Mark Goodman. He has a Ph.D. in exercise physiology and works as a consultant to media and television on maximizing sexual appeal. I'm fourteen. I want to maxi-mize anything about me, except my thighs, especially my breasts, and sex appeal?! The doctor is all smiles, he has dark wavy hair, nice long sideburns, a thick moustache and beard and big sensitive eyes just like Cat Stevens.

It was just one word that caught my eye. On page forty-six, in *Cosmo* magazine, one word that absolutely changed the entire course of my life. There was no fork on this path that diverged in the wood. No pondering, this way or that. I had chanced upon a one-way road. Mark was describing, in detail, *cunnilingus*. Up till now it was just me rubbing this little spot that felt good. Now, I had a picture in my head, a scene involving another person.

I hesitate. I think of school—the nuns. Suddenly Sister Rose pops out like toast, in her long black habit, right in my parent's bathroom.

"Leggo of my eggo!" I scream.

"You are turning your back against God and all that is sacred," she roars, pointing that ruler right at my crotch.

Then, I hear Cat Steven's voice, so sweet, so truthful, *"Morning has broken, like the first morning, blackbird has spoken, like the first bird. . ."*

Pond's cold cream beckons from the cupboard. I stare at Mark's face, his inviting smile, and Sister Rose dissolves like bath beads.

I read: *"A woman's clitoris can be described as her little nub of joy. It is a man's responsibility to understand what I call the woman's clitoral personality."* I stop breathing. My eyes bulge. Just a little pitter pats between my legs.

"Place your hands securely around her buttocks, grasp and pull her toward you and tease playfully with the tip of your tongue."

I'm so moved at this point that my legs are starting to shudder, so I slowly make my way over to the toilet to sit down. I'm gripping the Cosmo like I've never gripped the written word before. Mark discusses the clockwise rotation of the tongue interspersed with *sucking*!!

My bell bottom jeans mysteriously fall to the floor. My J.C. Penny white cotton briefs for girls creep down to my knees. I have a dollop of Pond's on my index finger.

I close my eyes tight. (If I don't see myself do this, then God won't see me either.) The Pond's stings slightly on my clit, my fingers twirl and twirl on my little nub of joy. In my fantasy, the tongue spins around and around. I'm making noises, brand new ones, ones I've never heard before.

Quickly, I reach over to the sink and turn on the faucet to drown out my moans.

I'm breathing so deep my belly extends like a balloon as those lips suck and suck so delicately.

"Sweet the rain's new fall, sunlit from heaven. . ."

My mind is like a movie screen. I'm lying, splayed across my bed, my butt is being held firmly, the lips come toward me, I raise my supine head in order to see—to reach my hands out to grasp my made-up lover, and it isn't Dr. Goodman, or Cat Stevens, or the bedpost. It's the model on the cover of the magazine, her name is Cindy, and she has long dark hair and she's wearing a black negligee and her lips are slightly pink from Estee Lauder's Cimmaron Rose.

I'm lost, swirling and swooning in my parent's bathroom in Pond's Now-Warm Cream.

I leap off the toilet, startled and bleary. Those lips in my mind weren't surrounded by a moustache or beard or even stubble. They were all hers, soft and full, slightly glossed with a touch of rose. I knew this was trouble, with a capital T that rhymes with P that stands for *pink*—lips.

I grab some tissues and wipe myself. I flush the evidence down the toilet. I flush twice, just to be sure. This sensation washes over me: on the one hand a feeling of such satisfaction, like putting that last piece into a puzzle, and at the same time, a desire to toss the puzzle into the air and start over.

I gaze at the cover. Cindy's poutier and bustier then she was in my mind. I stuff the magazine back where it belongs, hidden under my grandma's musty towels.

When I emerge from my parents' bathroom, into their bedroom, it feels as if I have new eyeballs. My little brother Fitz is sitting on their bed watching *Romper Room*.

"Are you a good dooby?" he asks, holding my mom's hand mirror toward me.

I don't answer. I ruffle my fingers through his hair, and turn the mirror toward him. "You are, Fitzy," I say. "You're my good dooby."

I hop up on the bed with him and he curls into my lap. When *Captain Kangaroo* comes on, Fitzy is silent and wide-eyed, he sucks his thumb and giggles when Mr. Green Jeans appears. I fall asleep during the storytelling, and wake up with Fitz pulling my hair, needing to go potty. I take him downstairs, to the kids' bathroom.

He sits unsteady on the edge of the toilet, his little boy stomach poofs out as he strains to make himself go.

I'm thinking, as I sit on the floor, hugging my knees to my chest, that Fitzy and I are both crossing over into new territory. We're expanding. Our bones and skin, our eyes, what we see and hear, and most importantly, what we know and understand. New shapes and words and sensations adding to the old, and there's no turning back.

Perched on the toilet, his legs dangling above the floor, Fitzy begins to hum, "*Row, row, row your boat,*" high and sweet, like a girl, and then points to me.

"*Gently down the stream,*" I sing, "*Merrily, merrily, merrily, merrily, life is but a dream.*"

A dream, Cup. If only I'd wake up and find you asleep next to me and an eager Mona tucked safely between my legs.

My forefinger is lodged snugly between the pages of *Portnoy's Complaint* when the doorbell rings. Unlike Mr. Portnoy, there's no spare anus around to lodge into. I open the book slowly and I'm punched by two big bold words: "WHACKING OFF." Shit, Mona.

I hear the door open and I assume it's Christie, here to keep herself company and continue pestering me like a reporter from *Hard Copy* about why you left, Cup.

"I'm in the bedroom," I yell, figuring Molly and Sadie will do their ferocious dog-being if it's a stranger.

I have the book draped over my eyes, and a wet washcloth over my groin and still no underwear. I moan as I lift the book, so Christie will know just how badly I'm feeling, and staring quizzically at the washcloth on my groin is Peter.

"Peter?" I say, "If I knew you were coming I'd have baked a cake."

He hands me one of the wrapped meals from Angel Food. "Someone died," he says, "so we had an extra." He bounces down on the bed. "You're tragic!"

I unwrap my meal. Chicken breast, green beans, sweet potato, and a brownie. "What are you doing here?" I ask.

"I came to cheer you up."

"I don't need cheering up." I start to pick at the beans one by one and pop them into my mouth.

Peter grunts. "Look, girl, you've got to forget that old snack, she's gone! Live like I do," he says, then grabs the brownie from my plate.

"Good idea Peter. I think I'll drive over to Griffith Park, climb through the bushes. Suck off some guy, then call it a night. No names, no phone numbers, no sticky sheets."

"Women," he snorts. "Look, Mia, here's my motto: What's too painful to remember, I simply choose to forget."

"I feel better, Peter, thank you."

"You do!?" he smiles widely.

"Yes, I've already forgotten that you're here. I don't know who you are. Now go home. I'll call you tomorrow."

He turns at the door for one last look at me. "Tragic," he says in dismay, "but I love you."

Two

My best friend, Jenny, told me that Dave Martino wanted me as his girlfriend. I'm meeting him behind school. We're sixteen. Jenny gave me a whole tube of bubblegum lip gloss to wear as a gift. Jenny has her very own cosmetics department hidden underneath her bed. Five-finger discount at Monkey Ward's.

"I like you a lot," Dave says. I burst into tears. I think Dave thought that was a good sign.

We're tucked behind St. Gerard's in a large bush. He's supposed to be at football practice, I'm supposed to be on my way home. Home is across the street. On one side of us is the O'Brien family, on the other side is the convent.

After he says the I-like-you stuff, his face comes at me real fast. He has peanut butter breath and he tries to stick his tongue in my mouth and he smears my bubblegum-flavored lip gloss all over my face. I'm still crying.

Dave pins me against the red brick wall. Underneath his practice jersey he's wearing shoulder pads and they practically puncture me. His hands are moving up and down my thighs.

I stare past him, through the bushes, and I can see Miss Cook down on the field coaching the girls' volleyball team. She's the first lay teacher at St. Gerard's. Besides coaching, she's also a math teacher slash girl's counselor. Every day I pass by her office on purpose and try to catch a glimpse of her. When she's in, and her door's open, I wave, and say, "Hi, Miss Cook."

She answers, "Hello there!" real excitedly. I'm sure she'd say, "Hello there, Maria," but she doesn't know my name because I have Sister Rose for third-level algebra and I don't play volleyball.

Dave's hands are inching toward the front of my school uniform and he goes for my mouth again. "Hey," I say, pushing him off, "I better go, Dave, my mom will kill me."

He says, "Yah, uh, okay, uh, see you, uh, tomorrow."

I run home and go straight to my parent's bathroom to check my Kotex pad. I wear them a lot, even when I'm not on my period. It's 'cause of the wetness. I'm so afraid one of my fantasies will happen at school and Sister Rose will get a look between my legs and she'll know. We don't have co-ed classrooms yet. She'll look in my school locker and see all the lipsticks I've got, and then they'll kick me out or send me on a short bus to a special school.

I'm dry as chalk. Dave Martino doesn't make me wet. My eyes are all puffy from crying. Any minute now Fitzy, or the twins, or Mom—someone will bang on the door. I take out the Pond's cold cream and smear it around my eyes. I use it a lot to hide when I've been crying. No one seems to notice.

"Maria? Is that you?" It's Joseph. "Hey, Maria, I've got something to tell you. Can I come in?"

I smear more cream around my eyes and open the bathroom door. I slump onto the toilet and Joseph hops into the tub.

"Are you okay?" he asks.

"Nope," I mutter.

"What's wrong kiddo?"

Joseph is nineteen. I like that he calls me kiddo. He's got real long hair which my parents hate and he wears an earring too, which they hate even more. He's the only person in the family I can really talk to and he still gives me all his books.

"There's this guy at school and he likes me but I don't really like him," I whisper. I'm staring at the floor and the Pond's gunk is flowing down my cheeks with my soppy tears.

Joseph is silent. He extends his hand. "Here, I want you to have this," he says. It's his leather beaded bracelet. "Give me your arm."

He ties the bracelet around my wrist and then hands me a wad of toilet paper.

"Listen, kiddo, you don't have to like anyone just because they like you. You'll know when the right person comes along."

I blow my nose. I curl my fingers around the bracelet. It's the coolest thing I've ever seen. "What were you going to tell me?"

"I'm leaving to join the Navy. I've got to get out of here," he says.

My belly wobbles and I feel sick.

"Don't worry kiddo, I'll be back to visit. I want you to have my books for safekeeping. Okay?"

I nod yes. I can't talk. Joseph climbs out of the tub, kisses my forehead, and leaves the bathroom. I'm clinging to the bracelet. I'll never take it off.

After Joseph leaves for boot camp I walk around feeling real homely and real ugly inside. I don't know how to make this glum wad in my belly go away. Jenny tells me I should go and talk to Miss Cook. We've been encouraged to use her services, but I'm afraid I just won't know what to say. You have to make the appointment with Sister Ruth. She's nice, but she looks at you with these big sad eyes, like she can just see there's real trouble inside.

I force myself to go up to Sister Ruth's desk and I say, "I need career counseling, Sister, I'm going to be seventeen in four months, and I have to start thinking more seriously about counseling, I mean college, so I thought. . ."

She's gazing up at me with a mixture of sorrow and "oh, you're so lonely," and I could feel little pools in my eyes starting to form and then suddenly Miss Cook walks in.

"Hello there!" she says, and places her hand on my shoulder. " I've wanted to meet you. I'm Miss Cook."

"I'm Maria," I mutter, my eyes glued to her brown penny loafers.

"C'mon in Maria," she says, and leads me into her office.

I sit down across from her. She's rummaging through a stack of files. "Oh, here you are!" she says. She flips through the pages going, "Hmmm, ohhh, good good, oh, I see you live right across the street!"

I nod and smile.

"I see you have three brothers and three sisters?"

I nod and smile.

"Which number are you?"

"I'm number three," I reply. I have to hold my leg still because it keeps shaking.

I can hardly look at Miss Cook. Her eyes are big and brown, with that warmth of being on the verge of tears, and when she talks they bounce with little sparks of delight.

She leans back in her chair, puts her hands behind her head, and looks directly into my eyes. "You've got good grades, a family active in the church, and according to your evaluations, very nice social skills."

"Yes, thank you." My bottom lip starts to shake. I bite down on it hoping to stop it before she sees. I'm blinking rapidly and feel my brow beginning to scrunch like it does just before I burst. A few stray tears escape down my cheek.

Miss Cook stands. "Maria, I need someone just like you to be my assistant coach for the volleyball team. What do you think?"

"Yes, thank you," I say again.

Miss Cook hands me some Kleenex and pulls out a book from her desk drawer. "Sweetie, I want you to have this book. It's very special."

Jonathan Livingston Seagull. I don't have the heart to tell her I've already read it. Joseph sent me a copy from boot camp. Inside he wrote: "Kiddo, Dream and fly! Love, Joseph."

"It's one of my favorites, Maria, I think you'll like it too." She winks.

She puts her hand around my neck and we leave her office and she keeps her hand there for few moments. "I'll see you every day after school for practice," she says.

"Okay, Miss Cook." I'm about to bust with joy.

"And Maria," she says, as I'm halfway down the hall, "you're gonna be okay."

I'm actually *skipping*—down the sidewalk, past the convent, across our front lawn. It's gone. My sadness is gone.

"Guess what?! Guess what?!" I scream. My mom is pouring a cup of dry oatmeal into a bowl of ground hamburger.

"Grab me a can of tomato sauce," she says, carefully eyeing the meatloaf recipe on the back of the oatmeal box.

"Mom," I say, handing her the can, "I'm assistant coach for volleyball."

"That's really nice, honey, grab me two eggs from the fridge," she says.

I crack one egg at a time on the edge of the bowl. I want to tell her everything I know about Miss Cook. How she's twenty-two and she graduated from Michigan State, and she has a huge green and white macrame wall hanging of a peace sign in her office.

My mom digs her hand in the gooey mixture and begins kneading the oats, meat, tomato, and eggs. I'm staring at the oatmeal box, at the picture of the happy old guy with long hair who looks like Ben Franklin.

She picks off the sticky blend of raw meatloaf from her hands. She pushes the bowl in front of me. "Finish mixing this," she says. "I'll get your sisters to set the table."

I want to tell her how Miss Cook said I was a good student

and that I had very nice social skills, and when she leaned back at her desk, I could see she was wearing a gold necklace, just like the one my mom has, the rays of sun came in through the window and made it sparkle when she rocked in her chair.

My mom leaves the kitchen. A few of the nuns are crossing the street to the convent. Sister Rose is scowling about something Sister Ruth is saying to her. I wonder if they're talking about me and Miss Cook.

I dig my hands into the bowl. I squish the mixture through my fingers and whisper to Mr. Quaker Oatmeal, his eyes seem to listen, and I tell him all about Miss Cook. How *I* know, that *she* knows about me, and how she said I was gonna be okay. I can't wait to write Joseph a letter.

Jenny never asked why I broke up with Dave Martino after one date. She doesn't have a boyfriend either, so when I'm not helping Miss Cook with the volleyball team I roam through the mall with Jenny stealing lipsticks. She's taught me the ins and outs of the five-finger discount.

Big news! Miss Cook asked me to come to dinner this weekend. For my seventeenth birthday. I can't believe she even knew or remembered it was my birthday. Since it wasn't on a school night, my mom said yes.

I'm wearing my real faded jeans, one of my brother Joseph's old shirts, and his leather beaded bracelet.

"Hello there, birthday girl!" she says, as she opens the door.

Suddenly, I have to pee very badly. It's the first time I've ever been in an apartment. She has two wine bottles dripping with candle wax on the table. Her carpet is rusty shag and there are posters of Joan Baez and Judy Collins on the walls.

Miss Cook is wearing jeans too, but hers are brand new. She's wearing a fuchsia T-shirt and brown sandals with little leather straps over her big toes. I've only seen her in beige and blue skirts, white blouses, and her brown penny loafers.

"I have to use your bathroom." My voice cracks a little. I clear my throat and cough.

"Are you feeling okay, sweetie?" she asks, gently touching my forehead.

I nod yes. She points me toward the bathroom.

"There are fresh towels in the cupboard. I'll pour us some wine." She laughs, "just one glass for you, you're underage."

I giggle in a really stupid way and lock the door behind me.

I open her cupboard. Jean Naté body splash. That's her smell. I rummage through her makeup bag. Maybelline Deep Bordeaux lipstick. There's an almost empty tube of it and I slip it into my pocket. Just a nub of maroon to keep.

I sit on the toilet and pull a slightly damp bathtowel off the shower door. I hold it to my face and breathe in.

Throughout dinner I'm aware of each and every noisy stupid word that flies out of my mouth. I'm trying to act confident and sophisticated, but so far, I've excused myself to the bathroom three times.

"So, Maria, I know you love reading. What's your favorite book?" she asks, just as I scoop a huge pile of wild rice into my mouth.

"Oy-oy Comploynt," I mumble as the sticky rice stays glued to the roof of my mouth. I gulp down my wine. "*Portnoy's Complaint*," I repeat. It isn't my favorite book but it's the only one that I can think of.

Miss Cook is wide-eyed. "Wow," she says. "That's quite a book. What are your thoughts about it?"

My thoughts? I'm about to excuse myself to the bathroom when a string of words, an answered prayer floats through my brain. "Deliciously funny," I sputter, "absurd, wild and uproarious, hilariously lewd." The book jacket. In an instant all those stuffed words are released from my brain like caged chirping canaries.

After dinner we're sitting real close on Miss Cook's green crushed velvet love seat, listening to Joni Mitchell's "Court and Spark." I've never heard this song before and Miss Cook keeps replaying it so I can get the words.

She leans her head back and begins to sing along, barely a whisper, so I lean carefully nearer, just the very tip of Joseph's shirt touching her.

"Dancing up a river in the dark, looking for a woman to court and spark. . ."

I want to call Joseph and tell him that the right one has come along. I feel deliciously funny, wild, and lewd. I don't know if it's the one glass of wine, or the incense she's burning, but I'm light-headed. It's a giddy sensation, my whole body tingles, and I feel dreamy and high.

Miss Cook surrounds my wrist with her hand.

"I love your bracelet, did you make it?" she asks.

She rolls her fingers underneath the leather strap, touching each of the colored beads one by one.

I can't imagine even a vowel coming out of my mouth. Just the feel of her skin against my wrist makes me shudder, like that zip of electricity up your spine. I'm sure my face is even a deeper red than her lips.

"Maria," she whispers, "you'll be a senior next year, then you'll graduate. What do you want to do after that?"

I can feel the heat of her words against my cheek.

"His eyes were the color of the sand and the sea, and the more he talked to me, the more he reached me. . ."

I close my eyes and turn toward her. The Jean Naté and incense swirl, and my lips touch hers; Maybelline Deep Bordeaux meets tropical fruit gloss.

Our breasts press together, our nipples land directly onto each other as if guided by invisible homing devices. We shimmy.

My tongue pops out and hers is there to greet it, just like I've seen in my head a thousand times and I'm glad I'm wearing a Kotex pad because I'm so wet and so happy.

The song ends, *"city of the fallen angels,"* and Miss Cook pulls away. She smiles at me and her eyes seem to dangle between tears and something else, maybe worry or regret, I can't tell. I'm too scared to say anything.

We hug at the door before I leave—longer then I've ever hugged before.

I walk the mile home real slow, replaying every single moment of my seventeenth birthday dinner with Miss Cook. I clutch the stolen lipstick in my hand, hold it like it's a precious gem.

I lace my fingers in Joseph's bracelet, remembering the exact feel of her skin brushing against mine. As I get closer to home, the smell of her fades, and I feel an unfamiliar ache in my stomach, like a craving or hunger, but deeper.

I see Mr. O'Brien first, crossing over to our house. It's dark, but I know it's him by the hard sound of his work boots, and the big outline of his body. I know something is wrong. Maybe my brother Paul got into another fight with Jimmy O'Brien. They're always drinking too much beer, then fighting over whether Notre Dame has a better football team than Michigan State.

Then, under our porchlight, I see them. Sister Rose, Sister Ruth, *and* Mother Superior. Oh, God, not her. She's so old and fat she never ever leaves the convent. I was supposed to be home by 11:00 and it's almost midnight.

I don't remember when I start running, but I push through the nuns and I hear what sounds like harsh laughter, and as I cross the threshold I see my mom on the floor, curled up, and my dad is holding her and they're both crying.

Everybody's standing around them: Paul, Beth, the twins, and Fitz, holding his Elvis Presley doll. Father Francis is hunched over and kneeling on the kitchen floor with a rosary hanging off his robe. His hands are fat and spongy, splotched with coarse dark hairs. I hate going to him at mass; when he puts the communion wafer in my mouth, his hands smell sour, like something spoiled.

Sister Rose comes up behind me and places her hand on my shoulder and quietly murmurs in my ear: "You're brother, Joseph, was in a plane crash. He's dead, Maria."

Fitzy grabs my leg and buries his face into my faded jeans. That deep ache ruptures inside my body, and all I want to do is disappear.

Father Francis and the nuns begin the rosary, *Holy Mary Mother of God, pray for us sinners, now and at the hour of our death.* They're all kneeling on the kitchen floor.

Fitz is wrapped around me and I'm afraid for both of us, because I feel as if I'm being pulled under. I need to hear a different prayer, something to drown out the vacant awful noise of them filling the house.

I close my ears, as if sealing an envelope, and turning inside of me, I can hear just the slightest trace of her voice, low and dreamy. *"Dancing up a river in the dark. Looking for a woman to court and spark. . ."*

I quit being assistant coach to the volleyball team. I couldn't face Miss Cook. I forced myself to stop replaying the pleasure I felt with her on the night Joseph died.

Jenny stopped stealing and stopped wearing lipstick. She joined Shilo, a Christian youth group that thinks Catholics are going to hell. I went with her to one meeting. I liked the holding hands part, but not the praying and especially the crying. Jenny cried while she prayed. I didn't.

"You must have some unrepented secret sin in your heart," she said.

Dave Martino never even looked at me. He was going steady with Lois Feldman, the most stuck-up person on the planet.

Sometimes after school I stood behind the bushes and watched Miss Cook coach. I avoided her completely. Once, she stopped me in the hallway and handed me a book, *Coping with a Death in the Family.*

"Maria," she said, "how are you, are you okay?"

"Yeah, I'm fine," I muttered to her loafers.

Luckily, the bell rang and I bolted. Before her hand touched my wrist. Before my eyes fell into hers and I collapsed onto the floor. Every day was a countdown. One long countdown leading to college and far far away from here.

I was the oldest living at home. I spent the summer taking care of Fitzy and keeping an eye on Beth. The twins merged even closer. Paul joined the Navy, replacing Joseph, and we hardly heard from him at all.

I read that book about death that Miss Cook gave me, and I knew one thing for sure. My family was left in a tangled pile of fuselage, and no one was picking through the remains to see if there were any survivors.

It was called a touch-and-go landing. A routine procedure. The plane touches down, then pulls up, then goes. Something went wrong. Instead the plane exploded, and fell to the ground—metal, bone, teeth fragments, burned carpet, shattered plastic serving trays, melted flesh and floatation devices, and my brother, Joseph. Beyond recognition.

Three

"You're falling apart!" Christie says, as she struggles to unwind Molly's leash from the tree she's frantically circling. Molly is a mutt on a constant adrenaline rush. Sadie, her mom, is slow and pokey and not the least interested in smelling the remains of the neighborhood dogs.

Since you've been gone, Cup, Sadie won't leave my side. We sigh together, big, long, sonorous sighs, sighs too deep for words. I think she's worried about me. She looks up at me with those sorrowful dog eyes, and I throw her a puppy cookie, and she yawns as Molly furiously grabs it and runs away.

Sadie is very empathic. Molly tries to remind me and Sadie that life is just a series of boundless opportunities. She's like a revved-up teenage boy, and Sadie and I are like two elderly spinsters sitting all cobwebbed on the porch, eager for life's last sunset to sink.

I'm next to Sadie on the curb, waiting for Christie to free Molly. Both Sadie and I are experiencing a slight measure of pleasure as Molly now starts circling Christie's leg.

"Come to the group with me," Christie begs, as she unlocks Molly's neck from her leash. Molly darts away quickly. Sadie sighs, rises and slowly saunters after her.

"She's a good mom, isn't she?" I say, as Christie collapses on the sidewalk.

"You're avoiding the topic!"

I'm working hard not to let a smile unfold across my face. Christie has just plopped down on a condominium complex of red ants. I chew my bottom lip and look away, focusing on the dim L.A. sky, the gray strands of smog capture the morning's sunlight. The color is like a ribbon of your lipstick, Cup, Revlon's Wine with Everything.

"I know it makes you nervous, Maria, but you'll see, the grief group is really supportive."

I put my hands over my mouth. Suddenly, Christie starts pounding her sweats with her fists and bolts into the air, stomping her feet against the pavement.

"I suppose you think that's funny," she barks.

I shake my head, my hands are still pressed over my mouth in order to subdue the sadistic glee in my belly.

She wants me to join the grief support group that our friends, Sharon and Lynn, therapists slash lovers, hold every week at their apartment. It's for *any* woman facing some kind of loss. Yikes!

I know Sharon and Lynn mean well. They actually sent me a sympathy card after you left, Cup. They said it was really really sad we hadn't had the chance to participate in their lesbians loving lesbians weekend workshop, *before* the breakup.

I just can't stand going to their apartment. They have a bijillion candles all over, tacky macrame plant holders, and overstuffed pillows everywhere. No couch, no coffee tables, no bed. Just pillows and exotic materials draped on the floor. And they always serve this really gross tea, some seaweed tofu-root concoction along with sugarless, wheatless, tasteless cookies.

Christie extends her hand toward me. "You need a safe place to feel," she says, as she pulls me to my feet. "What do you say?"

Sadie is leading Molly back to us. She brushes up against me, nuzzles her face into my leg, prodding me home. We both sigh.

"Christie," I say, serious as a judge, "grieving in their apartment with all those wimmin who won't shave on political ground, and meditating my ass into the bosom of mother earth is depressing."

She stomps her foot and makes that noise. "Fine, Maria, it's just like you to reject support."

"I'm in the AIDS caregivers' support group already," I remind her, although I haven't gone in months.

"It's not the same. It's not the same," she repeats, "it's not feminine deep healing work."

She makes it sound like some kind of vaginal cream.

"Christie," I snort, "for the last time—no."

"No wonder Cup left you," she bites.

"*How* dare you!" I say sternly. I like the appalled and astonished sound of those three words strung together. "How *dare* you!!" I repeat.

Christie's eyes hit the ground. I've brought the Vatican to its holier-than-thou knees. "I'm sorry," she mutters, "I'm sorry."

Christie can't hang on to anger for more than a few seconds. Righteousness, yes, she oozes it like sweat, but not anger. She even clips the thorns off the roses at her flower shop. She actually believes she's doing her customers a favor.

"I've got to get to work," I say. I grab Molly's leash and run ahead, leaving Christie alone.

I drag my barren crotch into the office and on my desk is a note from Esther. "See me—as soon as you arrive!"

"Good morning, Esther," I say, lagging at the doorway to her torture chamber.

"Maria, come in and sit down. And shut the door." She is pecking at a manuscript with her red pencil of death. She's the most anal-retentive person I've ever encountered. Pick, pick, pick. Talk a lot. Pick a little more.

She eases her reading glasses down her nose and intently stares at me, folds her hands together, and begins:

"Maria, as you know, I am very sympathetic to your. . .situation. I understand you had a funeral on Friday, but you have had so many personal days for funerals, and I don't think it sets a good example for your staff. After all, I've just appointed you the chargé d'affaires of the editorial department. It's not quite fair to those who don't have the need to take off so many days for their own very personal reasons. Do you understand?"

Esther loves using French and squashing the life out of the written word.

"Oui, Esther," I reply.

"Very good," she smiles. "Have you notified the staff of your new position?"

"I wrote a memo."

"Very good," she eases her glasses back up. "That will be all."

I slither out of my chair.

"Maria, one more thing. This article you edited on the automatic cardioverter defibrillator needs much polishing. I'll get it to you by the end of the day," she sighs.

"Oui, oui." (You tight-ass bitch!)

Esther resents having to promote me, but I've been here the longest and I'm the best editor on staff. On a scale of one to five, five being extremely cooperative, I've never made it past a two on Esther's evaluations.

Here's my memo to the staff:

"I am now the chargé d'affaires for the editorial department, which, as most of us who did not get expelled from school for selling drugs know, is French for 'the person in charge.' French is the language of France, a country in Europe that exports wine and cheese, has its very own Disneyland, and was once known as Gaul, until it was overrun by the Celts and Romans. France stands as a major world power, respected by all nations except for the fact that they actually think Jerry Lewis is funny. If this does not convince you of my qualifications, let it be known that I have been intimate with a French physicist, in the Biblical sense."

The last part of the memo is incorrect. Yes, I was intimate with a French physicist. But what we did together is right up there with eating shellfish in the Old Testament. Despicable! You remember that lost weekend, don't you, Cup? For three months, I spent every single night watching you sleep. You had been completely shut down since Mark died. I plastered, "Silence=Death" bumper stickers all over the bathroom mirror. You scraped them off with a razor blade. I couldn't understand why you didn't talk about him.

"Just give me some space," you said.

"Just give her some space," the support group echoed.

So, I gave you damned space. I went up to San Francisco and met Paulette. She was studying astrophysics at Berkeley. Paulette's English was horrible, my French even worse, but we were totally fluent in body language. Besides, anger makes the heart go wander.

The next morning, after she finished grazing between my legs, I said, "Paulette, I have to call my lover."

She just sorta laughed at me, handed me the phone and said, "Oui, mon ami."

I called you. Seven A.M. on Sunday morning and you didn't answer. Where were you, Cup?

When I got back you asked if I'd eaten.

"Just a croissant," I said, "I'm starving." You didn't inquire about my weekend and I didn't inquire about yours.

I didn't care. The important thing is that when you picked me up at the airport, you held on for those extra moments, and we made out all the way home, and went straight to bed. We licked and kissed and sucked and finally you told me how Mark didn't have the strength to pump his morphine and he asked you to help him die, and so you pumped, all night, enough for him to fade away.

You curled up next to me, like a little girl, and fell into dreams and all I could think was that you're an angel, Cup. This is how we mourn for our dead friends, endless nights of speechless, wordless licking. We're two baby cubs, cut off from our kith, sharing our saliva as salve. Who were you with that night, Cup? Fuck you for leaving.

Once safely back in my cubicle I decide to write a letter to Oprah. I know it's a long shot, but what the hell. I need national attention. I describe it as a reunion program. You know, like when they reunite long-lost mothers with the children they abandoned thirty-five years ago because she was dirt poor, without a man, and shamed into it by some minister. The mothers always say, "Not a day goes by I don't pray for my babies."

Well, it'll be me on the stage, telling my sorrowful saga and Oprah will pause for a commercial break, and then after the studio audience has wiped its collective tears, Oprah will say, "Maria, are you ready to see your vagina?"

I'll nod, wringing and wringing my sweaty hands together. And there she will be. MONA. "Welcome home, Mona," I whisper. We'll touch, tentatively at first, shyly, and she'll sit down and clip on her little microphone, and talk about why she had to leave.

"Caller, you have a question?" Oprah asks.

"Yes, hi, Oprah. You look like a million bucks. Now, my question is, why did Maria treat Mona so poorly? It seems to me, she used her, she depended on her too much."

Vagina experts, Sharon and Lynn, address the caller. "You see," they say in unison, "Maria is in a codependent relationship with Mona. Mona needs to feel separate and independent. That's why she left. To find out that she was a worthwhile vagina, without Maria."

Oprah: "Thanks caller. Next, we'll meet a man who says his love life has dramatically improved since, Ralph, his penis, gained weight. When we come back, what do you think about penis enlargement?"

I can hear Esther coming, her nylons are rubbing together. I cover my letter to Oprah as she tosses the manuscript onto my lap. Merde.

I stare at it. Defibrillator. A device that's implanted into the chest and restores normal rhythm to the heart. Like a trained bystander. That's what I need, Cup, a device or someone to massage the will to live into my heart.

Before I know it, the phone is in my hand: "Hi, Peter, it's me."

"Hey, how's my little Greek tragedy, have you plucked out your eyeballs yet?" he asks.

"No," I retort. "But I haven't slept with my mother."

"It wasn't my mother, it was my father," Peter laughs.

"Peter, don't joke."

"I'm sorry," he says. "How are you really?"

"Oh, it's touch and go."

Four

"What's up baby, you're sweet as sugar."

I'm trying to keep his hand from sliding between my legs. I work security for the dorm. The midnight to 8:00 A.M. shift on weekends. I had to have a job at college and chose this one because I figured it met an important goal of mine. The students are drunk and bleary-eyed when they come in. All they have to do is flash their student I.D.'s and I buzz the door. They hardly notice me. That's the goal.

I didn't count on Pea-Funk. That's his nickname. His real name is Horace, Horace Jays.

Around four in the morning on Sundays, it's deadly quiet. The only thing I can get on my transistor radio is Sister Kizzie's Gospel Show, live from the motor city, on WLIV.

It's about four when Horace shows up. He sits real close to me and says I'm the prettiest white girl on campus. His grandma knows Sister Kizzie personally. We laugh together as Sister Kizzie wheezes Jesus and advertises Mabel's Holy Face Cream.

So far, I've only let him touch my breasts. We don't kiss or anything. And, I know I'm not even close to being pretty enough for him, but he seems to like my company.

Tonight he wants more.

"Horace Jays, you don't have Jesus on your mind," I tease as I hold his hand steady, just below my stomach.

"C'mon girl, it'll feel real good. I can tell you need to feel good."

"I feel just fine." He circles my nipple with his free hand.

"I think you're lonesome," he says, "just let me put my hand down there a little, if you don't like it, I'll stop." He squeezes my breast.

I untie the string on my sweats. It's all I ever wear. Sweats and big shirts to cover up my body. I'm getting fat. My hair is long and thin and all split ends.

"There, that's real nice," he moans, as he slips his hand inside my underwear.

He slides his palm up and down very slowly. He throws his jacket over my lap as two students enter the door. I buzz them in, staring straight ahead as if fixated on my work.

I don't know how it is, but Horace is making me wet, and a sweet ache swells inside of me.

"Oh, baby, you are dripping!"

I close my eyes and before I know it, I orgasm. The next Saturday, I do the same to him. While I stroke him, he closes his eyes and licks his lips. I keep waiting for him to want to kiss me. But it never happens. When I see him on campus, he walks by me as if I don't exist. In secret, I pretend he's my boyfriend, and we're just playing a game, like hard to get.

After Horace leaves, I listen to Kasey Kasem's top forty. When Kasey finally plays the Bee Gee's "How Deep is Your Love," I think of Horace and his fingers inside of me, and I cry.

Somewhere along the way, I've lost track of my nice social skills. I read all the time and stuff myself with donuts. I get fatter. My split ends split wider. The only thing that seems to matter is the orgasm I have on Sunday mornings between 4:00 and 6:00 A.M.

My roommate's name is Holly and she has poofy hair, manicured nails, a sorority pin, and two best friends down the hall, Candy and Dory. The three of them are like a cheerleading squad: same height, hairdos, same swish of the hips, same peculiar manner of swooping their heads back and forth so their long curls wave in the air like pom-poms. They squeal when the new *Cosmopolitan* magazine arrives, memorizing beauty do's and diet don'ts. Basically, Holly uses her side of our room as a closet. Which is okay by me. This is my freshman year in college.

I choose the same shift for my first summer job at home—waitressing at Vinnie's Truck Stop. I like working midnight to 8:00 A.M. It's when most people's busy brains slow down while they sleep, and the quiet permeates everything.

After 4:00 A.M. it's quiet like that, when the 2:00 A.M. bar crowd finally shuffles out. The college guys that come in are always drunk, their necks are red and faces puffy. They bark their food orders at me, and I know, thank god, that not one of them wants to put his hand up my skirt and feel me.

Vinnie wants to, and some of the truckers, but I tell them I have a boyfriend from school. Hank. Hank Jays.

Vinnie is fat and greasy and he wears these gold rings and chains around his neck, and a St. Christopher medal blessed by the Pope. He brags about going to Vegas every Christmas and hiring a babe to "do him."

"She does it all, know what I mean?"

"Yes, Vinnie, I do," I reply.

I hate Vinnie. He has a fat gold ring on each one of his pudgy fingers and the thought of him running those fingers through my pubic hairs or his fat mouth licking me, makes the inside of my mouth warm. The way your saliva heats, right before you throw up.

"Chili Size, no onions," I bark, as I slam the check down in front of Walter.

"I don't make it without onions!" he barks back.

We go through this every Wednesday when Mrs. Stipple orders, Chili Size, no onions, coke, no ice, which I have to refill at least a half dozen times. All this for a quarter and one dime left under her plate.

"C'mon, Walter, do it for me, please?" I beg.

Walter winks and suddenly Vinnie is leaning against me, pushing his cock into my butt and holding me against the counter.

"Three bulldaggers just came in, table four," he whispers in my ear. "Watch yourself, they'll want to lick your boyfriend's pussy."

He wipes his mouth with the back of his hand. He's always pressing himself into me like this. I want to tell him to fuck off, instead I just squiggle away. I hate him. But I always get him his apple pie, and I put extra ice cream on top just to please him. I don't know why.

I slither out to the floor. It's her. Miss Cook, sitting with two other women. They're all wearing black jackets with *Kalamazoo Blazers* written in yellow satin.

"Can I take your order, ladies?"

I always say ladies and gentlemen. I think it makes people feel respected. I even say it to those drunk white assholes who snicker when I walk away. Their girlfriends have poofy hair, slim hips, manicured nails, and lots of jewelry. They sit in the bathroom smoking and smacking bigs wads of gum, always tearing apart someone they hate.

My eyes lock onto Miss Cook's. She doesn't recognize me at first. Her friend orders a Tuna Melt, extra mayonnaise. It's Miss Cook's turn.

"Maria, how are you?" she says too loudly.

I want to cry on the spot, crawl into her lap and say, not so good, not so good.

"Oh, Miss Cook, hello there," I say.

She's wearing the Deep Bordeaux lipstick. Jean Naté floats into my nostrils, mixed with the smell of fried onion rings.

"How do you like school, are your classes hard?" she asks.

I mutter incoherently and then spit out, "What can I get you?"

When I go to the kitchen with their order, Vinnie and Walter are smirking. Vinnie sticks out his tongue and twirls it in the air. It isn't pink. It's brown from coffee and cigarettes. I place the order and run to the bathroom.

I sit on the toilet and cry. Mrs. Stipple burps in the stall next to me, and I want to die.

I close my eyes and try to imagine Miss Cook's nipples greeting mine, her fingers tucked underneath Joseph's bracelet, and that rush of love I felt and how ever since that moment I've had this ache in my gut and no matter how many donuts I stuff down my throat that ache doesn't budge.

When I pick up the order, Walter's face is dripping sweat, heated by the vats of oil and sputtering burgers.

"Hey, kid. Ignore the asshole," he says warmly. "You're good people."

I look in his eyes, and he winks, then slaps the counter with his hand and growls, "It ain't gonna walk to the customers, get going."

As I give them their food, I try to focus on their plates so I don't have to look in Miss Cook's eyes. I place their check on the table.

"Ladies," I say, "I'm going on break, but if you need anything Nancy will take care of you."

Miss Cook reaches over and grabs my hand.

"It's good to see you Maria. Why don't you stop by the school to see me? I'm there in the mornings, summer sports."

"Sure," I say, and rush back to the kitchen, behind Walter's workstation and slump on top of an empty milk crate.

Walter hands me a patty melt, no onions, my favorite. "It's yours. Nancy fucked up another order."

I feel calmer as I eat. I peek out to the floor and see Miss Cook's table empty. Nancy walks up and hands me three dollars. "Big tippers," she says.

"Keep it," I moan.

From the front dining room Vinnie yells: "Hey, Mrs. Jays, bring me a slice of apple pie."

I get home from Vinnie's at 8:30 every morning. My dad has already left for work. My mom is still in bed, having stayed up most of the night planted on the couch, drinking wine, staring at the television.

I brew her coffee, and by nine, I wake her up.

"What are you doing today, Mom?" I ask.

"Groceries, I've got to get more groceries," she says.

"Do you want help?"

"No."

When she shops, she's gone for longer and longer stretches of time. So is Dad. I wonder what they do, where they are, whether they sit together at Joseph's gravestone.

No one's home to intervene. No one stops the twins from tormenting Fitz with a yell, "You brats, go outside and play or you're grounded!" No one keeps Beth from sucking in enormous amounts of sugar. My dad doesn't complain about money, or insist that my mom mix whole milk with Carnation powdered milk so it will last longer.

Sunday mornings are the worst. It used to be we'd all go to eleven o'clock mass together. We'd wake up to the comforting smell of bacon sizzling and we'd have piles of scrambled eggs and usually a raspberry coffee cake. Now, the standard line is: "You're on your own."

I take Beth and Fitz to Saturday night mass at 4:30. Well, actually, we go at four, I run in and grab the church bulletin (evidence that we attended), before Father Francis is there, brooding in the vestibule. Then we walk through the field behind the church to Tug's for candy and pop.

Tug has a gumball machine with speckled balls and if you get one to come out, you get twenty-five cents of free candy. This is Fitzy's favorite. He'll put his penny in and when an all red one or all green one comes out, Tug looks at me and winks and says, "Looks speckled to me, Fitz."

Tug's brother was killed in Vietnam, and since Joseph died, he'll send my parents a glazed honey ham or a dozen corn on the cobs or a pot of Tug's jug of chili. Every month it's something different.

Beth hangs out a lot at Tug's. I worry, because that's where she gets the Hostess Cupcakes, and fruit pies, and Twinkies. When I take her and Fitz on Saturday's, I make her buy Tab instead of Coke, and only one Hostess product.

"How'za my favorite customers?" Tug shouts when we walk in. He's got a huge deep voice and when he talks, his enormous belly hangs on top of the counter and rolls and vibrates. His white short-sleeved shirt is always stained with mustard or ketchup or pickle juice.

Tug picks Fitzy up and lets him stand on the counter and count all the stains, and for each one he gives us a free red licorice.

It's the best time of the week. Tug makes us feel special, and noticed, and it's sweeter than any hymn I've ever sung at church. I'd rather have a speckled gumball from Tug, than a stupid wafer from Father Francis.

When we leave, he'll peck Beth and Fitzy on top of the head, and say, "Bye lambykins." Then he'll rap the top of my head and say, "Keep up the good work, scholar."

It'll do, but it doesn't replace Mom. She's stopped making her rounds at night, she stopped checking in on Fitz, the twins, even Beth, though Beth thinks she's too old for it now that she's fifteen. So, when Fitz goes to bed, I tuck him in, kiss his brow and say, "Night punkin." Just like she used to do. We all long for milk, mixed with the powdered stuff.

About noon I go to bed. I sleep for six hours, until Fitz can't stand it anymore. He waits and waits for me to get up, and sits outside my bedroom, futzing with his airplane, crashing it into the door when he wants me to know it's time for me to play with him. Sometimes, I just lay there and listen to Fitz. He sings when he doesn't think anyone's listening. Lately, he's been humming the theme song of the show, *M*A*S*H*. Of course, it worries me. One, he hates when we're watching *M*A*S*H*, it bores him, and he whines continuously, "Is it almost over, Mia, is it almost over?" Two, the song is about suicide.

I finally decide to go see Miss Cook. I'm sitting on the steps of the church, overlooking the playing field, watching her. She has such a big laugh, so big, that when the church bells ring, her laugh rises up higher, like a big balloon filling the sky, and the ringing bells just fizzle.

I want to catch that balloon and be carried along, dreaming

and flying, wherever it leads. I stand at the top of the hill just as the kids she's coaching start to run off toward home for lunch. She tosses the last ball into a huge net and looks up toward me. I guess the noon sun is at my back, because she shades her eyes, turns away, and starts walking off in the opposite direction.

"Miss Cook!" I squeal. I run down the hill, catch my foot in a hidden dip in the ground, and tumble, head first, into the hot grass.

She runs up and scoops me in her arms. "Maria, I didn't know it was you, are you okay!?"

I look into her eyes, God they're pretty. I want to crawl up into her mouth and cry, not so good, not so good.

"I'm fine," I say, "I came to say hi."

"Oh, I wish I knew you were coming, I've got a softball practice to get to." She's still holding me.

"That's okay," I reply, sitting up, and easing out of her arms.

"Maybe we could have lunch sometime next week?" she says, brushing the blades of grass from my shirt.

"I'd like that," I squeak. (Where does my voice go?)

"You sure you're okay?" A spark flies out of her eyes.

(Not so good. Not so good.) "Yeah, I'm good," I say confidently.

"I'm glad you stopped. Come back, okay?"

I nod yes. She walks away dragging that big net bag full of red kickballs, and I sit still, the sun warming my hair, my butt and heart aching. I have green stains on my elbows and knees and I don't move for a long while.

The church bells ring four o'clock, and there's no laughter anywhere around to grab onto, so I head for home, up the hill, across from the church, next to the convent.

One thing hasn't changed. At dinner time we still pray before we eat. *Bless us, Oh Lord, and these thy gifts, blah, blah, blah, from thy bounty through Christ, our Lord, Amen.* Except now, there's one more line we had to learn. *May his soul and all the souls of the faithful departed, though the mercy of God, rest in peace.*

I mumble this part, it's like my mouth is filled with stones. I just don't understand, why this prayer for Joseph's peace, when those of us sitting around this table, barely speaking, would die to have some of that too. Mercy.

On Joseph's grave are several little bundles of flowers, arranged neatly in a semicircle. I'm hanging out with him. It's the last week of August, and I'm leaving in five days for my sophomore year.

I'm still wearing Joseph's bracelet. The leather is thin and frayed but the beads are all there. I want to talk to him, but when I try, it feels odd, as if by talking I believe he can hear, and if I believe he can hear, then maybe he could help, and if he could help, then why hasn't he?

I remember at the funeral home my mom stood at Joseph's closed casket and with one hand she stroked the sleek cherry wood, so gently, as if she were patting a newborn's head. In her other hand she held three coins, old coins from Europe that her father gave her when she was a little girl. He slipped them into her hand the day before he died. I know they're precious to mom because they were his, and he died when she was ten, leaving her alone with grandma who slapped then hugged then slapped then hugged. My mom was feeling slapped and she needed her father.

I wanted my dad to stroke her instead of standing off to the side with his auto plant buddies, sipping a Stroh's, and sharing Navy stories.

Every so often, his eyes would dart over to the casket, to Mom, and he'd shift his weight from one foot to the other, shake his bottle, his eyes drawn back into the fog of the foamy brew.

I wanted to shove him. To push him with the weight of my heart, slam him ferociously into my mother. Instead, I sat silent, stuffing prayers for the dead into my brain, behaving myself.

Paul was out in the parking lot, sucking beers and secretly believing he couldn't survive this blow. Beth, Fitzy, and the twins were at home with Sister Rose.

That's were I wanted to be. At home, in the bathtub, warming my body, erasing this chill from my bones, feeling my fingers run through my pubic hairs, softened by baby oil, but I was afraid, if I took a bath, I might slip under and forget to hold my breath.

I rearrange the flowers before I leave, placing them in a

closed circle, instead of a broken one. I'm on my way to see Miss Cook. "Watch out for me big brother, if you can," I say.

When the door opens, I want to rush at Miss Cook, fold myself around her and tell her everything. But I don't, because Miss Cook doesn't open the door, Angela does.

They live together. I excuse myself to the bathroom and rummage through the cupboards. Next to Miss Cook's Jean Naté is a bottle of musk oil. That's what Angela smelled like when she lunged at me, hello, and hugged my ribs hard.

Two slightly damp bathtowels hang on the shower door. I collapse onto the toilet.

My stomach is in knots all through dinner. I keep taking tiny nibbles off the vegetarian lasagne, and refilling my glass with Chianti.

"So, Maria, what's college life like?" Miss Cook asks.

"Great!" I say. "I have a roommate, Holly, and we do *everything* together. We're so close. We even wear each other's clothes."

I'm not sure why I'm lying, but as I continue, even I start believing my words. At one point Angela rises from the table, and when she walks behind Miss Cook, she pauses, glides her hand across Miss Cook's back, and then asks me if I'd like more garlic bread.

The next thing I know, I'm on the floor, kneeling in front of the toilet, vomiting. Miss Cook is wiping my brow with a wash cloth. "It's okay, sweetie," she says.

She pulls my hair back in a ponytail and when I finish, we sit on the bathroom floor together. I can hear Angela, in the kitchen, washing the dishes.

"I'm sorry, I'm sorry," I say.

She tells me all about her and Angela. How they met at a softball game and they've been living together for six months. She asks if I love Holly that way too.

I throw up before I have to answer. Then, I leave.

Angela crushes my ribs again at the door. Miss Cook walks me outside. "Take care of yourself," she says, and then kisses me, lightly, on the lips.

As I drive away, I say, "I love you, Miss Cook." I say it to the car, the street, the hot night wind, and to Joseph, in case he's listening.

The day I leave, my mom gives me a huge bag of groceries

and walks me to the car. "Mom," I say, "keep an eye on Beth, she's eating too much, and Fitzy wants to be an altar boy after his first communion this year."

My mom leans down and kisses my cheek. "I'm so glad your father and I don't have to worry about you, you're the smart one," she says.

As I pull away, I reach into my backpack and pull out a tube of my mom's Estee Lauder's Cimmaron Rose. I hold it tightly in my hand and I whisper, over and over, *worry about me, worry about me.*

I carry a big heavy box filled with Joseph's books into the dorm. I knock into three guys, one of them is Horace. He doesn't even see me. His friend grunts, "Watch where you're going." I have a new roommate, her name is Mandy, she left me a note saying she's partying down the hall, come and say hello.

And, I have a new job. Usher at the school's theater. Walk people down an aisle, in the dark, and show them to their seats. They'll hardly notice me. That's still the goal.

My first class is Introduction to Psychology with Dr. Hilda Rothman. I slip into my seat just as class begins.

She's probably in her sixties or early seventies, short and round with a ball of tightly curled gray hair. She's wearing a big, maroon, man's sweater over plain blue polyester slacks, and those thick-soled orthopedic shoes that old ladies wear.

"Most people know nothing at all about the forces that make them miserable," she begins, "and most people are, in their own secret way, miserable. You've heard the saying, lives of quiet desperation. You are here to learn about this. About desperation, and why you feel miserable."

Her words zip fast from her mouth and I'm furiously trying to keep up.

She has round bifocals that slip down her nose every few minutes, and she pushes them up, over and over. After she writes on the board, she wipes her hands across her sweater, imprinting her chalky handprint like a child's fingerpainting. Two guys behind me snicker.

There's about sixty people in class. Every seat is taken. I'm sitting in the front row, near the exit, so I can vanish quickly. She's been talking for fifteen minutes when James walks in. He sits on the floor next to me, crosses his legs, Indian style.

He has curly black hair and he's wearing baggy shorts, a

loose corduroy shirt, and sneakers. He opens his notebook, and inside with the loose sheets of paper are a bunch of dandelions.

I guess I am staring at his lap because suddenly, he hands me a dandelion and smiles. He has these blue eyes, like I've never seen before. I want to pull them out and wrap them in a scarf, carry them around in my pocket like rare stones.

I pick up my pen and continue taking notes. She lectures for two hours. Every so often, she turns around and glances at the wall clock and gasps, startled by the time, as if she is running behind and with every fast word she tries to catch up with the sweeping second hand.

I get most of what she is saying, but I can't stop thinking about his eyes, the blue of them so startling yet familiar.

She ends her lecture at the precise moment class is over. "So, by the end of the semester you will achieve an understanding of your own personal misery, and this insight will enable you to function in a healthier manner. Will you be happy?" She smiles, a little grandma twinkle in her eyes. "Who knows? Next class, all about suicide."

I'm about to bolt when James asks me to go to the Quad with him for a cup of coffee. At first I think he's joking. He's so beautiful.

"I've transferred," he says. "It's my first class here. I'd love to talk about the lecture with you."

How does this happen? Beauty and brains. My roommate, Mandy, has long rolling locks of black hair, manicured nails, perky breasts, slim hips, and a wardrobe right out of the pages of *Cosmo*. And she's smart. She likes me because I'm the first person she can talk to about important things.

Non-beautiful people have no trouble exploring the deeper hidden mysteries of their existence. That's all we've got. Beautiful people gathered together just keep slamming into each other's flesh, scrutinizing and admiring and awed by the image. They can't go deeper. They don't have large pores, the portals to the soul.

You ask beautiful people, "How do you like Camus?"

They reply: "My mother used it, but it dries my skin out."

Ugly folk will tell you all about Sisyphus and that mountain, the rock, the push, the meaninglessness. Who's better off?

As James and I walk across campus I'm feeling some strange shift occur inside of me. I feel as light as an autumn leaf, gliding effortlessly, buoyed by the wind. The strangest part, though, is that as we walk, his shoulder will brush against mine, or our palms lightly meet midswing, and that's when I feel it, from my bones out—James and I are from the very same tree.

I get back to my room and Mandy is polishing her toes, little poofs of cotton stick out between each one.

"Mandy, guess what?!" I say, tossing my books to the floor.

"You've met a gorgeous guy and you're in love!" she says.

"No, I'm not in love, but I did meet a guy, his name is James and he's *real* smart and he's. . . beautiful."

"Mia, is he handsome or beautiful?" she asks, as she extends her leg out, grabs her foot and pulls it to her mouth, blowing the wet nails dry.

I'm a little perplexed. "Well, I guess he's both."

Mandy jumps off her bed, bounces on her heels over to her desk and pulls out a joint.

"This calls for a celebration," she says, twirling the joint between her fingers, "you've got a crush."

I giggle in agreement, but I know it's not a crush. It's something else I feel with James, some secret link between us. I do have a crush, though, on Mandy, and she has a boyfriend, Clay, who's a tennis instructor slash terminal senior at the college.

Mandy pays attention to me. She has taught me how to pull my hair back in a French roll. She lets me wear her makeup and lipsticks. She says I have lovely eyes, and never ever mentions that I could stand to drop twenty pounds.

She lights the joint and sucks in on it hard as if desperate for oxygen.

"Mandy," I say, "what do you think makes people miserable?"

She's blinking her eyes rapidly, as if her lashes are wings and she's about to take flight. She raises her chin up and blows a huge plume into the air, the white smoke shoots through her lips, glistening with Cover Girl's Bedroom Rouge Velour. She hands me the joint.

"They don't believe in God," she says.

I take little tokes in, just sips off the joint, because it makes me too nervous. "*You* believe in God?"

"Hit me," she says, nodding her head yes. I put the joint into my mouth, suck in and blow smoke up into Mandy's nose.

"How do you believe in God, Mandy, tell me?"
She's fanning her face rapidly, still holding her breath.
"GOD!" she bellows, as the smoke pours out of her. "God is everything—this joint, this room, your books, sex with Clay, my love for you, that's God."

My love for you. I'm blushing. I feel a wild womping tornado twirl in my stomach. *My love for you.*

Mandy collapses back onto her bed. I've got the joint between my fingers.

"C'mere," she says. I stamp out the joint. She scooches over to make room for me on the bed.

This is why I like to get high with Mandy. She loves to cuddle when she's high and tell me all about sex with Clay. Every so often, I yawn, pretending to just barely listen so she won't catch on that a damn choir is caroling between my legs.

She wraps her arms around me. "Listen, Mia, if you're gonna have a beautiful boyfriend, you need to learn something, and I'm gonna teach you."

I'm the iceberg hitting the Titanic. I'm a deluge of fire engulfing the Zeppelin. I'm an earthquake, a monsoon. Mandy has her tongue in my mouth and she's teaching me how to kiss, and if I can just stay conscious and keep breathing, maybe this feeling will last forever. I'm Lake Superior.

Five

I fell asleep watching reruns of *Real Stories of the Highway Patrol*. I had the worst dream. I was the lead story in my very own episode. Mona is found in a ditch along the Golden State Freeway. She has been stabbed repeatedly, but Officer Krupke said it was apparent she put up a valiant struggle. They put her in a little triangle-shaped body bag. There are no leads. I'm running and running, searching for the brute who has done this. Suddenly, I see them. Sister Rose, Sister Ruth, and Mother Superior. Huddled on the porch. I push them aside, and rush into the house. It is empty. Sister Rose hands me a bedpost. Pray for us sinners now and at the hour of our death, Amen.

Then, kaboom, the channel switched. It's *Rescue 911*. I'm rushed into emergency. The physician on duty takes one look at me. "I've never seen anything like it," he says hopelessly.

A swarm of nurses surrounds me. "Let's defibrillate," the doctor roars. He grasps two round smooth metal discs. He smears a dollop of Pond's cold cream on them, rubs them together, and yells, "CLEAR!" The nurses back off.

Volts of electric waves like bullets are shot through my crotch. They all gaze horrified at the machine. Nothing. Not a blip. Nary a quivering line on the monitor.

He screams again: "CLEAR!!" ZAP! Silence.

A weeping nurse gently spreads a towel over my groin. "We tried everything, honey, I'm sorry."

I beg them to throw me in a body bag.

When I wake up, I'm sweating and my heart is pounding fast. I bolt upright in bed, and search for your sweet sweet face in the dark. I reach out for you in the haze of half-sleep and grab Molly's wet snout. I want to open your legs wide, pull your crotch to my mouth, tease you, the way you like. Bait you with a quick suck, then roll my tongue down to your anus, back up, plunge in hard. Over and over, bait, suck, roll, plunge, until you grab my head, hold it steady, rocking your hips, "Stay, there, right there, don't stop," you'd moan, and I don't, I go and go until you and Amelia soar to the heavens.

"Sweet pea," you'd say, "what could be more loving than planting your lips on a woman's cunt?"

"Nothing, Cup. Nothing at all."

I pour myself a big glass of scotch and decide to clean the house. Sharon and Lynn sent over some eucalyptus oil with a note. "Use the oil mixed in water and wash all surfaces while praying. We ask the great mother to clear this home, this hearth. To brush away the losses and erase all negativity from this place so light and healing energy may bathe this dwelling."

I decide to use the vacuum instead. I really try. I aim the hose, like a rifle, at the dustballs swirling under our bed, but somehow, Cup, I can't evict them. Not yet. Maybe they carry flakes from our skin, cast off while we made love. Remnants of our life. They're the only pieces of you I have left.

When I'm in our home, my heart hangs strangely inside my body, like an old wire hanger, tired and bent from the heaviness of a thick winter coat. I'm so weighted down, at least I know I won't slip and fall. This load plants me so firmly into the ground that I feel as if I'm being buried alive, inch by inch.

I'm down on all fours peering under the bed and I see two little furry legs sticking out underneath a pile of blankets. Cupcake, your teddy bear. I can't believe you swiped our vibrator but left Cupcake. I pull him out. I reach under the bed again searching for more of you. Perhaps you left a clue behind, a way for me to find you. My fingers lock onto a strap and I tug and tug and then yank at it so hard it comes flying at my face and wallops me in the nose. It's Camille Paglia—our leather harness and dildo. The prickly dildo we bought at the Pleasure Chest because it guaranteed unsurpassed stimulation. If you enjoy being scoured by a wedge of barbed wire.

I've got your teddy bear in one hand and Camille in the other and I'm so damn lonesome that I strap Ms. Paglia onto Cupcake. Don't give me any grief over this. It's creative visualization. Sadie looks down at me as if I've lost my mind.

"No, Sadie," I say defensively, "I haven't lost my mind, it's my vagina that's missing."

I decide to call Christie and ask her to sleep over.

When she walks into the bedroom, and sees the teddy bear with cock lying on the floor, she doesn't say a word. She picks it up, unstraps the dildo, then asks if I've been drinking.

Boy, sometimes Christie surprises me. She just loses that Vatican thing and becomes so understanding. "Yes, I have been drinking," I say.

She gets me two aspirins, tucks me in, and crawls into bed with me.

We spoon in our sleep, finding those old familiar places where our bodies fit. In the middle of the night, I wake up sweating scotch, my mouth as dry as chalk.

I gulp down two glasses of water and when I crawl back into bed, I bend down to peck her cheek, just a thank-you peck, and we start kissing.

I slip my hand between her legs from behind and she's already wet. I slide two fingers inside of her. She sucks them in and rubs herself, my mouth is pressed over her shoulder blade. I listen as she orgasms, soft and hushed like always, and I hold on for dear life and start to cry.

We fall asleep like this; wetness dripping from my eyes, my nose, and between Christie's legs; our body fluids shared and staining the sheets.

Christie drives me to work in the morning because, frankly, I feel as if I cannot operate heavy machinery.

"Maria, please come to my office," Esther whines, and without waiting for a response, she sashays away from my desk. Her nylon-thigh-rubbing makes my stomach queasy. She's probably going to chastise me about the memo.

I slump before her highness, and wait for the lecture. She's shaking her head, staring at a manuscript with a mixture of disgust meets horror meets you're so pathetic.

"I just don't understand, Maria," she sighs. "I try to teach, but nothing sinks in, I am constantly finding errors."

"What is it, Esther?" I say, my voice as dull as the pastel porcelain figurines of happy-faced storybook children spread out on her desk. I want to smash them.

She begins reading: "The mortality rate of rapid ventricular tachyarrhythmia is high comma 400,000 persons a year comma survival is dependent on trained bystanders comma or persons learned in cardiopulmonary resuscitation."

It's my article. I see myself pick up Little Bo Peep and she's shattering the head off of Little Jack Horner, sitting in his corner.

Esther drones: "Doctor Lumby spells out in detail comma the latest technologic advancements of the automatic cardioverter-defibrillator." She grunts. Not deeply and passionately, but more like a prude taking a shit.

"Now, Maria, what is wrong with that last sentence?" She points the red pencil of death at me, aiming it between my eyes.

Gretel and Little Bo Peep are making out in the woods, while Hansel corners little Jack, they jump over a candlestick and realize that it feels really good, and they all live happily ever after.

"I don't know, Esther," I say.

She pauses, holds her head in dismay, as if she has just witnessed a drive-by shooting.

"Dog puppy," she says, and raises her eyebrows. "Dog puppy," she repeats.

(Briefly comma I'm Glenn Close with a knife pointed toward a trembling Mona comma I seethe comma quote I will not be ignored period end quote.)

"Spell. . . out. . . in. . . detail," Esther says. "That is a perfect example of a dog puppy. Spell out, alone, is sufficient. Period. Now, take a memo."

I pretend to scribble furiously as she talks. I try to find a tiny morsel of empathy or compassion for Esther, but I can't. I really hate her.

"Kneel down," she says, and for a split second I think I have finally found a smidgen of common ground. Esther is a dominatrix. "Kneel down," she repeats. "Now, as you know, the act of kneeling assumes higher to lower."

"Yes ma'am," I reply. For a brief moment, I'm actually enjoying Esther.

"Brief moment," she barks, "a moment is assumed to be brief."

(This is getting spooky.)

"A bolt of lightning," she gleams. "Maria, have you ever seen lightning manifest in any form other than a bolt?"

"Well, yes, Esther. Back in Michigan we had lightning storms that lit up the whole sky, as if you're standing in a dark room and someone flips on the light switch." I gleam.

Esther winces, like she's just sniffed sour milk. "Please continue writing. Three, partial truth or partially destroyed. Four, over exaggerate. And, five, personal opinion."

I stop listening as her lips continue flapping. For a *brief moment* I see Vinnie *kneel down* at Esther's crotch. They are both struck with a *bolt of lightning, partially destroying* their brains, and a vulture *swoops down* to *completely finish* them off.

Again, I slither out of my chair, and just as I am about to

leave, I turn and say: "Esther, I *mean it, sincerely*, it is my *personal opinion*, but I think it is *absolutely essential* that I reveal to the staff the *true facts* of our *meeting together*."

She's a bit baffled. She squirms in her seat and then waves me out.

Approximately one minute and thirty-five seconds later she approaches my desk. "Maria, you were deliberately using dog puppies when you left my office. All I ask for is mutual cooperation."

"Esther," I cry, "*mutual* cooperation?! Think about it."

She storms away from my desk, her thighs scraping together like fingernails down a chalkboard. Humorless, tight-ass bitch. I'd love to shove Camille up her ass. I guess I make Esther's vagina, I call her Gigi, very squeamish. Oui, oui. Esther-cunt is a dog puppy.

I'm spinning in my cubicle. I start writing out another Mona episode I'm developing called *Tales from the Clit*.

"It is dark, only a slip of the moon to light the earth. In the distance the outline of a prehistoric rock, as big as a mountain. At first, specks of light, hundreds of specks, like fireflies bouncing. A shout here, a murmur there, a woof woof woof. Closer the dancing lights move, beams illumine the brush, the desert brambles, and stone.

Hundreds of footsteps connected to the specks. It's a search party of volunteer eyes peering desperately through the brush, ambling toward the apocalyptic Ayers Rock.

Woof woof woof. I am Meryl Streep wearing a black, bowl-shaped wig. My eyes are bloodshot, my sweatshirt stained with blood and tears. The Australian black sky is ominous, the taste of dirt in my mouth.

I gaze at the Aborigines huddled around a fire, their smiles burn like embers. They are silent, mocking my frantic search. I am certain they must know the truth, the whereabouts, the fate of my beloved Mona. Suddenly, a howl pounds the night sky, from deep within my chest cavity: "A DINGO ATE MY MONA! A DINGO ATE MY MONA!"

I'm so pathetically desperate, Cup, I call Paulette in San Francisco.

"Paulette, open your golden gates," I say.

"Mon ami," she sings, "come see me." Her English is better.

I'd like to cum, period, and I'm thinking about flying up, and touching down. Since we're officially separated, I'm a free bird.

I feel like a vulture, famished, angry, unloved. I want to swoop down and pick at flesh. An hors d'oeuvre will do.

I can't bear this absence of touch. I need water and light and tenderness. It's hard to feel tender toward a vulture. They eat dead things. We just breathe the dead and eat each other.

What did my parents do after Joseph died? Did they suck and stroke or were their tongues like weapons, swiping each other with silent accusations: "You never told him you loved him." "You shut him out when he grew his hair long." "He went into the Navy because you wanted him to." "You killed him." They lost a cub. Did they cling to each other, staining the sheets, sharing their body fluids? Dad, what could be more loving than your lips on Mom's weeping cunt? Nothing, nothing at all.

The arctic circle has nothing up on my Mona. My anti-vagina needs antifreeze, and Paulette is willing.

She picks me up at the airport and whisks me off to her favorite French restaurant. She greets the waiters with a slight brush of her lips and orders us a seemingly endless amount of cuisine.

I discover that Paulette is one of those people who order piles of food and just pick at it. I'm from the clean-your-plate school of chow.

Also, now that her English has improved, Paulette is quite a blabber. I need that. Someone to fill in the empty space, and the endless droning of my heart.

If Albert Einstein had a wet dream, it would be Paulette. She's the Brigitte Bardot of astrophysics, with a heap of dirty blonde hair, pouty full lips, and a range of body movements unsurpassed by even Marcel Marceau. I'm mesmerized.

"Tell me about your work," I say, and instantly she begins weaving theories about the delusion of apartness, the merger between what is seen and the seer. Her full peach lips deliver a veritable feast of astrophysical poetics that leave me in a salivating stupor.

Of course, I'm being influenced by the full-bodied deep Bordeaux wine that accompanies our meal, but Paulette has me slithering.

"You see, Maria, the space surrounding a black hole is said to reach infinite curvature."

It's as if there's a 976 sex operator in my ear, translating every word into some kind of pornographic event.

A buttery, garlic-laced snail meanders on my tongue and slowly crawls down my throat.

I can't keep my eyes off her lips. "This is commonly known as the Big Bang theory, what we now call a harmonious black body curve," she swoons.

Her lilting French accent leaves my dull Midwestern self wilting.

"My specialty," she says, "is measuring the many body problem, the gravitational pull of three or more objects."

I lean closer over the table and imagine crawling, like a snail, inside of her mouth, leaving a trail of buttery wetness on the white tablecloth between us.

The primordial vacuum. The birth of a new universe. Unimaginable galaxies on the other side of space and time. Her words come at me like asteroids.

"Have you heard of the concept, quantum leap?" she asks.

"Yes, fascinating," I chirp.

"Well," she whispers, leaning over her full plate of untouched duck paté, "what is even more enticing. . ."

I'm bending toward her, the gravitational pull unbearable.

"Yes," I whisper, as if holding onto the very tip of her tongue.

She pauses. Licks her lips. "What is enticing, Maria, is quantum tunneling through the barrier of dark matter."

I groan. Loudly. Then try to recover quickly with a hack-hack-hack that Heimlich's monsieur escargot off my tongue, across the table, and right on top of Paulette's paté. She grabs the saliva-soaked snail quickly, and sucks it down with a red wine chaser. Oh, to be red wine.

I want to be swallowed. To vanish in her dark matter, off to a new universe, on the other side of space and time. Far, far away from you, Cup, and out of death's reach.

"Shall we go back to my place, Maria?"

(Mon Dieu!!) "Oui," I say, and I follow her out of the restaurant, and I kiss the waiters just like her.

She has a new apartment and in her bedroom she has created what can best be described as an altar, a high holy place of worship. Huge antique candleholders surround a four-post cherrywood bed. Lush rugs abound, and the bed is spilling over with down-filled pillows.

I sit on the bed and suddenly I feel like a black hole. I don't know what to do. Paulette is lighting the candles.

"Paulette," I say, "undress for me."

She follows my instructions silently. The only thing I know to do in this moment is to be the chargé d'affaires.

Her breasts salute the air, defying all known laws of gravity. I tell her to turn around, slowly.

I'm stalling for time.

"Paulette, I want to ask you to do something for me."

"Anything, mon ami," she replies.

"Get on top of the bedpost and make love to it as if it were me."

She smiles. "Sure, my love."

Are all French woman so compliant, or just physicists who understand how simple, strange, yet unexplainable all interactions are? I watch, breathless, as Paulette straddles the bedpost and rubs herself deeply into the smooth cherry-wood ball. I think of my white painter's pants, *Cosmo*, and Pond's cold cream.

She gazes at me, pinches her nipples, licks her lips, her tongue darting into the air rapidly, expertly.

I think of sending Mona a postcard from San Francisco. "Having a wonderful time, wish you were here!"

Our dinner table conversation crawls through my wine-soaked brain cells. I'm reviewing the "many body problem," as Paulette explained. The difficulty of calculating the gravitational interactions of three or more objects. As I study her gyrations, the waves of energy she creates by means of a consistent vibration on the bedpost, I figure the equation looks something like this: $(Maria + (-Mona) \times Paulette/Bedpost) =$.

When I get to "equals" I'm stumped.

The candles' light and her wetness create the illusion that waves of energy emanate from the sleek cherry ball. The gravitational interactions dissipate the delusion of apartness. I am part of the bedpost and the candle and Paulette. The observer marries the observed.

To gaze at a woman overflowing with self-given pleasure is to witness the sudden unexplainable brightness of a star—a supernova. I can feel Paulette's protons spinning and tunneling through the dark matter between us.

It's a fusion, so robust that the moment she orgasms, the Seven Sisters weep for joy, Orion cries victory, and the Southern Cross flares. I bathe in the glow of French stardust.

I'm not wet. No ping-ping-ping between my legs. I orgasm by proxy and for a few flickering moments, there is no death inside of me.

(Mona, Mona little star, how I wonder where you are.)

Cup, death has slipped between our sheets. We've been connected like two crumbling pages in a book, pressed against each other in the dark, our words fragile as ashes, spilling over and fading into some empty black body. Ashes, ashes, we all fall down.

Paulette climbs down and lays on top of me. "What do you want?" she asks.

"A pocket full of posey," I say. That's what I need to sweeten the air of disease and decay.

In the morning I take Paulette to her lab to measure quarks. As she brushes her lips against my cheek, I ask her, "Paulette, what do you think of Jerry Lewis?"

"A comic genius," she says, "why do you ask?"

"Just curious," I smile. "It's a theory I have about physicists."

"Silly American, come back and see me. There are three more bedposts."

I take a hike up the thighs of Mt. Tamalpais. San Francisco looks like a jewel, sparkling below. The green of the earth abounds, and I want to dive into its belly and swim.

I climbed up here with you, Cup, and we threw ashes from her summit, rolled in leaves and the clouds were like Gods and we sang to them, *wherever you're going, I'm going your way.* I squat on the rock we made love on.

A few hikers amble by, their faces red, slapped fresh by the wind. I pick up two stones and rub them together. The waves of friction create heat and I press them to my cheeks and tears meet stone meet flesh.

My shape is changing, worn down; whittled by life; like a rock; the steady stream of days upon days pour over me. When we rub and grind each other, our shapes change too; smoothed, then roughed, then smoothed again.

A gust of wind slaps my face and I think how faith is like a gust, sudden and brief.

I stand and hurl the warm stones into the air and watch a part of myself soar away, dreaming and flying. I'm waiting, Cup, just waiting round the bend.

Six

I'm home for Christmas break and all I want is to go back to school, back to Mandy and James, and Dr. Rothman's fast lectures.

Beth is in deep shit. Dad is yelling at her in the basement. Yelling louder and more furiously then I've ever heard before. Mom is there too, punctuating his rage with her own. I hate them.

Beth stole my mom's old coins and took them to Tug's to buy Hostess cupcakes. Tug accepted them, and then called my mom this afternoon and told her he had her coins. I know Tug wouldn't have called if he thought Beth was going to get hurt. She's sixteen, fat, and getting more and more withdrawn every year.

When Dad got home from work, they took Beth down to the basement. Fitz and I are on the couch. He's holding his Elvis doll over one ear, and pressing the other ear onto my leg. He's eight years old, but at this moment, he seems like two.

"You're a liar and a thief!!" my dad wails.

"I didn't take them, I didn't take them," Beth cries.

Then I hear it. A whack. Then another and another. He's hitting her with his belt. I've never heard them hit so many times in a row.

After several eternal minutes pass, my mom and dad come upstairs and tell Fitz and me to get to the table for dinner. My dad cracks open a Stroh's.

"Go sit down Fitz," I say. "Don't worry, you're not in trouble."

Beth is sitting in the farthest corner of the storage room. It's the part of the basement we huddle in during tornado warnings. Boxes of Joseph's things from the Navy are piled next to her. Lying on top of the boxes is the perfectly folded flag that was draped over Joseph's casket.

Her pants and underwear are pooled at her feet. Her face is shuddering. Her bottom is covered with long swatches of red welts from the belt. Her chubby legs are trembling too. She doesn't look at me when I sit down next to her.

Her eyes are so swollen, like my heart, and I want to rock her in my arms, because I know why she stole those coins. She stole them to buy sweetness 'cause there's nothing but sorrow in the house. She eats sugar to forget, like how I rub myself in the dark.

"Stupid, stupid, stupid assholes," I growl. It's cold in the storage room, so I take the flag and drape it over our laps.

We sit silent, the stars and stripes covering our legs. I think about Mandy, and look for God. I reach under the flag and rub Beth's chubby thigh, slowly.

"Beth," I whisper, "I want to show you something." I ease my hand up between her legs, and gently let my fingers run through her soft hair. She doesn't stop me.

"Do this," I say, "do this when it hurts." Her hand meets mine, and together we rub and rub and pretty soon she's not crying anymore, she's smiling, and we laugh, the flag as our blanket, covering our laps, our secrets, and her sore bottom.

My mom comes down and brings us two plates of food. Creamed tuna on toast, no peas, just the way I like it.

"Clean your plates, girls, then come upstairs for dessert. Your dad said we'd wait for you."

Beth won't look at her. My mom hasn't said a word about the flag.

As she's about to step out of the storage room, she turns and says to Beth, "It's cherry pie, punkin, your favorite."

Their eyes meet for a heartbeat, Beth mutters, "Okay," and my mom looks at me. "Fold that thing up when you're done."

When I return after break and walk into my dorm room, Mandy's side is completely empty. On my bed is a note, a joint, and a tube of Bedroom Rouge Velour lipstick. She eloped with Clay on New Year's eve. He got a job in Orlando, Florida, teaching tennis at a retirement home.

"Mia, I love you, and you're a great kisser! Mandy."

For those long gruesome months—January, February, March—a chill set in, like the thin layer of frozen snow that blanketed the campus. I felt like a Janis Ian lyric, ravaged-faced, lacking grace, inventing lovers on my own. And Mandy, with her clear-skinned smile, has married young and retired.

Erupting in my belly was that same sinking ache, and if James hadn't been here, I would have crawled around campus, my chin scraping the ground, scavenging for donuts.

James began calling me Smudge. It had to do with the blotches of newsprint on my face from the newspapers I read. I still stuffed words into my brain.

Lots of times that's exactly how I feel, like something smeared. Except when I'm with James, and we talk about moving to California. Then I look into his glimmering sapphire eyes, I actually feel hope. We moved out of the dorms and got an apartment near campus.

It's March and a thick cloud cover is rolling in from the north. The prediction is for over a foot of snow, a March nor'easter. James decides it's worthy of a celebration, especially if classes get cancelled tomorrow. We set up a picnic in our apartment. Apples, wine, cheese, a couple of Hostess twinkies.

We're a little high when the phone rings. James is dancing around the room and singing "*I'm the poetry man, I'll make you feel all right.*"

Whenever the phone rings I want it to be Mandy. I haven't heard from her in months, except a postcard from Disney World: "God is Mickey Mouse," she wrote.

"Hey Fitzy, how are you?" It's almost midnight, too late for Fitzy to be calling.

"When are you coming home?" he asks.

"I don't know, Fitz, are you all right?" I can hear him fidgeting on the other end. "Where's Mom and Dad?"

"They're sleeping," he whispers. "Why do you have to live there?" he asks.

"Fitzy, did you get in trouble?"

"Nope," he replies, his voice fading even more.

"Fitz, what's going on?"

"Sing to me," he says, "like when you sound like Elvis."

"Okay, how about 'Love Me Tender'?"

"Nope, sing the other one," he murmurs.

And so I sing, "Heartbreak Hotel," low and deep, like Elvis: "*I'm so lonely baby, I'm so lonely, I'm so lonely, I could die.*"

When I finish, there's a long silence between us, and then I think I hear Fitz say bye, but I'm not sure. The phone went dead, just as I whisper, "Night punkin."

James comes up behind me. I'm sitting stroking the phone in my lap.

"Hey, Smudge, who was it?"

I should have told Fitz I was coming home soon, but I don't want to go back there.

If I don't get out, I think this mitten-shaped state is going to clench into a fist and smother me. Paul went AWOL and we haven't heard from him in over a year. The twins are sealed off on their own planet and Beth just orbits haphazardly through space, eating and rubbing herself in the dark. It's touch and go.

James wraps his arms around me. "What is it, Smudge?"

"Nothing. Nothing at all." I lean into him. "Sleep with me?"

"Sure, Smudge."

I want to erase home, forget they exist, and leave Michigan altogether.

I only go home for quick visits, long enough to touch down, pull up fast, and go, hoping not to explode.

Fitz avoids me during spring break. He's just turned nine years old, and I feel that some part of him is slowly callousing over; the tender soft child part that would suck his thumb when we snuggled, or ask me to sing, in a deep voice like Elvis. He seems stiff and cautious. Maybe he's just getting too big, but he won't cling to me, or sit outside the door waiting for me to wake up and play.

My mom took a job as a bank teller. The recession cut into my dad's auto plant, so whatever mysterious thing he spends his time doing there now, he can't do it overtime. Beth is working at Tug's after school. She's still eating as much as ever, and I can't get her to tell me much at all about boys or school or friends. The twins' bedroom door is covered with handwritten signs: Keep Out! No Trespassing! Don't Even Think About Coming In! They've developed their own spooky silent language. When I come home, they look at me, then at each other, raise their right hands in unison, and nod twice. I guess it translates as hello.

It's a Saturday morning. I wake up to the sound of thumps, one after another, loud thumps outside my window. It's a small dirt-patch hill where my dad has tried forever, it seems, to get something to grow. He'll lay grass seeds then carefully frame it with string and sticks to keep our feet from trampling through.

It's his spring ritual. Usually the robins and sparrows will eat all the seeds, or the day after he spreads them we'll get one of those torrential spring rains and everything is washed away. One year, the sewer backed up and they had to dig into this hill to get to the line. Hopeless spring ritual.

I climb out of bed and put on my shorts and a T-shirt. The thump-thump gets louder as I round the back of the house. It's Fitzy standing at the bottom of this little hill with a huge pile of big rocks at his feet. Big, like heavy stone loaves of bread.

"Fitz, what are you doing?" I ask, as he brushes past me, retrieves the backyard garden hose, comes past me again without a word, stretching the green snake as far as it will go.

"Good morning, Fitz, what are you doing?" I repeat.

He shoots me an annoyed look, as if I've interrupted the creation of some monumental work of art.

The dozens of rocks piled at his feet came from the carefully landscaped shrubs in the front yard. I figured by the size of the load, it must have taken hours to move them. No wheelbarrow in sight. My dad will be furious if he catches him.

"Are you helping dad with a project, Fitz?" He carefully surveys the dirt pile. He scratches his head, like my dad does when he's puzzled.

Fitz's face is covered with dirt, his T-shirt dripping in little boy sweat. His hands are red and raw and sticking out of his jean's pocket is one of my dad's handkerchiefs.

"Can I help?" My voice is tinged with frustration.

"Nope," he mutters, still not looking at me.

"Are you building something?"

"Nope."

Fitzy pulls out the hankie, and wipes his brow with a grown-up sigh. I decide to perch myself on the ground, letting him know I'm not giving up.

He bends over slowly, his tongue hinged over his upper lip, and he picks up a rock, groans, musters up his nine-year old might, and lifts it over his head. I'm about to rush to him, terrified that the rock will drop to his head, but something tells me to sit it out, let him do it, and pray instead.

His thin, taut arms are shaking under the weight of the rock, as he takes careful aim and heaves it toward the ground with a deep grunt. It's a man sound, not a boy's, and in it I hear something that frightens me, like a fury too large to be inside his small bones.

As the rock lands with a muffled thump, and dirt scatters, Fitz quickly runs, grabs the hose, and sprays a hard stream of water at his target.

He digs his little toes into the muddy mess, drops onto his hands and scoots up the incline to inspect what I now see is a battered and drowned population of ants. This patch of hill is covered with mounds of ant homes.

"Oh, you're killing them, huh?" I say, trying to disguise the wad of worry about to spit out of my mouth.

He wipes his murky hands across his jeans and looks back at me —blankly.

"Your turn," he says, and skims down the hill quickly.

I follow his lead. He points to the rock he's chosen for me. I grunt, just like him, as I raise it toward the sky. I take careful aim at the village of hopeless innocent women and children ants below, and push with all my might. Fitzy leaps, his legs shaking, and he squeals frantically, finishing off my air strike with a flood of water.

By the time we obliterate the last village, we are both mud and sweat-soaked, our energy spent. The hill is pocked with big rocks, and streams of dead ants slowly ooze down the hill on rivulets of mud.

"Wanna put Dad's rocks back now?" I ask.

Fitz shrugs his shoulders.

"*We* might get in trouble if *we* don't," I add. He doesn't respond, just stares at his labor. "We can walk to Tug's after we finish, I'm buying."

"It's gonna rain," he says, "so we gotta hurry."

We walk barefoot to Tugs, through the field behind the church, where Miss Cook's laugh rose like a balloon.

Fitz got a Slo-Poke sucker and Mountain Dew, so I got the same, feeling a need to mirror him, if only to help me feel closer. I want to crawl inside his head, his body, track that fury down like a cop searching for a criminal.

Heavy clouds begin colliding and forming in the sky above. We sprawl on the grass and watch them roll over us, both of us dazed, our tongues wrapped around the sweet caramel and chocolate.

"Guess what?" Fitz whispers, bouncing the cold bottle of Mountain Dew on his tummy.

"What, Fitz?"

"Now that we killed those ants, the grass will grow. They've been eating dad's seeds."

"Oh," I say, "is that so?" I don't want to utter a word about the robins and sparrows, for fear Fitz will want to exterminate them too. "That's really smart, Fitz."

He's staring up at the sky. He scrunches his brow, child cogitating. He points up. "That's the kind of cloud I am."

The sky has darkened. A large coal black mass is spreading, casting a long shadow over the field where we lie.

"What kind is that?" I ask.

"A nimbus," he says. "They bring the storm, when you hear thunder and stuff, it comes from there."

"Where did you learn that?" I ask, a slight quiver in my voice.

"They bring hail too," Fitz says, "sometimes as big as a softball." His face is still blank.

"Why do you want to be a nimbus cloud?"

He glares up at the gray and says, "Cuz people get scared of 'em, and don't like to see them coming."

Drops of rain start falling, sloppy wet drops, enough to camouflage the pools of water forming in my eyes. That wad of worry in my mouth bubbles as I take in a big swig of the yellowish soda.

"There was big hail last month," Fitz says, "and I tried to catch 'em and put 'em in a jar, but they melted too fast."

"Too bad, Fitz," I say, opening my mouth for rain, to erase the syrupy sweet taste of the Mountain Dew, "I'd liked to have seen them."

A crack of lightning hits, so loud my ears feel as if they've been whacked. Fitz doesn't flinch. "We better get home, Fitz," I say, as the sloppy wet drops thicken, pouring down and stinging my arms as they hit.

"Let's race!" he squeals, and darts quickly ahead.

I run faster than I ever remember running, just so I can keep up with Fitz, stay at his side, feel his body fly through the air next to mine. When we hit the porch, both of us collapse in a heap, breathless and drenched. Fitz is finally smiling, but something is different, even his smile seems stiff.

I leave the next day. I wait an extra two hours for Fitz to get home from altar boy practice so I can say goodbye. The only info I could pry out of Mom is that Fitz got caught stealing an issue of *National Geographic* from the library. An issue about clouds. Father Francis had him clean the rectory for four

Saturdays in a row as his punishment.

I'm picking through my mom's makeup bag when I hear Fitz come home. His steps rush up the stairs, into his bedroom, where Joseph used to sleep, and I hear the door slam.

"Fitzy," I say, knocking on his door, "it's Mia, I'm going now."

He doesn't respond. My hand is on the knob, I turn it slightly, and it's locked.

"Fitz, I gotta go, but I'll come back soon, or maybe you can come see me, how's that sound?" Still, nothing. "I love you, Fitzy."

On the drive back to school, I think about Fitzy, and wish that he was three again, and he needed me to help him go to the bathroom, and I could sit cross-legged and waiting, watching his feet dangle and swing above the floor, as we sang, *merrily, merrily, life is but a dream.*

Seven

James and I are pulling an all-nighter for exams. It's the last stretch before our Go West freedom ride to California.

I've got my nose stuck in a book: *Abnormality and the Life Cycle*. We're in Dr. Rothman's advanced seminar, and in addition to the exam we have to write our own psychological theory. I'm calling mine *Meaning and the Accumulation of Experience*. So far, all I've got is the title.

I'm underlining in dark blue what I've already highlighted in pink. James is dancing around the room to the radio and balancing his textbook on his head, believing he can absorb the material. The DJ breaks in and tells us that John Lennon has just been shot. He's dead. James stops dancing. I stop underlining, and the radio gently weeps, "Hey Jude."

It's the forty-five record that Joseph played for my parents. He brought his phonograph into the kitchen while we were getting ready to eat. Beef stew over rice.

"Mom, Dad," he says excitedly, "I want you to hear this."

There's a lot of commotion in the kitchen. A flurry of voices competing for attention: "Pass the stew. Get the milk. I don't have a fork. Hush up you twins, or else!"

The song begins. My dad freezes, midbite on a chunk of dripping beef. My mom pauses too, just as she's about to pour me a glass of milk.

You were made to, go out and get her, remember to let her under your skin, then you'll begin, to make it better.

We are all silent as church pews, holding ourselves still. I'm leaning my head against my mom's pregnant belly, wondering if the new baby inside could feel us linked by the sound. The baby's going to be called Fitzgerald or Jacqueline, after the Kennedys.

And anytime you feel the pain, Hey Jude, refrain, don't carry the world upon your shoulders. . .

Joseph is standing by his record player, a light of ease and joy in his eyes. Just last night was the big fight between him and Dad about his hair. He's letting it grow straight, and it just brushes slightly onto his shoulders. My dad is threatening to take him to the barber this weekend.

Joseph argued that Brother John at church has long hair and

64

a beard. My dad called him a hippie, not a priest. I love Brother John. He picked me to read the words to "Bridge Over Troubled Water" during the students' mass this month. He looks kind, like Jesus, not scary, like Father Francis.

Then the song builds, growing louder, less restrained, full of some kind of erupting feeling that makes us kids squeal inside. The Beatles scream, *Judy, Judy, Judy, Judy, Yow! Yow!*

My dad clamps his teeth on the chunk of beef. "I've heard enough," he says, chewing. "Turn that thing off."

Mom pours the milk in my glass. "That's a real pretty song, Joseph," she murmurs to the pitcher of milk, not looking at Dad.

"Sit down now, we forgot to say grace," my dad says. I'm pushing all the peas in my stew to one little pile at the side of my plate. Joseph slumps in the chair next to me.

"Bless us, oh Lord, and these thy gifts," we pray in unison.

Joseph, head bowed, glances over at me and winks. "Which we are about to receive." I wink back, and feel a funny glee run down my spine. "Through Christ, our Lord. Amen."

After we eat the stew, my mom dishes out German chocolate cake, and Paul starts humming, real soft at first, "Nah, nah, nah, na-na-na, nah." Joseph joins, then me, and Beth. The twins are smooshing their cake all over the trays on their matching high chairs.

My dad rolls his eyes, smiles, then pushes away from the table carrying his cake and coffee into the living room where Walter Cronkite's voice is droning gravely about a faraway war.

Mom rubs her belly, standing over us as we continue the collective hum. We fill up with cake; Beth and I do the dishes; the boys take the trash out; and we retreat to our rooms waiting for a kiss on the forehead, "Night punkin." These thy gifts.

James and I curl up on the couch in our living room. We light candles, share a joint, and listen to the radio throughout the night. People gather in New York's Central Park. "*All we are saying, is give peace a chance,*" they chant, over and over, pounding sticks and spoons, beating a rhythm of hard sorrow.

I can feel that ache inside; it swells with a craving, a frightened loneliness, even though I'm being held by James, my one best friend.

I see my mom and dad curled up on the floor, drained of their faith in an instant. Paul is wandering out in the world like a migrant worker searching for life. I'm having a hard time remembering his face.

I want to steal a cigarette from Joseph, find his frayed leather bracelet, buried in my shoebox of fragile mementos. I want to stoop low in Joseph's closet with my eager fingers paging through the books we shared. I want the flowers on his grave to disappear, the broken circle, like a dinner plate, repaired easily with glue. In this awful moment, I have an ominous feeling that the road ahead is more menacing than promising.

I think of Miss Cook and the giddy high tingle in my body when we kissed, the enormous rush of a wave when Mandy put her mentoring tongue in my mouth. More than anything, I want a woman to court and spark, and I know from my bones out, James wants to spark a man. These are the secrets we haven't yet spoken to each other.

As if my pores have been oozing all these thoughts, James draws me closer, my legs wrap around his, and we grope one another like pillows, suck with our mouths, pacifying our bodies' hungers. "I love you, Smudge," James whispers. His glimmering sapphire eyes are so welcoming, and I still want to wrap them in a bandana and carry them in my pocket.

When he falls asleep, I watch him dream, and I sit in the dark trying to imagine no heaven, no hell below, above us only sky.

Dull and exhausted, James and I trudge into Dr. Rothman's class in the morning, just as she's handing out the exam. Her tightly curled ball of gray hair is mussy, her sweater wrinkled, and one of her orthopedic shoes is untied. It looks like she's been up all night too.

She places the exam face down on my desk and for a moment we look at each other and she pats my hand. I turn it over and there's one question: "Select a Beatles song and analyze it by discussing elements of human development. Cite references from the text."

There are places I remember, all my life, though some have changed. . .

The last stop before California is my high school reunion. James is my date, and I know he'll be the most beautiful man there. My parents are leery of James. They sat me down and talked about the sacrament of marriage, how they didn't have sex until their wedding night, and that night, before they consummated it, they asked God to bless their union.

"Of all our kids, Maria, we expect you to use good judgment," my mom said.

"We're just going to share an apartment in L.A.," I said. "That's all, just roommates."

My dad huffed and puffed. "I know men, and they don't just share apartments with women, they have sex on their minds."

"Why buy the cow if you can get the milk free?" my mother added.

"Which one of us," I asked, "is supposed to be the cow?"

That didn't go over too well.

"Can't you find a couple of nice gals to live with?" my dad pressed.

"I'd love to, Dad, and maybe once I'm in L.A., I will find the right woman for me to live with." I'm skating on thin ice, and loving it. "I promise both of you, I'll look for *gals* when I get there."

"Sex!" my dad insisted. "Sex is all that young man has on his mind."

What they don't know is that James and I figured it out. We know we come from the same tree and we're going to L.A. to find our fruit.

My reunion is being held in St. Gerard's cafeteria. James is wearing a pair of leather pants and a white T-shirt with a deep blue vest. He looks gorgeous, and I'd have probably worn sweats if it hadn't been for him.

Instead, he put an outfit together for me: His cowboy boots with extra socks stuffed into the toe. A pair of tight Levis, and a white sleeveless T-shirt with one of his purple vests. I had the vest all buttoned up and James shook his head in dismay. "Show off those boobs," he said. "The women will die when they get a look at those." And because I was feeling sentimental, I wore Mandy's Bedroom Rouge Velour lipstick.

For the first time in my life, I feel my sexual appeal is truly enhanced. Dr. Mark Goodman would be proud. When we walk into the cafeteria, arm in arm, I feel downright cocky. I have my line rehearsed: "This is my boyfriend, he wants to be an actor, we're going to live together in Los Angeles."

The cafeteria is dark with a swirling ball of light hanging from the ceiling, throwing bullets of color all over the room. My high school chums are awkwardly bouncing up and down to the music, and suddenly I'm feeling sick.

I start to turn around, but James grabs my arm tight. "C'mon Smudge, you're the best looking woman in the room, be proud of yourself." He presses his lips to my cheek.

Dave Martino rushes toward me and I slam my mouth shut to avoid a repeat of his peanut butter tongue smearing my lipstick. "Dave," I say, "how are you?"

"Maria, you look awesome," he says. Dave hasn't grown much since high school, except pudgy around the center. We slow-dance together and I learn he's selling La-zy Boys at his dad's store. He presses his body close to mine. My crotch is about five inches above his hard on.

James saves me from Dave's erection and we slip out to the field behind the church and smoke a joint.

"I hated it here," I say.

James takes a long toke off the joint and holds his breath in as the blue of his eyes catches bits of moonlight.

"It's gonna be great in L.A., right?" I ask. He bends down, picks up a lone dandelion, and hands it to me.

"Smudge, we're adventurers, Huckleberry friends, we're gonna find love in L.A." He smiles and drapes his arm around my neck. "Let's go dance," he says.

I slip my fingers in his belt loops.

When we walk back in, the DJ is playing "How Deep is Your Love," and I think of Horace's long dark fingers slipping inside of me. Then, I almost pass out.

"What is it, Smudge!?" James is holding me up. Across the room, Miss Cook is serving fruit punch. It was her laugh I heard first, that big laugh of hers that slammed the wall like a basketball bomb against my heart.

"Oh my god," I gasp. "It's her, Miss Cook is here."

James looks across the cafeteria. "Well, Maria, I think there's someone you need to go see." He nudges me. "Don't worry about me, I've got my eye on a couple of cute football players." He nudges me again.

I slowly move through the bouncing bodies. An invisible string pulls me toward her. Our eyes lock. I reach my hand out to her and Miss Cook hands me a glass of punch. Boom boom boom goes my heart. Ping ping ping between my legs.

"Maria," she says, "I was hoping you'd be here."

(I love you, Miss Cook.) "Me too," I squeak, "I mean, you too, I was hoping you'd be here, Miss Cook."

Her soft brown eyes light up. "Call me Pam," she whispers. Gulp gulp gulp goes the punch.

James practically squeals when I tell him Miss Cook invited me over. He takes the keys to our motel room and says, "Now, Smudge, play a little bit hard to get, but not too hard, have a ball with the teacher." We hug then, holding on for those extra moments, and he says, "I love you, my Huckleberry friend."

When I walk into Miss Cook's apartment, I go straight to her bathroom and rummage through the cupboard. The bottle of Musk Oil is gone. Angela left Miss Cook, I mean, Pam, for a basketball player, some big gal named Hilda from Kalamazoo.

When I enter the living room, Miss Cook has lit candles all over. The music is turned low. It's Helen Reddy's greatest hits. She hands me a glass of wine, and we sit on the love seat.

I feel so filled up with words and they tumble out like gymnasts, twirling and spinning in the air. She listens so intently, and when she laughs, she dips her head back slightly, and I want to plant my mouth on her neck.

She asks me real important questions about life: the mountain, the rock, the push, the meaninglessness. I discover that lesbians *and* people with large pores discuss these things.

At around four in the morning, a shift occurs. Her hands begin massaging my legs, my arms, as if that's what her hands were meant to do. I want to crawl inside her eyes and swim.

Boom boom boom between my legs. At four-twenty, she leans toward me and kisses my lips, lightly at first, Deep Bordeaux meets Bedroom Rouge, and then her tongue presses into my mouth, and I can feel it, a lesbian is pushing through the birth canal.

Our tongues play with each other like long lost pals. Our shirts levitate right off our backs and drop to the floor.

When she presses her breasts to mine, I feel quaked. I am Lake Superior! I scream in my head.

She sucks and licks and twirls my nipples. The little bunnies never knew they were destined for such a wild ride. Every pore in my body is a bell being lifted and struck.

I slip my jeans off. Miss Cook slides her hand down and murmurs a huge sigh, "Ohhhh, soo wet." Before I know it, Mona and Deep Bordeaux are getting acquainted.

Helen Reddy is singing, "You and Me Against the World," for the tenth time, and I'm gyrating under Miss Cook's, I mean, Pam's tongue, and for a split second I flinch when the little girl's high voice on the record says to Helen, "Tell me again, mommy." A flicker of shame.

Then, from my belly, up my throat, into the air comes a gruntish moan, a sound I've never even imagined, and I cum!!

I sob, like a baby swatted on the ass. Pam wraps herself around me like a blanket, "It's okay, sweetie, it's okay," she says.

I guess she knows it's my first *real* time. We kiss and kiss and do it again and again. I'm happy as a grass-fat cow, spilling with free milk.

In the morning, I'm wide awake as Miss Cook sleeps. I'm wondering what I can put in her bathroom cupboard. A half-used bottle of Mandy's foundation. The Blue Jean perfume Fitz gave me for graduation. My lipstick collection.

When she opens her eyes, she smiles and asks when I'm leaving for L.A., and maybe she could come out to visit sometime.

(I don't want to go to L.A. anymore. I'm in love.) "Tomorrow, I mean, today, I leave with my friend today."

"Too bad," she says. "I guess we'll have to plan a rendezvous."

You and me against the world sputters through my head. I'm suddenly feeling sick, like I've eaten a rotten peanut. I jump out of bed.

"Will you look at the time," I say, gasping at the clock like Dr. Rothman.

I want her to ask me to stay. I go to the bathroom and swipe a sample-size bottle of Jean Naté.

We hug and kiss at the door, and almost end up on the floor, but I pull away. "I need to leave," I say. "Bye Miss, I mean, bye Pam."

I stop off at Joseph's grave. The air is chilly and I plop down on the grass, a thin crunchy layer of a September frost. There are no flowers keeping him company. I hum a few bars of Hey Jude and leave.

It's a Sunday morning. Beth is probably at Tug's, eating a dozen Hostess donuts. My parents are asleep. Did they lick each other in the night?

Fitzy has quit being an altar boy. Father Francis told my parents that Fitzy was deeply disturbed. Fuck Father Francis and his sour old self. Fitzy listens to Alice Cooper all the time. He didn't come to my graduation, he just sent the bottle of perfume with my parents, and so far, this visit, he's avoided me.

My mom and dad have thrown up their hands. They say for a twelve-year-old, he's become nothing but trouble. He may have to go to a special school on a short bus.

I stood outside his bedroom door yesterday. He was blasting his stereo and inside I could feel it, a storm cloud so immense and threatening that I didn't want to go near him. Just like he said about the nimbus, "People don't want to see them coming." Fitz has become an empty jar filled with hail, and I don't know how to get him to melt.

When I get to the motel room, James is still asleep. I sit on the bed and he scooches over to make room for me. "How was it, Smudge?" he asks groggily.

"It was wonderful, James, I'll tell you all about it, but I need to shut my eyes."

I curl up in his arms and just a few drops fall down my cheeks, as I slip into dreams, imagining no heaven.

We took off in the morning and drove fast out of Michigan. We whizzed past grazing grass-fat cows that stood huddled on piles of browned leaves that carpeted the fields awaiting fire's smoke. Along the freeways, the bare branches of maples and oaks stabbed at the gray sky. They looked like hungry arms reaching toward the low, rain-heavy clouds. They made me sad. I felt hungry too, grasping onto Miss Cook, wanting to be fed.

Eight

I knew Peter would love to hear my Paulette supernova bed-post adventure. Peter appreciates a good trashy story. We're at the French Marketplace, a busy West Hollywood diner filled with queers, drag queens, and old Jewish ladies.

I tell Peter about my San Francisco treat *before* Christie arrives. She doesn't like to hear about my experiences with other women. Her main interest in my life is to point out that I have "issues:" intimacy issues, sexual issues, family issues, codependency issues, death issues, issues about my issues.

"You didn't have her do *anything* to you?" Peter asks in disbelief.

"Nothing, just a peck on the cheek," I reply.

"I don't believe you," he says, as Christie slides into her seat.

"Sorry I'm late guys, we're planning a fund-raiser for the Hate Crimes National Committee," she says.

Peter is scheming, I can tell by the shit-eating smirk he's wearing. "Don't go there, queen!" I threaten. He loves to stir up Christie's righteousness and get me in trouble.

"Christie," Peter chirps, "I want to ask you a hypothetical question."

I wallop his shin under the table. He doesn't flinch.

"If you were with a gorgeous, brainy beauty and she was willing to do anything your little box of delight wanted, would you go for it?"

Christie's face sags in that way that announces the unfortunate arrival of moral authority. "Number one, Peter, your statement is sexist and you are objectifying the act of lovemaking, making it sound like some kind of sport. I decline to answer your question."

I'm sketching on my placemat, hoping to stay as far away from this conversation as possible. I've got a pretty decent likeness of Mona in a casual pair of slacks. Underneath I write: "Mona wore khakis!"

Christie glares at Peter like a librarian. "Listen," she says, "we're starting a fund for Timothy Michael, he was the guy killed in Maine, we're trying to force the police there to investigate his death as a gay bashing, and I'd like to ask you two to help organize with me." Peter and Christie keep talking, while I draw furiously.

Now, I've got Mona on a little red scooter, whizzing past smiling grass-fat cows in the Italian countryside. She's wearing a white nun's habit, her sleeves flapping like peace flags in the wind. A guitar is strapped to her back and she's singing: "Domineeca, neeca, neeca!" The Singing Vagina.

"Sure, Christie, I'll help," I say, "it's an important issue." I'm relieved to change the subject.

"Speaking of issues," Peter sings, "how *was* your trip to San Francisco, Maria? You haven't even talked about it."

"Yeah, Maria," Christie chimes in. "Did you do anything interesting?"

T.J., our waiter, swoops up and, as usual, demands we order. "What do you want, I don't have all night, I've got plenty of customers willing to eat and pay and leave, not wait for latecomers to arrive!" He runs his hand through Christie's hair.

"Sorry, T.J.," Christie replies, as she places a flyer in his apron pocket, "it's a worthy cause."

"Don't worry, doll," T.J. swoons, "I got to hear all about Maria's little buttery French roll spinning on the bedpost in San Francisco, oui, oui!!"

Christie makes that noise. (Fuck you. I'm disappointed. You're so pathetic.)

I've sketched Mona in black, on a country road that runs along a bleak and dismal field, her little hands are pasted to her face, and she is wailing. It's an existential moan of deep despair. The Vagina Scream.

After dinner I go home and take a long, soothing bath. I linger in the bubbles, shave my legs until they're shimmering and smooth. I cut my toenails and then decide to clip my pubes, slowly. I slide into a dreamy state, so much so, that I forget what I'm doing and I gaze down at my pubes through the hot steam and staring back at me is the head of Sinead O'Conner.

I towel off, apply lots of cream to my legs, powder my ass and under my breasts, and slip on a pair of your flannel boxers, Cup. I climb under the sheets, saying to myself, "Self, let's get all bunchy under the covers and get a good night's sleep."

The cool sheets greet my warm body like old dear friends. "Self," I say, "let's just enjoy the silence."

Sadie and Molly are in the kitchen, asleep on the floor. I can hear Sadie snoring.

"Self, aren't we content, don't we enjoy the quiet time? Happy happy happy."

(No significant or meaningful thoughts about you, Cup. Your lips, your long legs, that damned sweet face. No thoughts about Sinead all fresh and powdered. No thoughts of the Magic Wand muscle massager slash vibrator I purchased this morning at Thrifty's making sure the checker saw me rubbing my sore neck whilst scrunching my brow in pain as I handed over my American Express card. No, none of this.)

I grab *Portnoy's Complaint*—it's still whining on my nightstand.

I open it up to no place in particular. A section called, "THE MOST PREVALENT FORM OF DEGRADATION IN EROTIC LIFE." Mr. Portnoy is lying in bed reading Freud and whacking off. *"Yes, there in my unbuttoned pajamas, all alone, I lie, fiddling with it like a little boy-child. . .tugging on it, twisting it, rubbing and kneading it, and meanwhile reading spellbound through Contributions to the Psychology of Love."*

My free hand slides across your—*the* empty side of my bed where I had casually placed the muscle massager after plugging it in to make sure the electrical components were sound.

So, I'm reading the book, whine, whine, whine, and I slide my palm a little further and casually clasp my hand around the sleek handle of Magic Wanda.

I flip the switch, to low, and the speeding hum begins, the comforter shimmies, I read, Sadie continues snoring, drip drip drip from the bathtub faucet.

Wanda shudders in my grasp, I flip the switch again, to high, having surpassed *low* years ago. We move closer. The erotic thudding of my heart fills the room.

I casually raise my leg like a drawbridge for her, closer, slowly, turn the page.

Twenty minutes later I flip off the switch. Drip drip drip from the faucet. Snore snore snore, Sadie *and* Mona. I stare at the page before my eyes, seething.

I glare down between my legs and see Sinead holding a picture of the Pope and I tear it to shreds. Wanda goes back to Thrifty's tomorrow. The drawbridge closes.

"Don't play me for a fool," Mona echoes from afar.

Cup, if you've ever spent twenty minutes with a Magic Wand burning between your legs with nary a ping, then you know it's bad—really bad.

God knows what slime you're staining the sheets with. Some boozed up broad-minded bisexual who can only suck back with vodka on her tongue? Or that loony artist who paints eggs gleefully sliding down fallopian tubes? Or, is it that old Dr. Virginia Hamlin? Oh, how I hate her let me count the ways. Your aged college professor who took you under her claws when you were a freshman.

I hate her blue-blood East Coast attitude. How she glared at me behind her bifocals when she came to visit us, letting me know she's sucked your clit too, but her lips were more refined, literary, nay, genteel, than my old white trash mouth.

She said her dog was "hirsute."

"Come again," I replied.

Then, you leaned over and whispered in my ear, "It means hairy."

I looked at her sagging face and said, "Like your upper lip, Virginia?" Okay! I know I was *way* out of line, but her goddamed dog was *shaggy*! Like the movie. They didn't call it "The Hirsute Dog."

Vagina Ham. The old gray mare, she ain't what she used to be. Sucking on a couple of dried up old prunes imitating labia? Where the hell *are* you Cup?

Molly farts in the kitchen. I throw caution to the wind. No more pussyfooting around with technology, time to tug, twist, rub, and knead.

I let my fingers creep slowly down the flannel shorts. It's a little startling at first, as if I'm palming an eighteen-year-old boy's head at boot camp. I lazily circle and circle, round and round.

For whatever reason, Roberta Flack pops into my head. *Strumming my pain with my fingers.*

This is useless. There is not going to be a sudden unexplainable brightness of a star, no supernova, not even a bitsy flying flicker from a bad match.

I'm lying in bed whacking off reading about Mr. Portnoy lying in bed whacking off reading about Freud who was probably whacking off when he wrote his damned contributions to love.

I pick up the phone. "Come spoon with me," I say.

Christie hesitates, still peeved, I'm sure, about Paulette in San Francisco. "I'll be right over," she says.

Sometimes there is God. God like a gust of wind, sudden and brief. Christie and I spoon. Snoring Sadie and farting Molly lean against us in bed. They are all breathing, sleepy and deep, while I watch them, wide awake, feeling grateful; my crotch, raw and itchy.

I wish you were here, Cup. I'd ask you to tie me up. I can't ask Christie to do this. For her, bondage equals oppression equals misogyny equals satanic ritual abuse. I never argue with her politics. I wish I could tell her what happened between us, Cup, but I'm afraid if I do, she'll go too.

I want to be tied up, Cup. You can even the score. Dish what's been dished out.

Tie me up, face down, my arms and legs outstretched just enough for my muscles to tighten, my joints to ache. I want you to put a gag in my mouth, shove it in deep enough so that my throat hurts, saliva drips from my wide-opened lips, my jaw locks and cramps.

I want you to leave me this way for as long as you want. Moments. Hours. Days. Once in a while, release the gag and drip cool drops of water into my mouth. Give me hope, puny hope, then shove the gag back in.

Say anything to me. Tell me I'm worthless, beautiful, stupid, brilliant, a fucking cunt. Whatever, it's all true at one time or another.

I want your tongue to trace trails on my body, like a homesteader heading West. Your teeth to plant in my skin, along the trails, marking territory, ownership, *this land is your land, this land is my land.*

Do whatever you want to me, and when you finish, say, "Goodbye my love." Then leave. Then come back. Then stay.

I have to move Molly out of the way. She's planted herself between Christie and me, nuzzled into our spoon like a knife.

I'm thinking of you, as I run my palm down Christie's back. Her spine is like a familiar book to me, like words caught forever in memory. Her cheeks are cool and I run my hand between her legs and she moans, already wet, even before I slip my fingers inside. My hand is still, her wetness seeps between my fingers, under my nails, salve on the palm. She squeezes and pulls, the way she does, like she'll never let go; a frightened child clutching a blanket to ward off the blackness in the night.

After she orgasms I watch her dreaming and I've got these

words looping through my brain. *Sail on silver girl. Sail on by. Your time has come to shine. All your dreams are on their way.*

"See how they shine!" Peter is showing me two glossy heart-shaped stones. He invited me over for breakfast. He got the stones from Lydia, a self-proclaimed healer who volunteers at Angel Food. When she's not lecturing or traveling or writing, then Lydia shows up to pass out meals to the dying.

"She handed them to me," Peter exclaims, "and told me she felt called, as if I needed them."

"Peter," I whine, "she's a hoax, a fraud, don't you know that?"

"Christie likes her," he relents.

"Oh, what an endorsement, Christie wraps garlic around her cat's neck to keep satanic abusers from kidnapping her!" I pound my fist on Peter's couch.

He's silent. I pick up my coffee mug and cradle it in my lap. "Look, Peter, I'm sure she meant well, but I've seen her praying over dying people who can't even speak. How the hell does she know they want her prayers?"

He's staring at the stones in his hand. "Maria," he says, quietly, with more fear in his voice then I've ever heard. "It's a bad day on Wall Street."

"What?" He puts one of the heart stones on my leg.

"My numbers are dropping like a bad day on Wall Street, the market's crashing. It's the Depression, when pathetic men fling themselves out of tall buildings."

I hold his hand.

"Mia, I want you to be my executor, for everything, you're my best friend and, in case I get sick, I want you to be there." He picks up a thick file of papers from the coffee table. "Everything's already drafted, I just need you to sign, if you want."

Peter's a lawyer with two specialties. He spends most of his time defending guys charged with lewd conduct. Guys who haven't learned how to discern a cop's dick from a fag's. And he drafts living wills for the dying.

He's looking me squarely in the eye, scanning my face for hesitation or lies.

"Sure," I say, "don't worry. I'll do it."

I'll do it, Cup. I'll check the color of his stool and urine.

I'll change his diaper and hide my gag response because the shitting is endless and I'm so tired of the smell. I rub Peter's leg. "I'll do it," I repeat.

"I'm going to work with her, Maria, just one session," he whispers.

I want to scream, no! I've come to see health care providers as cruise missiles dressed in white. Lydia, big blonde buxom straight Lydia, is worse. She's a stealth bomber with a halo and a smile promising eternal life for 120 bucks an hour. "Okay, sweetie," I say, "I'm here for you."

Suddenly, Peter jumps off the couch, shattering the sorrow that's wedged between us. "Wanna play cards?" he hoots. He rushes to his bookshelf, grabs a deck of cards and tosses them into the air. "Fifty-two pick-up!" he laughs, and the cards fly to the ceiling. On the face of them are fifty-two naked and buffed men and they swirl through the air and fall to the ground.

I join him on the floor and we roll over the cards, as if we're in a field of flowers, spinning with all those beautiful paper boys, and we laugh so hard we cry.

Nine

California is so unlike Michigan. Instead of being afraid that a mitten will clamp down on me and smother me to death, I'm afraid of brand new things. The speed of it all. The constant hum of patrolling helicopters, the frantic buzz on weekends that surrounds our apartment.

I'm up on the roof of our building. It's December and it's hot. I'm not used to L.A. yet. I'm tanning myself by the pool. A pool on the roof? That's as weird as stars in the ground—and L.A.'s got those too.

I hate tanning, but it has to do with being surrounded by palm trees, I feel I'm obligated, in some way, to lay out in the sun, though I hate the heat of it and the oily mess. It's late afternoon, so it's really a half-hearted sun.

James and I have been in West Hollywood for three months and I still don't have the courage to go to the only bar advertised for lesbians. The Palms. That's what I need—palms and lips and breasts.

James is waiting tables and I got a job as an editor for these really awful medical journals. Now, I stuff my brain with dull words and my body with donuts. This time, though, I'm not getting fat. I work out every day, do a thousand jumping jacks and jog with James down Santa Monica Boulevard. I'm depressed.

When we jog past the Palms, I can smell the scent of sweaty women tinged with smoke and beer. Like Jean Naté, it draws me, and I vow, each day, to take the plunge, walk in, sit at the bar, act like I know what I'm doing, and find anyone, except a man, wearing lipstick.

James and I are sharing an apartment. Below us is Matthew. He's taken us under his gay wing. He runs a little French restaurant on the boulevard where James works. Matthew reminds me of Brother John. He sorta looks like Jesus too. And he has the same warmth, a way of making you feel safe.

When I was in sixth grade, Brother John took us on a field trip to Michigan State's agricultural school. We learned that you have to plant corn close so they can pollinate, so they can grow. If you plant them too far from each other, they'll die. The leaves must touch. Then we went out to a huge field of corn and I wandered off alone, staring up at the enormous plants, making sure they were all touching.

Pretty soon, though, I got all turned around and mixed up and I couldn't find the rest of the class. I was sure they forgot me. I sat down, the giant stalks staring at me like monsters, like the apple trees in *The Wizard of Oz*. I covered my head with my hands because I was sure they were going to heave ears of corn at me like big yellow bullets. Then, like a miracle, Brother John appeared, and at first I really thought he was Jesus. He picked me up and carried me on his back and I got teased by the other kids, but that didn't matter, because I got to sit next to Brother John on the bus ride home.

That's how it is with Matthew. People want to be near him. In the restaurant, I watch him, and it seems that the moment he greets a customer or instructs an employee, he suddenly radiates, and those around him glow too. He's like a firefly. A sudden burst of humming light, just when it seems there's only darkness to latch onto.

Last night, I was all dressed and ready to go to the Palms, and I made it as far as the courtyard of our building, turned left, up the stairs toward the roof, instead of right, toward my car, and slumped down on a chaise lounge.

It was dark by the pool, and I was muttering vulgarities to myself, like "You chicken shit." I finished my tirade with, "I'll give you something to cry about," and like a sudden breeze, Matthew was there, with a glass of wine for me, a single rose, and a book of poetry.

"Maria, something told me you were up here," Matthew said, handing me the rose. "You look wonderful, are you going out?"

"No," I muttered, "I'm too chicken."

"Well," Matthew said, "I could use some company myself."

I immediately forgot all about my chicken-shit self. Matthew is like an older brother, the kind of brother that Joseph was, exposing me to new words and thoughts. I even get full access to Matthew's collection of books, and the best part is that no one can stop me from reading them.

"I have a poem I think is for you," he said. As he read, the words seemed to link us together like a new skin. "*I like for you to be still, and you seem far away.*"

Maybe it was his voice, how he handed each phrase to me

like a gift and for a few moments, I felt as if we had been lovers long ago. *"Let me come to be still in your silence."*

At the end I was crying. That longing inside of me spilled out and I told Matthew all about this woman I have a pathetic crush on. I don't think she knows I exist. There's a little flower shop in the lobby of the building I work at. Her name is Christie. I know that because I snuck a peek at her name tag while I pretended to be reading greeting cards. I also saw her do the sweetest thing. She clips the thorns off the roses. I melt.

I browse in her shop on my lunch hour. I wither when I watch her wrap bundles of flowers in paper. There's a soft butchness in her hands and when she lifts a heavy crate filled with potting soil, and the muscles in her arms flex, I want to be that crate. I want to be an earthworm in the dirt and get shoveled into a ceramic vase, have her dip her hands into the soil, and touch me. Instead, I creep out without saying a word.

"I'm thinking, Matthew," I said, "that sometime next week I'm going to actually buy some flowers from her, day lilies, or maybe lilacs. Next week, *for sure*. What do you think? What should I say to her?"

I was pulling the petals off the rose he gave me. Matthew reached over and laid his hand on mine. *"One word then, one smile, is enough*—she'll love you."

"Who do you like, Matthew?" I asked.

He blushed, pulled the last petal from my rose and whispered, "Peter."

"Peter?" I said. "He's a big flirt."

"I know, I know," Matthew said in dismay. "I'm sure there's some deep sick reason why I want him."

I'm surrounded by a lot of Peters in West Hollywood, patrolling gay men; tight-jeaned, muscled, and oozing a kind of rabid hunger. When I walk down to Matthew's cafe at night, I pass clumps of them, and they're hissing with a fierce pleasure, that scares and seduces me at the same time.

I feel invisible when I pass through, as if the presence of my breasts, my just being a woman, as opposed to just dressing like one, is as unimportant as a discarded cigarette butt. The entire street is like one massive erection, and from the bars, roaring rhythms spill onto the sidewalk like semen.

I always breathe a big sigh of relief when I enter the cafe because I'm welcomed here. James hoots when I walk in,

"Mia, my Huckleberry friend!" and he kisses me and orders me a basket of fried zucchini. Peter is the bartender slash law student, and he always has my white wine spritzer ready.

I sit at the bar huddled with a handful of old queens who feel as cast off by the buzzing frenzy as I do. And Matthew, with his hum of warm light, helps ease our loneliness; a loneliness that feels as permanent as a vital organ.

From up on the roof I can see the ocean. The sun is a huge flaming orange ball sliding low, succumbing to dusk. Down on my street, I see the form of an old man walking his dog. Both limp. Two young guys brush past him without a glance or a hello. The dog screams as the man jerks the leash hard because the poor dog stopped to sniff the remnants of another dog. That man wants to be sniffed too. The leaves from the palm trees spit and crackle in the hot wind. I want to lean over the edge of the roof, extend my arms out, and push the palm trees together, so they'll touch, so they'll grow.

The next week I linger in Christie's shop after work. Everyone is gone. "Take your time," Christie says, as she locks up and hangs the "closed" sign in the window.

I'm standing in front of a bunch of baby's breath. She's clipping the thorns off her roses, and I can feel my knees go slack.

"I hate baby's breath," I say, "especially in high school, for the stupid prom, all the stupid girls put it in their stupid piled high hairdos." I hope my dislike for the prom might give her a clue.

She laughs and says she feels the same way. "What kind of flowers do you like?" she asks.

I'm dumbstruck. All I can think of is the common ordinary kinds. Carnations. Marigolds. Roses. "Well, uh, I like," I fumble, "day lilies!" I hoot. My hands are so wet I can water the entire store.

She walks back into the cooler and comes out with a bunch of day lilies. She wraps them in newspaper—pages from the *Lesbian News.*

"Do you read it?" she asks, scanning my face for any hint of aversion.

The flowers are strewn before me on the counter. My fingers are nervously breaking off stems, pulling on petals. "Sure, all the time," I quiver.

"Maria," she says, "the lilies!"

(She knows my name.) My eyes bulge.

"Oh, your name," she smiles, "I have my ways. I've had my eye on you ever since I first saw you." I think she's blushing, although next to my heated face anyone would look downright ghostly.

(My eye on you. My eye on you.) I want to run home and tell James and Matthew, rush into the cafe and buy a round of drinks for the old queens.

"Come back to the cooler. We'll get more lilies, but no ripping." She takes my hand and leads me into the walk-in refrigerator. I'm sweating despite the brisk air blowing down on me.

One after another, she hands me day lilies, and they pile high in my arms and then, she turns, presses real close to me, and we kiss, the day lilies sandwiched between our breasts. Oh, to be a day lily.

Ten

"You have dogs, don't you Maria?" Sharon asks.

"Yes, two hounds, Molly and Sadie," I answer.

"Studies have shown," Lynn recites, "that single people should have an animal to love."

"Persons of age in rest homes too!" Sharon chimes in.

I'm struck with an image of Mona, haggard and hunched over in a wheelchair, a gob of saliva drips down her chin. She's discarded and ignored in a corridor filled with other dried-up prunes. In a place called Sunny Valley Old Genitals Home. I hope someone cares enough to hand Mona a little pussycat.

I'm at a workshop with Christie, it's one of Sharon's and Lynn's special weekend package deals. Two for the price of one. It's called, "Shun that Shame."

I'm here out of obligation. I feel every time I ask Christie to come over and sleep with me I owe her something. She finally stopped hammering me about the woman's grief group, so I didn't feel I could get away with saying no. It's that Vatican thing.

We have to focus on one incident in our lives where we felt total humiliation. They have developed a process they call "REWORD!" Relive Experience. Write Occurrence. Read. Dramatize.

Their theory is that by immersing oneself into the one memory as opposed to skimming over the vast array of shameful moments, you can get to the core, the kernel of shame and begin to heal.

First, we have to go around the room and talk about our fear in coming to the workshop.

"Tell us, Maria, what is it you fear most today," Sharon asks.

"Well," I say, "I fear most the fears I fear I'll fear far into the future." Sharon and Lynn nod their heads in therapeutic unison, as Christie jabs me with her elbow. She knows I'm joking.

Next, we have to write out the exact occurrence, in detail.

"This must be hard for you," Christie whispers to me, "you have so many issues."

That's when I decide to make up a story. I am not about to

spill my guts with these strangers, and especially not with Christie. Even though it's been over eight years since we were lovers, Christie somehow has appointed herself guardian over my psychological well-being. For eight years she has sent me every flyer announcing yet another workshop by Sharon and Lynn promising to get to the core of my pathology.

Here's my story of invented shame. *"I was eight years old and I was at church with my parents. I looked down at the floor, and stuffed under the kneeler, I saw a white envelope. I extended my little leg over and pushed the envelope toward me with my black patent leather shoe and dropped my coat over it. I reached down while everyone was saying the Our Father, and I slipped the envelope into my coat pocket.*

When I got home, I ran to the bathroom and opened it up and inside were four crisp dollar bills. On the envelope was written: Catholic Charities. The money was for the little black kids in Africa with swollen bellies who needed more bowls of rice. I kept the money. I tore up the envelope and flushed it down the toilet.

I went outside and played hopscotch with my little sister Beth and I was so excited. I had a secret. I took Beth to the candy store, Tug's, and I pulled out one of the dollar bills and she asked me where I got it and I told her I found it in the street and then bought her a huge amount of candy to shut her up.

I felt so guilty. I didn't know what to do. I went into the bathroom again and I tore up the rest of the dollar bills and flushed the green bits down the toilet and then I got real scared that the police could trace the bits of green to our house, our toilet, and my parents would get in real bad trouble for throwing money down the drain."

When it's my turn to dramatize my scene, I play the little girl in the pew. I play the eyes of Jesus looking down at her from the crucifix. I start really cooking as the torn-up envelope and get a rousing round of applause on my dramatic interpretation of a toilet. When I get to the part with Beth, I suddenly feel totally responsible for her eating disorder. Buying her candy with my hush money. It's awful.

Next, we do the reliving part silently with a guided imagery called "A walk in the park in the dark to the shame." Then the group starts exploring my story, and I begin to feel woozy.

"What issues have emerged from this experience?" Lynn asks.

"Well," I said, "I feel this experience gave birth to many issues. Spiritual issues, money issues, of course, eating issues, ya' know, buying all that candy, the thrill of it, and of course, authority issues, fearing the police."

"And? And?" Christie presses.

My gut is heavy at this point, heavy like eating way too much Mexican food and wanting to vomit. I feel humilated. I'm lying to these people and some of them have cried for that little eight-year-old in patent leather shoes.

"Don't push, Christie," Sharon chides, "Let her go as deeply as she can."

I bolt from the room, rush to the bathroom, and throw up. I want to shred myself into little bits and flush me down the toilet. I need a Miss Cook to wipe my brow, to tell me it's gonna be okay, sweetie. I'm a sham at shunning the shame.

When I get back to the room, Lynn is leading the last exercise. The big reward part. Everyone is in a circle, and it's broken, because they've left a spot for me, and this makes me want to cry, or confess, but I do neither, I take my place, cross-legged, and close my eyes.

Lynn repeats, "See me, feel me, touch me, heal me." After her, each member is supposed to repeat it, individually, and then as a group. Over and over. See me, feel me, touch me, heal me. I lower my head when it's my turn, wave my hand as if I'm too pained to utter words.

The worse part is that I'm snickering. I actually want to laugh. I'm not stupid. I understand the process of defense mechanisms. That maybe I really am so filled with shame that I have to push it away and instead react inappropriately.

I glance over at Christie. She looks like she's praying. Another member is weeping. Sharon is barely able to eke out the words, she seems so moved.

Inside, I start to imagine a different exercise. All of us doing the hokey pokey, turning ourselves around. That's what it's all about. I have to suck my tongue like a hard candy so I don't burst.

Finally, it's over. My tongue is weary from being sucked and bitten.

Sharon and Lynn pull me aside, thank me for my honesty, and invite me to their lesbians-loving-lesbians workshop.

"Sometimes we make exceptions and let a single woman in," Lynn says.

"Oh, that's really great," I reply. I feel like something smeared; the worst kind of smudge; something vulgar, a gob of phlegm on a sidewalk.

"Most relationships," Lynn continues, "get to a point where the fear of abandonment leads to an even deeper fear of being swallowed up, which leads to an even deeper fear of annihilation of the self."

"Is that what happened with you and Cup?" Sharon asks. They both look up at me with mournful eyes.

"In a nutshell," I mutter.

Christie, bless her, slides up next to me.

"Christie," I gasp, grabbing her arm, "you gotta get me home, I don't feel so good."

"Take her home, Christie, and give her that massage," Sharon instructs. "It will help to release some of the feeling."

When we get in the car, Christie throws a pile of newsletters on my lap. I can feel her need to talk about the workshop, so I begin flipping through the pages.

She glances over at me as she drives, and points to the page. "That's the one, read it," she says.

When they discover his body, it is bloated from river water. His skull has been crushed with a blunt, hard object, probably a rock. His ribs were cracked and broken. His face was so badly beaten, it took the police two days to identify him. At first, they didn't report that he had also been penetrated anally with a large, sharp object, maybe a knife. He may have been dead before he fell off the bridge. He was twenty-seven years old. A hairdresser from Portland, Maine. Friends described him as fun-loving. He began the first AIDS support group in the state. Police conclude that it was probably a sex trick gone bad, or drug-related. His name is Timothy Michael. Hate Crimes Update

I want to change the channel, flip the switch, turn the page, but it's too late, the words are crawling through my brain like a worm: *May his soul and all the souls of the faithful departed, through the mercy of God, rest in peace.*

Still stuffed in my head are these old puny prayers for the dead. I need a squall of hope, a tsunami of faith, a gust of God. Even a fork in the road will do. This way or that? Some divide in the wood, so I can swerve off this path and head in a new direction. God, Cup, I miss them all so much.

I reach over and grasp Christie's thigh.

"Thanks," I say, "for making me pay attention."

"To what?" Christie asks.

"Being alive," I whisper, "just being alive."

I have Christie drop me off. I need to be alone and I'm feeling really guilty about lying at the workshop.

About four in the morning I wake up when I hear a loud banging on the front door. I was having a dream about Cup. We were up in San Francisco on the summit of Mt. Tamalpais, and we have a box filled up with someone's ashes, and we're supposed to toss them into the air, the trees, the ground blanketed with pine needles. I have the box cradled under my arm, and when I open it, the ashes are gone. The box is filled with lipsticks. Some red-faced hikers approach us. They all come up behind me as I'm scavenging through my collection. Deep Bordeaux. Bedroom Rouge Velour. Bubble-gum Gloss. Tropical Fruit. Autumn Smoke. Cup's Wine with Everything. They form a circle, lift me high up above their heads, and just as they're about to throw me off the summit, the banging wakes me.

I open the door and Peter flies past me and rushes to the bathroom. He smells like Tequila and smoke. Molly and Sadie sit outside the bathroom door as Peter wretches. I perch myself on the floor next to them and Sadie and I sigh; a sigh too deep for words.

I rap lightly on the door. "Peter, are you okay? Do you need anything?" It is quiet, all around us, I can't even hear the whir of the distant freeway.

He leans up against his side of the door. "Hey," he says, "I got laid tonight."

Sadie and I roll our eyes to the ceiling. Molly wags her tail as if to say, atta boy!

"Was it a date or a bush?" I ask.

"Just a fuck," he replies, "and I paid for it too."

"Peter, I'm going to make you some scrambled eggs and toast, then you're going to sleep on the couch."

Molly and Sadie follow me to the kitchen. I love how dogs just accept circumstances so easily. No fussing or arguing. As far as they're concerned, four in the morning is as good a time as any for table scraps.

Dog-being is better than human-being. Dogs are forgiving.

Humans remember and cling to the teeniest tiny detail of a
fight, a fear, a hurt. Not dogs. They aren't interested in ana-
lyzing, punishing, accusing, or replaying the events in super
slo-mo. Dogs are boundless love and tireless licking.

"Soft or hard?" I say, as Peter walks into the kitchen.

"He was hard!" he grunts.

"The eggs, Peter, the eggs."

Molly plunks her forepaws onto Peter's lap as he sits, her
tongue like a desperate salve facing a gaping injury. Sadie
drops to the floor at my feet.

"Do you have any aspirin?" Peter asks, his fingers rubbing
his temples so fervently a genie may pop out.

"On the counter," I point to the batch of medicines. All
painkillers and sleep agents. I've collected most of them from
the dead. It's a hobby, like my assortment of lipsticks, except
the medicines are more functional. I only use aspirin, but I like
having the strong stuff around, just in case life gets too thorny.

Peter is staring down at them as if he's struck gold. I walk
over with the pan of scrambling eggs and hand him the aspirin.
"Your head," I say sternly, "is drugged enough."

He drops four aspirins into his palm and sucks them down
quickly.

I scoop the eggs onto three plates. One for the dogs too.

"So, you get fucked lately?" Peter mumbles, a big gob of
eggs in his mouth.

My face sags like Christie. "Peter, please, it's four in the
morning, that's disgusting."

"Oh, get off it!" he grumbles. "Don't give me that
Pollyanna pure shit, I'm just asking if you've been *fucked*!" he
growls.

Yikes! Sadie creeps under my legs and rests her snout on
my foot. Peter is stabbing at his eggs, intent, it seems, on
wounding something. I'm too tired for this.

"Peter," I say carefully, like I'm about to dismantle a bomb,
"do you need something from me?" As soon as I say it, I know
I've snipped the wrong wire. I sound like Sharon and Lynn.

He leers at me, a sinister film coats his eyes.

"I don't need *anything* from *anybody*!!" His words are a
scalpel slowly incising my skin.

I want to pick up the plate of eggs he's scooping into his
mouth and throw it across the room. He's just a child launch-

Elise D'Haene

ing a tantrum. I try to focus on this thought to keep myself from splattering the walls with scrambled yellow goop. In this moment, I'm going to be a forgiving dog. But, I am *not* going to lick Peter.

I stand and carry my plate to the sink. "I'm going to bed now. You know where the blankets and pillows are."

He doesn't even look at me as I leave the kitchen. Molly and Sadie follow me to the bedroom. Both of them not wanting to get too close to the storm cloud brewing inside of him.

Peter is like Fitz in this way, with these sudden bursts of meanness, although Peter's bursts are usually diluted through a bad-boy sexual depravity. There were times when Peter would jam his obscene escapades at Matthew like a crude fist and I hated him.

I wake up to the sound of the freeway and a whirring helicopter nearby. It's dawn. Thin lines of light pour through the room with swirls of lazy dust circling within. I climb out of bed and slip my shoes on.

The three of us tiptoe quietly into the living room. Peter is asleep. For now, the nimbus inside of him has dissolved. Sadie is blocking Molly from jumping up onto the couch.

I bend down and lick Peter's forehead, "Sleep tight, punkin." As I lick, my tongue glides over a tiny nub. I gaze at it like a microscope. It could be a pimple, I think, just a pimple. I inspect his ears, his neck. I lift the blanket slowly and look at his ankles. Those lesions always seem to show up there first. There's two little purpling bumps, just like the one on his forehead.

I want to grab a deck of cards and toss them into the air. That's how this grief feels to me. Like a game of fifty-two pick-up. Each card is a different reaction, response. Coping with terminal loss is not like the books say. Not like some goddamned ladder with five simple rungs. Denial. Bargaining. Anger. Sorrow. Acceptance.

I hurry out of the house with Molly and Sadie at my heels. I haven't run in a long while, but it seems the only thing to do. If I can exhaust my muscles and my heart and fill my busy brain with mood-enhancing endorphins, then maybe I'll be able to just go to sleep. And if I can't, I'll use a chemical agent that will put me out for awhile.

Each fast step I take is a tossed playing card. Each playing

90

card is a response, a feeling, a reaction to death. I hear them in my head like a mantra: Denial. Anger. Bargaining. Sorrow. Acceptance. Numb. Fucked. Psychotic. Happy. Horny. Giddy. Suicidal. Homicidal. Grateful. Despairing. Lousy. Low. Shitty. Bored. Empty. Depressed. Prayerful. Loving. Really Fucked. Disgusted. Raging. Lonely. Overwhelmed. Really Horny. Disbelief. Mute. Miserable. Anguished. Panicked. Breathless. Blessed. Calm. Seething. Phoney. Relieved. Cursed. Horrified. Sad. Joyful. Sick. Guilty. Really Fucking Horny. Really Lonely. Really Fucking Lonely. Leave this Card Blank. Blank. Blank.

It's a vengeance run, and I round the corner and leap onto a dirt fire road that winds around the hills. Sadie and Molly are barely keeping up. I can hear their long tongues wagging and panting behind me. Sweat drips and my breasts are throbbing because I'm not wearing a bra. I feel as if I'm chasing something, the wind, maybe, or a gust of God.

I hit a dip and tumble headfirst into the dirt and my legs slam down on top of an overgrown cactus. Molly and Sadie collapse next to me.

A trail of blood eases down my shin, and Sadie laps it up with her long pink mother tongue. Her language. A dialect of stroke and suck. Our language, Cup—silence equals death.

"Anyone wanna play fifty-two pick-up?" I mutter to the unfolding smog, to the dry brush, to Joseph, to anyone, in case they're listening.

Eleven

I'm lying naked in bed, picking at my belly button. I'm supposed to be getting dressed for my dinner tonight. I'm back in the same apartment building I moved out of when Christie and I got together. It's been two months since I left her. James has his own one-bedroom next to mine. Matthew and Peter live together upstairs, not down, and I'm in a single apartment. Single. It's such a wicked word. I'd rather be known as efficient.

James is sitting on my bed rubbing my feet with rose oil. I'm staring at the postcard I got from Disneyland. In the photo is Minnie Mouse dressed as Cinderella. It's from Mandy. "God is Minnie Mouse," she wrote.

Mandy's been transferred from Disney World to Land. She's divorced from Clay and tracked me down through my mother. We're meeting for dinner tonight.

"Does she know you're gay?" James asks.

"Nope," I mutter, bending the postcard in half and digging it into my belly button to scoop out the lint.

"Well, Smudge, you never know, maybe she's a sister."

"I doubt it, she really liked sex with guys."

I still have the note she left on my bed when she eloped with Clay. It's in my mementos box, the paper frayed and thinned from age. "Mia, I love you, and you're a great kisser!"

"I'll help you pick out an outfit," James says, and he hops off the bed and begins pulling clothes out of the closet.

"I think, Smudge," James sings, "you should go for it. It can't hurt to have a litte creature comfort if Mandy's willing."

"We'll see," I sigh.

"I can come with you if you'd like," James says. His words are soothing, a quick spray of fast relief to my sore heart. He places my outfit on the bed, then lies down next to me. I wrap my arms around him and hold him close.

"I'll call you if I need to," I mutter. "Besides, I thought you had yet another date with this mysterious man I've never met."

"There's no reason for you to meet him," James says. "It's not love, Smudge, it's creature comfort."

"Yeah, but you must be developing toward some kind of relationship," I press.

"No, Smudge, we're just enjoying sex with each other," James says.

I grab his cheeks in my hand and hold his face close. "I spill every picayune detail of my love life, and you never tell me anything."

Even when we shared the same apartment I would hear James crawl in late at night with some guy and in the morning he'd be gone. Only traces of the encounter were left strewn across James' bedroom: empty wine glasses, lubricants, poppers, messy sheets.

"When I fall in love, Smudge, you will be the first to know." James pecks my forehead and leaps off the bed. "Enjoy yourself, my Huckleberry friend, don't take it too seriously. Remember," he says standing at the door, "creature comfort, it's natural."

I'm meeting Mandy at Matthew's restaurant. I need to be close to my friends, and I'm hoping she'll just figure out I'm gay, on her own, so I don't have to make some big old declaration of my sexuality. I'm feeling insecure enough as it is.

Thank God Christie had already moved her flower shop to another building *before* we broke up. I don't know what I'd do if I had to pass by her every day at work.

She calls me once a week to lecture me about my problem with intimacy. Christie says I'm ambivalent about commitment due to some unresolved issues with my family of origin. It's annoying how she can string a few words together like a psychological fortune cookie. My entire existence is abbreviated and I always end up feeling like a rotten peanut. Ate it anyway.

Now there's a pharmacy in her old space, and sometimes when I'm pathetically sentimental, I go in and browse, replaying every detail of our first kiss. I stand in front of the adult diaper section where the walk-in refrigerator used to be, where the day lilies were squashed between our bodies.

I decide to get to the restaurant early, sit at my table and try to appear as self-confident as I can. I wonder what Mandy looks like. How has she changed? I've finally lost the extra twenty pounds I was carrying back in college. My hair isn't all split ends anymore. Besides the dark circles under my eyes from lack of sleep, I think I've improved.

"Hey, Maria," Matthew says as I walk in, "I've got your

table all ready." He slides his hand around my waist. Matthew is getting really thin. He says his stormy relationship with Peter has made him an emotional bulimic.

I don't understand why they stay together. I hear their rumbling arguments above me. Peter tossing lies at Matthew like garbage. Matthew taking it until finally he snaps and all that warm light inside of him flares like a brush fire. Besides lies, mostly what Peter gives to Matthew is the latest sexually transmitted disease. Herpes. Gonorrhea. Anal warts.

"You need to eat more, Matthew," I say as I slide into the booth. "Your likeness to Jesus is bordering on the crucified version."

"Well," he laughs, "if Peter would stop betraying me, I may not need that hammer and those nails after all."

I'm sipping my wine when Mandy walks in. I recognize her right away. She still looks like an advertisement for Revlon's Bedroom Rouge Velour. Matthew approaches her and leads her toward me. My legs start shuddering under the table.

"Mia!" she squeals, "you look great!" She leaps at me, throws her arms wildly around my neck and kisses my cheek.

Matthew drapes a napkin onto her lap as she sits. "Mandy, I'd like to buy you a drink," he says. "Maria's guests are VIPs here."

She beams. "Gin martini, dry, two olives," she orders. "What a great restaurant, Mia! God, you look fabulous."

"You too," I say, placing my hands on top of my knees to keep them from quaking the table.

Mandy has stopped smoking joints, but she sure puts away a lot of gin. Throughout dinner, she oozes closer and closer to me in the booth. She uses her hands to punctuate her words, slapping my leg, squeezing my arm, tapping my shoulder. At one point, she holds a plump olive between her teeth, pushes out the pimento with her tongue, then briskly slips the olive into my mouth. Here's the strange part, I didn't want to be that pimento.

We leave the restaurant and go back to my apartment building and I take her up to the roof.

"I love your friends!" she exclaims, dripping her body onto a chaise lounge. "Maria, are you what they call a fag hag?"

I'm unfolding a chair and practically drop it in the pool. "No, Mandy, I'm more like a fag than a hag." I keep futzing with the chair, my back to her, waiting breathless for a response.

"Let's swim," she says, stripping her dress off in record time and diving, naked, into the pool.

She emerges, glistening and wet, and I'm thinking this is a real life "Bo Derek" moment. The only problem is that not once through the entire evening have I felt even the slightest ping of attraction. Not even when she glossed her lips at the table.

I lay back on the chaise lounge she's abandoned. "I'm not ready for a swim," I say, as she bobs up, then dives back in the water like a dolphin, her pale butt sailing above the blue for a split second.

Someone has left a towel hanging on the railing and I grab it when Mandy climbs out, all soppy and gin-buzzed. I close my eyes and hold it out, but she grabs my hand, not the towel, and spreads my legs to sit down between them.

"So, Mandy," I chatter, "do you still believe in God?" I'm hoping to derail the train that's fast approaching.

"Mia," she drools, inching closer, "I've always remembered our time." Her hand is coasting up my leg.

I feel like a cat staring at curiosity. "Mandy," I chatter, "don't you want to see James?"

"I came to see you," she says. Before I can ponder this way or that, Mandy's tongue is coming at me as quickly as that olive. She tastes like gin and chlorine, and despite my misgivings, it does feel good to have her arms groping me, her body pulling at me with longing. Creature comfort.

Once in bed, I feel horribly self-conscious. I haven't been with anyone since Christie, and it feels wrong somehow. Mandy's like a child on her first trip to an ice cream parlor. This is the tenth time she's gone down on me, foraging between my legs as if determined to taste all 31 flavors. I just stare at her head, separating sections of her dark hair like long rows of wheat, to keep myself occupied. One hundred hairs to a bundle.

My clit is so exhausted that I'm thinking about filing a disability claim for stress. I flip Mandy over, sit on her butt and massage her lower back. Every so often, I slip my hand between her legs and she moans. Her damp cunt is like a bowl of warm vanilla icing. I'm sexually diabetic and all I want is to give Mandy a good ride, and send her back to the happiest place on earth.

I'm missing Christie. I stare up at my dresser. The light from outside is casting its glow upon my family photos. My mom and dad are beaming back at me while Mandy bucks my arm. Fitz dressed as a pirate for Halloween when he was eight years old. Before that nimbus cloud took him away. Mandy is moaning and I'm reviewing my family of origin. Oh well, now is as good a time as any for self-reflection.

Fitzy has had three DUIs, and he's only sixteen. One day he seems to respond to me, we'll talk for hours on the phone and I'll finally convince him to go to AA meetings and then I won't hear from him for a month, sometimes longer.

He's also been caught setting fires out in the woods. My mom and dad have given up. He's not allowed to even go to the house unless he calls them first. The rest of them have scattered across the state like blown leaves.

Paul's now a born-again Christian married to Tanya. He's studying to be a minister, the spooky kind who speak in tongues. Beth is as big as a house, pregnant and unmarried. The twins got scholarships to college for synchronized swimming.

Christie's right. I'm unresolved about a lot in my family, but I'm happy to be far far away. I became a cirrus cloud, slight and fading, just a scuff mark on the sky's ceiling, and I've drifted outside of my family's orbit. And my baby, Fitz, is roaming the state, becoming an even larger nimbus cloud, leaving a riot of hail in his path.

My weary hand is about to drop off when I notice that Mandy has fallen asleep. I slip my fingers out carefully, not wanting to rouse her from slumber.

It's as if an emotion-filled U-Haul has pulled up and put something inside of me. Attached to my rib cage, it feels as permanent as my loneliness, but bigger, taking up more space. It's not a refrigerator, but it's making my insides feel chilly and dead.

Mandy is snoring, a gross snore, like someone who's had too much to drink. I stare down at my crotch, my vagina is filing a complaint with the Society for the Prevention of Cruelty to Sexual Organs. I imagine her weeping, dialing one of those 800 numbers. "If you're eighteen or older and feel sad most of the time, have trouble sleeping, and lack motivation, please call for a free evaluation." That's when it comes to me.

Melancholy. Despair. Glum. My vagina is glum. I moan. "Mona," I whisper. I name her Mona.

I climb out of bed and walk over to James' apartment. It's three in the morning. I peer into the window to see if any lights are on. I crawl back up the stairs to the pool, my arm aching, my head spinning, my vagina moaning. I slip onto the chaise lounge when I hear it. Sex. Across from me on the other side of the roof. The sound of sex. Good sex. Rough and playful. Not like the awful, low tone of the sexual dirge I'm plucking.

Two men are boffing each other, having a gay old time and I'm about to pitch myself over the railing. They're really going at it now. The grunts and yelps and wet smacking of the fuck echoes and bounces off the apartment building next door. I start to cry. I wrap Mandy's wet towel around my ears to block out the sounds. Suddenly a huge wave of water showers my body as the two men dive into the pool. They leap out in unison and standing before me, semi-erect and dripping, are James and Peter.

All three of us gasp. Their exhilaration shrivels as quickly as their retreating balls. They look at me dumbstruck, like two little boys caught in the act. I've still got the towel wrapped like a turban around my head.

I stare at James. All I can think about is Matthew, alone, sleeping below us, or pacing the floor waiting for Peter to come home.

Peter reaches toward me and grabs the towel, then wraps it around his waist. James is silent.

"Lighten up, Mia," Peter says. He tosses the towel back at me, then dives into the pool.

I scowl at him, then look back to James who is shivering from the cold. "So *that's* your creature," I say harshly, then quickly turn and rush down the steps back to my apartment.

Twelve

It is like a chain reaction. A procession of dominos tumbling. An invasion of body snatchers. Socks disappearing. Flies dropping. Ordinary men conducting ordinary lives. I get my photos processed at Jim's Camera. Jim died. Ryan and Paul run a bakery. Then it just closed, so I've resorted to buying my bread at the grocery store. At night, the boulevard is limp, no longer a grand erection spilling semen. The old queens gathered at Matthew's bar stop gathering. Younger guys take their bar stools. Words are whispered: "He's gone." "How did it end?" "They committed suicide." "He went back home to Kansas." "They're in the hospital."

Pharmacies sprinkle the boulevard. Vans with medical words painted on them weave through the streets. Page after page of colorful advertisements in our newspapers: immune-building vitamins; home health care; pretty smiling doctors with their pretty smiling staff welcoming more patients—they understand your special needs; hospice care; Being Alive. Billboards with half-naked men promoting a brand new wing at a hospital instead of a Gay Cruise Ship.

I'm up on the roof with Matthew. It's noon and the sun is beating down on us. Matthew thinks if he sweats enough during the day, he'll stop waking up in the middle of the night drenched. He's got it too. His thinning was only partly due to the chaos of Peter. The doctor called it wasting. HTLV. That's the name of the virus. They don't know how to stop it.

Matthew is drinking an immune-building milkshake. He drinks six of them a day.

"I hope my energy is better tommorrow," he says. "Wait till my family gets a look at me."

We're flying to Boston to tell his family he has the virus. He hasn't seen them for over five years and Matthew decided introducing them to Peter *and* telling his family he's dying would be too much. That's why I'm going.

"Maria, I keep having this dream," Matthew says, "in black and white, that I'm London. . ."

"You're *in* London?" I ask.

"No, I *am* London, and these sirens are blaring and I'm being bombed by an endless stream of air strikes. I just know

I'm going to be completely destroyed, and there are no allied forces coming to my rescue. And all the people who live on me—you, Peter, Christie, James, the guys at the restaurant—all of you are going to be destroyed too." He closes his eyes. He's tired all the time.

I don't know what to say. It's touch and go. I feel we're all in a tangled pile of fuselage and nobody cares, nobody is investigating the cause of the disaster, or searching for the black box that contains our screams. We're alone, the survivors picking through the dust for fragments, remnants, anything we recognize.

I scan faces for spots, scrutinize coughs, measure body dimensions. My eyes are instruments, tools for detection. My arms too. How much space does Matthew fill when I hug him? Arms around his torso and my hands would touch. Then I could hold my wrist behind his back. Now, I can reach past my elbow.

Reagan is invading Granada. Everybody's talking about it. When he comes on television as the Commander-in-Chief, my saliva heats, and I want to blow chunks in his face. He has a tight ass, like my boss Esther, and I hate him. Bodies are being invaded all around me. Nobody's talking about it.

Peter has stopped lying to Matthew. I've never seen him show fear until now. Peter has the virus too, but no symptoms.

My armpits are dripping and I glance over at Matthew and he's shivering.

"Matthew," I whisper, shaking him awake, "let's go inside."

I put Matthew to bed. Peter is in their kitchen making more milkshakes. Peter and I have called a temporary truce, a cease-fire. It's still awkward between us. After I discovered Peter and James together that night, a thick tension swelled between us. For three months I could hardly look James in the eyes. A brand new distance was between us. Then Matthew got sick and James moved to San Francisco. He just fled. He met a man at the restaurant, Gaspar, who asked him to come up and start a catering business. I walk around West Hollywood with my chin scraping the sidewalk missing my old friend, wishing I could have bridged the gap before he left. Especially now. Death is everywhere.

"Peter, Matthew is asleep, I'm gonna go pack for our trip. I'll be back tonight," I say.

"Do you want a milkshake?" Peter asks. "I'm trying a new recipe."

"No thanks, I gotta go."

"Okay, see you later," Peter responds. "Have a good one."

This is pretty much the extent of our interaction. Polite. Pleasant. Swirling underneath our bland exchange is a loud chorus blaring with accusations. I want to blame Peter for Matthew's sickness. I don't care how repentant Peter appears, I just can't seem to make it go away—this hatred gurgles in my stomach.

Matthew and I have a three-hour layover in St. Louis. We grab a cab at the airport and ask the driver to take us down to the waterfront. I had read an article in the airplane's travel magazine that said the waterfront of St. Louis was being renovated with flower shops, coffee bars, theaters, and art galleries.

Matthew and I looked at each other and said, "Queers!" We told the driver to pull up at the flower shop.

When we walk in, two guys are spritzing a wall of flowers and we know we've struck gold.

Sure enough, they're lovers, and across the street is a dyke that sculpts naked ladies and gets top dollar for 'em, too.

We are treated like regular queens from the city of angels. We share the international queer language full of big bawdy laughs. Big laughs, and now death too.

The coffee bar queer tells us about a St. Louis legend, Randy Sue, who insisted he was to be buried in a Donna Karan black cocktail dress and one tasteful strand of real pearls.

"That girl looked like she stepped right out of *Vogue* and into the casket—fabulous!!" Our guts bust with a loud roaring laugh and our eyes tear up.

Matthew's energy is holding up well. He excuses himself to the bathroom and one of the flower queers follows him in and I think Matthew got a blow job. His face is beet red when he returns to the table. Matthew will do this now, every once in awhile, to even the old score with Peter.

All I get is a quick feel down my leg by the sculpting dyke.

When we leave she hugs me tight and her hands trickle over my boobs. "I'd like to do your breasts sometime," she says.

We fly out of St. Louis with a key to the city. On take-off, I think about Randy Sue and ask her to keep us safe. Matthew grabs my hand and clenches it the whole way to Boston. When we land, we hold on tight, and wait for our fellow passengers to murmur a collective sigh, signaling a safe return to earth. Both of us are crying, knowing we'd rather be flying far far away.

The silence at Matthew's family home in Boston is downright spooky. His parents are in their seventies and they seem as if they come from another era. Everyone is so well behaved. Everything is so precise. I'm afraid to move for fear I'll knock something over or make too much noise.

It makes me long for the sounds I grew up with. Screaming kids playing kickball. Televisions turned up loud. Arguments erupting around the dinner table. Life noise. I'm so tense, I've been eating Tum's by the handful.

We've been here for two days and are supposed to leave tomorrow. Matthew hasn't told them yet. He says he's waiting for the right moment.

There's been no mention of the soaked sheets from the bed where Matthew is sleeping. The long naps he takes in the middle of the day. The pile of medications he has left on the counter of the guest bathroom. Nothing.

We're having another formal dinner. Matthew and I went out and he bought me a dress. I didn't realize that some families actually change their clothes for dinner.

"Matthew, it's good to see you have a healthy appetite," his mother says. She hands me a platter of roast beef and red potatoes.

"Thank you," I mutter for the hundredth time.

"You always were such a finicky eater," she continues. "That's why your father and I were so surprised you went into the restaurant trade."

It's happening. My stomach flips, my spine tightens. I want to scream. It feels as if we are being slowly taken over by a tangled mass of silent weeds winding around us; obstinate and willful, they threaten to clog our voices. CAN'T THEY SEE HOW THIN HE IS? HE IS SICK!

I smash my potatoes with my fork, stabbing at them, and focus on the sounds coming from the housekeeper in the kitchen. The clamor of shifting plates and glasses is like tiny reassuring sounds of life. I look up at Matthew. All that warm light inside of him is fading. He's pushing his food around on his plate.

"Matthew's restaurant is one of the most popular in our area," I say, anxious to slice the silence.

"Is that so?" his mother responds.

There's another long lull in the conversation. I see a mask of resignation shroud Matthew's face.

"I'm sick," Matthew murmurs. These two small words suck the oxygen right out of the room. His father stands abruptly and I just about fall out of my chair. He picks up his plate, still covered with food, and walks into the kitchen. The three of us don't move and then we hear a scraping followed by the garbage disposal. Matthew is staring down at his plate, shaking his head.

"Mother, we're taking an early flight back—tonight."

That was it. We packed our bags and left for the airport. The night we return, I walk the boulevard, thankful to be amongst queers, a soldier returning to the front lines feeling relieved.

I decide to stop in at the Palms for a drink. I desperately need to talk to someone. Someone who sees what is happening. I keep waiting for big green trucks with red crosses to circle our streets, pass out soup, tell us to hang in there. Instead there are white roach-coaches selling bean burritos for a buck.

I sit at the bar and no sooner have I taken my first sip of scotch than Christie walks in. We haven't laid eyes on each other since I broke up with her. She's here with her therapist friends, Sharon and Lynn. They both smirk at me and I feel like the loser on *Jeopardy*.

They rush off together to the bathroom, leaving Christie and me alone, sitting at the bar. I imagine them huddled in the bathroom stall paging through their *Diagnostic Manual of Mental Disorders*—looking me up.

"So, Christie, how are you?" I ask. I twirl my finger in the ice cubes of my drink.

"Great. I'm really discovering a lot about my internal world," she says.

"Oh," I respond. I hate these moments. Here is a woman whose clit I've sucked and I can't pull out one coherent sentence of normal conversation. Just a puny "oh."

"Have you been with anyone. . .since me?" she asks.

"No," I answer, "I haven't been with anyone." (Except for Mandy.)

"I'm surprised," Christie says, a tinge of anger in her voice.

"I've even named my vagina Mona," I giggle nervously. "You know, Mona, like all those dismal 'm' words: moody, moan, misery, melancholy, morose." Scotch splashes out of my glass as my finger spins rapidly.

Christie grunts and looks away from me toward the dance floor.

"Mopes," I add, "I could have named my vagina Mopes." She's still not looking at me. All I want to do is lay my head in her lap and tell her about Matthew and the awful ache of being with his family. It's as if my words are stuck inside the thick arteries of my heart. If I let one word go, I might cause an eruption. "Can I buy you a glass of wine?" I ask.

"Sure," she sputters.

"Christie, speaking of discoveries, do you know what a butt plug is?" I ask. (I don't know what demon dyke is striking me with hoof-in-mouth disease. The very moment the question hits the smoky air I know I've made a mistake.)

Christie's brow is wrinkled as if she's just witnessed me declared winner of a puking contest.

"A butt plug!?" she snaps. "What are you into now?"

"I'm just asking," I say defensively. "I found a box of them in Peter's bathroom. They're little baby dildos." My finger is spinning so rapidly that scotch splashes my jeans.

"That's gross," Christie grunts.

"It's not gross, Christie. I thought you were supposed to be liberal and open-minded."

"I am, but that's not natural." Christie lifts her spine, assuming the Buddha position, centering herself for the duel.

"Well, Peter said we are frightened by our assholes. We become what we fear," I retort. (I can't believe I'm quoting Peter's philosophy of sex.)

Now is definitely not the time to tell Christie I actually tried a butt plug. I pushed it up inside of me when I masturbated and the clitoral tom-tom extended into a whole percussion ensemble that pounded deep within. I even went to work with a plug in. Spice up the doldrums of medical editing. Nobody asked, "What's up your ass?" Too bad.

Christie is glowering. I'm sure she's anxious to tell Sharon and Lynn how sexually depraved I've become. We're both staring straight ahead. The bottles of booze lined up on the wall behind the bar look like a firing squad. I close my eyes, imagine being blindfolded, awaiting a flurry of bullets to rip through my chest. That's when I realize that something has changed inside of me. It's about living—I'm not sure I want anything to do with it at all.

"Christie, I just got back from Boston with Matthew. He told his parents that he's sick."

She sighs and turns slightly toward me. "How did it go?" Her voice loosens.

"Not so good," I mutter. I turn a bit too, letting my knee connect to hers.

"What about James, do you know about him yet?" she asks.

"No. I'm too afraid to find out."

"You've got to ask him, Maria, he's your best friend," she says.

"I know." My bones are all wobbly, exhausted from my trip with Matthew. I feel as if I'll drop to the floor like spilled beer. I hold on to the bar like a panicky kid on a roller coaster.

"How is Matthew?" Christie asks. She slides her palm down her leg. Her fingertips just lightly form a bridge between us.

"He only weighs 125 pounds. He's disappearing." My jaw droops with my words. "He's dying." I can feel my whole face—cheeks, eyes, brow, chin—sliding down, a sudden avalanche of weary flesh unable to stay fixed. I catch it all in my hands, holding the pieces of my face together like fragments from a broken vase. "Ohh, I'm so tired all of a sudden." My neck gives, withers like a weak stem.

Christie glides her hand up my spine and digs her fingers in deeply. A wave of relief buzzes down to my toes. "Are you okay?" she whispers. She slips off her bar stool and stands close in between my legs.

"Come home with me," I say. "Please, just for tonight." I reach my arms around her. She's so warm.

Then her arms circle me and our lips find each other; tongues push deep, hands run free, slip up and down between skin and denim.

"Let's go," she says.

*****

"James, how are you feeling?" I ask. I'm circling, in blue, a phrase in a boring manuscript I've been editing. The phrase is *T-cell immune surveillance system*.

104

"How are you feeling" has become a loaded question. A question about death, not mood. I've circled it with James. What are you up to? What's new? Is it happening there too? Each time we speak, the words cling to my tongue like leeches: How are you feeling?

T-cell surveillance system. I imagine big burly men in dark glasses, like bouncers, like bodyguards, investigating anything suspicious. Scanning with infrared the perimeter of the body; alarms ring when invasion occurs.

James is silent. "How are you feeling?" I repeat.

"Well, Smudge," James says, "I'd like you to come up for a visit, how about this weekend?" He didn't answer my question. He's being invaded, I can feel it. An alarm goes off in my brain.

"Sure, I can leave tonight." I'm circling fast now, with my blue pencil, the word *T-cell*, it's supposed to help the body fight off disease. I wonder what "T" stands for. Tranquility. Terrific. Trustee. Thank you, cell.

I run to Esther's office. "I've got to go. My friend is sick."

She draws in a huge breath and sighs disapprovingly. "Maria, this is becoming a habit."

I have to bite down hard on my bottom lip because the word "bitch" is inside my mouth waving a machete. "I'm sorry, I'll make it up. It's almost five anyway," I say. "At least I don't smoke."

She waves me out as if I'm something unpleasant—her crotch, for example.

I go to my apartment to pack. I get to the airport three hours before my flight and wait. I can't read, or think, I just let the endless transitions of people scattering to places across the globe fill my eyeballs. I become so hypnotized, I almost miss my flight, and I'm the last one to board the plane.

I notice you right away, Cup. I'm in 28C and when I pass by your row, you're leaning against the window, with a backpack on the seat next to you. I want to be a backpack. Our eyes lock for that splendid long moment signaling recognition. *Yes, I'm one too!* I actually smile, before my eyes drop to the carpet in the airplane. Then, I knock into a flight attendant who's searching for more space in the overhead compartment.

I spend the entire fifty-minute flight waiting for you to go to the bathroom. Hoping for another look. Now you fill the screen in my brain. The airline magazine is featuring an article on the Russian River. I imagine a river swim with you, sleeping under the redwoods on a mattress of leaves, slapping our wet bodies together like seals at Goat Rock. Hurtling through the air at such great speeds seems to boost my carnal cravings.

I lose sight of you when exiting the airplane, and then I spot you standing under the BART loading zone sign. I quickly get out of the taxi cab waiting line, and deliberate on the benefits of public transportation.

"It's so much easier taking a bus to the subway to get around," I say to you, as I drop my bag very near to your backpack.

"Visiting?" you ask, as you lightly brush a few windswept hairs from your forehead. You're wearing a familiar lipstick. It's in the Revlon family, in their Red series. Romantic Red. True Red. Twilight Red. I can't quite place it.

"Yes, my friend, James. He lives in the *Castro*," I say, hoping to dispel any questions regarding my sexuality. Queer language is so subtle, with secret shadings and nuance that only those who belong to the family can understand.

"I'm staying there too," you say. "I'm visiting my ex."

"How ex is *she*?" My boldness is staggering. She. I've completed the inquiry.

"High school sweethearts," you answer, "which makes her very ex!" I laugh too loud in response.

The bus pulls up and we sit next to each other. You hug your backpack the whole ride, glancing over at me as you talk. I can see the roadside passing quickly and I pray for a traffic jam. San Francisco's clouds swell in the distance.

"What do you do?"

"I'm an editor for medical magazines," I respond, feeling self-conscious about the dullness in my voice. I wish I were an artist. A film director. A writer. I think about my boss, Esther, and I feel doomed to a life of thighs tingling at the sight of an error.

The bus squeaks to a halt. We've arrived at BART. I'm looking forward to the next jaunt into the Castro with you, I've got so many questions to ask, but so far they've been pressed against the corners of my brain like shy wall flowers at a dance. You step off the bus first, and a woman screams, throws her arms around you, and grabs your backpack, and with a familiar sling, it tumbles across her shoulder.

"See you," you say, as you glance quickly at me, and you and the scream drift into the crowd.

I nod and smile. I don't even know your name. It's dusk and I have no idea how to get to Castro Street.

"Bon jour, Maria!" Gaspar swoons when I enter the Häagen-Dazs. In addition to catering, he and James are assistant managers. He plucks both of my cheeks with his lips, his scruffy beard tickling my face, and then James emerges from the back room carrying a cylinder of Rocky Road. He takes my breath away. A vital moment when I see those sapphire eyes like gentle prayers. He's thinner. (Just look in his eyes.)

"Smudge, you're here," James sings. "I told Gaspar you probably fell in love on the plane and that's why you're late." He slides the ice cream into the freezer, lit up and shining like a spaceship filled with spirals of color. I walk behind the counter and wrap my arms—my tools for detection—around James' stomach. He's thinner.

"I love you," I say, burying my face between his shoulder blades. He smells sticky and sweet. "I did fall in love, but I lost her at BART."

"If she's meant to be," Gaspar says, "you will collide once more." He hands me a cone of butter pecan.

"She'll be waiting round the bend, my Huckleberry friend," James sings.

I sit and wait for James and Gaspar to finish their shift. I stare at the customers, the bustling street of queers.

I watch James' slender arms dig deep into ice cream, his muscles twitch, his tongue hinged over his lip as he concentrates on creating a ball of sweetness. Each time the little bell rings when a customer enters, I pray that it will be her, walking in for a cone too.

"Enjoy," James says to the pierced leather queen as he hands him a strawberry sundae. I look behind James at the clock up on the wall. My eyes follow the sweeping second hand, and I gasp, like Dr. Rothman would during her fast lectures. How much time do we have? I hate that it's twirling so fast.

In the morning, James and I hike up the thighs of Mt. Tamalpais. So far, he hasn't mentioned those letters followed by the word *positive*.

Hints of fall surround us. The light has softened, the ground is covered with pine needles and the first dead leaves. Colors of autumn are sprinkled lightly like spices throughout the woods below. I miss this change of season.

In L.A., seasons are muted, slipping into each other quietly without much notice. A dip in temperature, more rain, and like a magic show, the mountains reappear. Always, though, the palm trees stand their ground, like the tallest soldiers.

James and I have brought apple cider and warm donuts for our hike. Climbing the mountain with him, I feel that old welcome ease, the brush of our hands together, how chummy our bones are.

He seems strong. Matthew could never make this hike, he's become so short on breaths.

"Do you love Gaspar?" I ask him, as we lay out our tablecloth on the ground. We're at the summit, a scattering of great rocks perched on a lookout.

"We're lovers, on and off, but great chums mostly," James says, placing his tongue through a donut hole and twirling it like a tire.

"I like him, James," I say, pouring cider into blue tin coffee cups. The oxygen is startling up here, and my lungs feel giddy.

The air seems to cool as we sit, a thick cloud cover rolling in off the Pacific, diminishing the sweeping rays of sun to thin streaks of light bouncing against the vast forest below.

"How is Matthew doing?" James asks. He sits cross-legged and motions for me to lean against him. His arms extend wide, and he pulls me close to his chest.

"Not so good," I say, leaning into his chest. I can feel it. Our bones murmuring a sad language.

"And Peter?" he says hesitantly.

"Peter is Peter," I respond. "But, I have to say he's good with Matthew now."

I massage James' long arms, listening to his body with my hands. The thick veins in the crook of his arm are warm to the touch. They're holding something that doesn't belong there, a virus I want to erase. He's positive. I close my eyes tightly like a child praying. I don't know anymore what should be said, what should be kept in silence. His body is being invaded.

"I'll be all right, Smudge," he whispers, his face so close that a drop from his eye travels down the canal in my ear. Like wine to the tongue I take it in and imagine that lone tear sailing and gliding into my bloodstream.

"When did you find out?" I ask tentatively.

"A month ago," he says.

I think about the night Peter and James were together. "Was it Peter?"

"Don't," James says. "There's no way to know." He grasps my hands. "It's not important."

I hold a warm donut and wrap my lips around it and suck in a huge bite. It doesn't budge the ache in my belly. I hold it to James; a communion wafer, and he bites too. "Bread of life," I whisper.

"Nose to the wind, Smudge, fall is coming," James says. "You can smell it." He pauses to sniff the air, the blue of his eyes are rooted with a knowing, a dim knowledge of his death. He hands me a deep red leaf that's fallen. I run my finger up the red spine of it, the veins that shoot out are still moist, holding water.

I can't really smell fall approaching because my nose is filled with the stuff sorrow creates, and the tears fall fast. "Those are nimbus clouds," I say, pointing to the sky. "I like to see them coming."

Against the dark clouds, a hawk sweeps through the air. It is just a speck of black, buoyed by the wind, eyeing the movement of life below, and setting its course for home.

Gaspar was right. If we were meant to be, we'd collide again, Cup. And we did, in the aisle on the plane back to L.A. Thank God, it was you that bumped me. If I don't feel a nervous rush of love or anything extraordinary, it is because my load is heavier, and it isn't the dozen donuts James and I ate.

I'm wishing the plane will get caught in between the two cities, trapped in another time zone, slip into the past or the future, anywhere but in the here and now. Maybe I'll find Joseph, maybe he escaped into that sphere before the plane exploded.

This time, you ask me to join you in the empty seat next to yours. It's the window seat. As we rise above San Francisco, I can feel my body filling up with low blue notes, some deep sad song without words, just gloomy chords cascading through my veins. I wonder if you can hear it.

"How was your friend?" you ask. "James, right?" You're still hugging that backpack.

"Not so good," I say, some of the blue notes drip off my tongue. "He's positive." I look down at your backpack and you've got a big sticker on it that I didn't notice before. "SILENCE = DEATH. ACTION = LIFE."

"I'm sorry," you murmur, and you tell me the same about your friends. Then we sit in silence as the engines, having climbed high, ease to a low humming that resonates with my body's song.

I lean my head against the window and fall into the hum. When I wake, your hand is resting on my sleeve and your head on my shoulder. I don't know why, but as I watch you sleep, I imagine holding you in my hands, like a hefty mug filled with something warm and soothing.

I take your hand and you link your fingers in mine and in this moment I know that we belong together. You don't open your eyes. It's as if you want me to fall into sleep with you. You carefully slide your hand down between my legs and you keep it there. Where it belongs. I feel as if we are suddenly hinged by some dark secret vision of the future. My eyes are drawn to your lap, to the bold words stamped in black and white. SILENCE = DEATH. ACTION = LIFE.

I look out the window and see L.A. gleaming below. It's a maze of lights that hiss and buzz. You and I are just a speck of silver above the frenzy, gliding toward home. I can feel the heat of your sleepy breath on my neck. I want you in my hands. "Cup," I whisper, "I'll call you Cup."

Thirteen

What I said: Esther, I quit my chargé d'affaires position. It's too much pressure and I'd like to do my editing from home for awhile. If you don't mind, of course.

What I thought: You fucking bitch, wipe that Nazi smirk off your fucking face.

What Esther said: Well, Maria, this comes as quite a shock.

What Esther thought: You no brain plebeian employee, I should just fire you.

What I said: Yes, well, as you mentioned previously, I have had to take too many personal days, and I feel it isn't fair to the others.

What I thought: Fire me bitch! (Authority issues.)

What she said: I'm sorry Maria, I've got to let you go.

What she thought: I make myself wet, I'm so powerful. You swine!

What I said: How dare you!!

Thought: Free at last!!

*****

That bitch Lydia is having Peter inject himself with bovine hormones. She's suggested he lay off all antivirals, and has him on a regimen of herbs, vitamins, and extracted oils from plants. The bovine goo is a secret method she came across in Mexico. It makes him sick for forty-eight hours. Flaring headaches. Knotting intestines. Cramping muscles. His skin is pocked with several small lesions, as if a team of cleated football players has used his body as a playing field.

"It's called mushrooming," Peter says. "For awhile the lesions burst and flourish, but Lydia says that's normal."

He is lying on the floor in his apartment, a cold compress on his forehead, two ice bags under his arms to reduce the fever.

I came over to tell Peter the dismal news. One, I'm unemployed, and two, I got a postcard from Cup. I'm clenching it in my hand. An urn of ashes is sitting on Peter's coffee table. It's Matthew.

"Peter, don't you think I should talk to Lydia?" I say. "I am your agent for health care."

"No, I don't want you to," he answers, extending his muscled arms into the air. "Look, Mia, my muscle mass has increased on this stuff."

"Mushroomed?" I spit. I want to shove a bovine cowpie down Lydia's throat. "Peter, since when do you follow someone's direction blindly, you never listen to anyone!"

"I'm transforming," he coos wickedly.

"My ass!" I snap.

Peter lifts the compress off his eyes and glares at me. "Please leave your ass out of this discussion," he says. He eyes the urn. "You can take those with you," he says.

"Why?" I'm starting to hiss inside. He's pushing me away.

"I don't want any negative energy in my space," he answers, staring at his flexed bicep.

I want to dump Matthew all over Peter, shroud him in the gray dust. *Give me patience.* I'm remembering how tired I became when Matthew was sick and how I marveled at Peter's patience.

Matthew had *cryptosporidium*, a pesky bacteria that swims in the drinking water, and his diarrhea was out of control. We had just gotten Matthew bathed and dressed to take him in to the hospital.

He was standing at the kitchen sink crying. Suddenly, Peter starts undressing. He pulls off his cowboy boots. Then his jeans and underwear. I'm thinking, now is not a good time for sex, Peter. Then he unzips Matthew's jeans, pulls them down, and I see it. Matthew had soiled his underwear—again.

Peter warmed a cloth with water, washed Matthew, and then Peter dressed him, in *his* underwear, jeans, and even his boots. Just like that. No words between them. I stood silently, hiding my gag response because the shit was disgusting and I was so tired of smelling it.

I get on my knees, bend over, and lick Peter's forehead. He doesn't say a word. I walk to the door, turn before I leave, and say, "Peter, you're tragic, but I love you. Call me if you need me."

"She's a legitimate healer," Christie says. "I've seen her do some amazing work."

Christie is holding Matthew in her lap as I drive us back to my place.

"Christie, please, just because someone calls themselves a healer doesn't mean they have special powers!" I bark. I slam my fist on the dashboard.

"Hey, Maria, don't take your anger out on me," Christie says.

"I hit the dashboard, not you." I round a corner too fast, and skid on the shoulder, jerking us like bumper cars. "Sorry," I say, as I hold my arm out, bracing Christie and the urn.

"You sure are in a huff," Christie whispers as we walk in the house.

"I just feel like shit." Molly and Sadie jump up to greet us, their hopeful tongues and tails wagging and waving like parade-goers.

We go to the bedroom and I collapse. My head is pounding. I'm prostrate on the bed. Christie begins rubbing my feet, noodling my toes with her knuckles; some new massage technique that's supposed to really get to the pain.

"He's such a stubborn ass. That hurts!" I yell.

"Sorry," she says, rolling her fist up my instep. "There's lots of stored negativity."

"Ouch!" A pain shoots up to my hip.

"There's your problem area," Christie responds, as she presses again.

"Ouch! Godammit!" I jerk my foot away. Sudden tears spill fast down my cheek.

"I should have warned you," Christie says. "This foot massage can tap into a lot of stored-up feelings."

"These aren't stored, Christie, they're brand new!" I snap. I begin sobbing and Christie hugs me.

I'm clutching Little Bo Peep in my hand. I swiped her from Esther. I'm thinking about sending an anonymous ransom letter: "If you ever want to hear a peep out of Little Bo, then send a bijillion unmarked dollars."

"I got a postcard from Cup," I grumble, hoping the angry sound of my voice will dam up these tears. I use my pillowcase to blow my nose. It seems that I've lost track of the proscribed utility of objects; using the electric toothbrush as a vibrator; pillowcase as Kleenex; puppy cookie as donut; teddy bear as surrogate lover; and dildo as drain plug. Necessity is the mother.

"Where is she?" Christie asks, a tinge of apprehension slips into the air.

"In Maine," I say, "With that half-baked Vagina Ham."

"Is she coming back?" Christie says, stroking my legs.

"She didn't say."

Christie is relieved for the time being that you are still her-story, Cup. She moves her hands up to my breasts and starts to circle my nipple. I push her hand away.

"No!" I yell as Christie begins to slide her other hand down my belly.

"What's wrong!?" she asks, startled, drumming her fingers on my stomach like a desktop.

"I can't Christie, not now." My eyes meet Sadie's. She's looking at me like a disapproving mother.

Christie jumps off the bed. "I'm tired of this," she says. "We only do it when you want to." She scurries out of the bed-room and goes into the kitchen.

Sadie hops to the floor. Molly follows her and they head for Christie in the kitchen. "Hey," I yelp at them, "where are you going?"

Sadie looks back at me. I feel like an adolescent and Sadie has just grounded me for a month.

I slide my hand under the pillow. Cup's postcard. I've already memorized it and analyzed every crossed "t" and dot-ted "i" for clues. It says: "Sweetpea, Sorry I haven't contacted you sooner. I've been doing a lot of thinking. Still not ready to talk. Take care of yourself. Cup." It was mailed from Kennebunkport, Maine. I know there are at least three bushes there I despise: George, Barbara, and Vagina Ham.

Stellar location. The home of pansy-ass cowards. There's no return address, but Vagina has a bed and breakfast just south in Ogunquit. We went there together three years ago. On the plane trip to Boston where she was going to pick us up, all you did was go on and on about how intelligent, witty, urbane, Ms. Ham was. By the time the plane landed, my working class, "ain't-I-just-a-piece-a-white-trash" self-esteem was skidding on the pavement. I longed for a K-mart where I could hear, "Attention shoppers, Kraft Macaroni and Cheese, four-for-a-dollar, aisle sixteen."

Nobody dying of AIDS at your little haven by the sea? Must be slow going, Cup, shuffling along the cobblestones with her walker. Be careful not to lose your footing or accidentally get tossed off a bridge like a crumpled beer can.

I can hear Christie in the kitchen banging the cupboard doors. I'd better go in and make peace. I don't think I could handle her absence, especially now that Peter's sprouting spots and losing helper cells.

I'm unemployed. Mona is probably living under the Witness Protection Program with a new name. Cup has taken up with a resident of Sunny Valley Old Genitals Home. Sadie and Molly are in the kitchen, probably discussing sending me off to some special school on a short bus. I've become nothing but trouble. Maybe I should sign up for Sharon's and Lynn's workshop and manufacture more lies about myself.

Maybe I'll just call Paulette and go for another bedpost. *Merde!* I throw Bo Peep across the room and she shatters into the wall. Christie, Molly, and Sadie come rushing in.

"Don't worry," I say. "Just an accident. C'mon, I'll make us dinner."

Once in the kitchen, I pull out the large bag of dog food. Molly and Sadie are panting at my heels.

"Maria," Christie pauses, then ever so carefully, as if aiming her words into the eye of a needle, she says, "Sharon and Lynn have a workshop this weekend called, 'Hopeless, Less and Less.'" She smiles at me as I pour kibble into the dog bowls, "Do you get it, less and less?"

"You know, Christie," I say, scavenging through the refrigerator for a half-eaten hamburger, "I'm really sick and tired of workshops, but thank you for asking."

I pull at the meat, thinking about Lydia and her damned bovine gunk, and dump the meat onto the kibble.

"I thought the last one was very successful for you," she persists. "You had never ever shared that story of stealing the money before."

I'm down on all fours watching Molly furiously inhale her food while Sadie just picks at hers. "Uh, huh," I drone.

"I think you really identified a lot of your issues," Christie presses.

Bits of kibble spill to the floor from Molly's bowl. I scoop them up and she whisks them off my palm with a quick swipe of her wet tongue.

"Drop it, Christie," I say.

"That experience you had as a little girl," she continues, "stealing the charity money. I've been thinking that maybe it has a lot to do with your not getting enough attention as a child."

I'm handing Christie provisions from the refrigerator for our dinner. Turkey, bread, mayo, lettuce.

"Uh, huh," I sigh, as I begin piling meat onto the slices of bread.

"So, what do you think?" Christie relents.

"About what?" Molly and Sadie are pooled at my feet, now interested in the main course.

Christie is inching closer. I feel as if she's a huge can opener trying to pry me open. I cross to a cupboard to look for potato chips. I know I don't have any chips, but I have to divert myself from Christie's inquest.

"Your *issues*," she whines. I hate the way she says "issues"; it sounds like a noise made when you smell sour milk. Ewww.

I'm staring in the cupboard. Aunt Jemima and Mr. Quaker Oats are scolding me. "Christie," I pause, "I made it up." I pull in a huge parcel of air, and hold my breath.

"What did you say?" Christie says, steady as a judge.

"I made it up," I repeat. "It never happened."

I can feel her approaching from behind like an angry cop and I'm about to get kicked. The silence is so earsplitting, we could use a big, big chain saw to cut through it.

Sadie and Molly have maneuvered toward the dog door. Sadie is staring straight ahead, as if we've both been caught rummaging through the teacher's desk. Her eyes are as wide as saucers.

Christie's hot breath is at my neck. "Turn around and look at me," she grumbles, a low thunder. I start counting, one thousand one, one thousand two, waiting for the bolt of lightning to strike.

My eyes meet Christie's. Fear meets Rage. Boy, do I wish I had a pair of scissors to clip her thorns off.

"That story about stealing the money was a lie?!" she thunders. "You sat there all weekend and lied?!"

"Yeah," I mutter to her hiking boots, "I thought I should tell the..."

The sharp sting on my cheek doesn't register until I see the hind ends of Sadie and Molly scurrying out the dog door. The second blow to my face seems to cause an explosion in my brain, like a stick of dynamite has been planted secretly into a filling in my tooth.

The room spins, and I hear a thud. Loud, like dropping a box filled with heavy books to the floor, except it's my head. It's dark, hazy, and I feel as if I'm slipping into sleep.

I hear Christie's voice, like a distant echo. "I'm sorry, I'm sorry."

When I come to, I'm lying in bed, a cool cloth on my forehead and Christie is rubbing the side of my face with an ice cube. The first sensation is on my nipple, where a cool stream of water drips down and greets my tit with a "howdy doo" that makes it leap to attention.

By instinct, my fingers grasp my nipple, and I start to rub and squeeze; encourage the erection to continue.

(Under normal circumstances, any stimulation to my tit produces at least a ping ping between my legs. It's a direct line. Now, though, I can hear this bitchy voice whining, "The number you have dialed has been disconnected or is no longer in service. Please hang up!")

I'm still in a haze. Christie is sitting on top of me, her eyes spilling tears. Her nose is all red and she's biting her lip. She looks like hell.

I'm about to ask her what's wrong, when I remember, vaguely, the slap, the dogs' asses disappearing, the thud, the blackness.

"Did we have an earthquake?" I ask.

Christie is shaking her head no, but she can't get a word out because her sobs are filling her mouth. Her belly is shuddering.

I reach for the ice cube, and I place it in Christie's mouth, draw her hand down to my breast and together we rub. I pull her face toward me, and suck her cool tongue deeply into my mouth. My gums like magnets, drawing her as far down my throat as possible.

Her chest and belly are pressed against me, bouncing with sorrow, and she sucks back harder than she's ever sucked me before. Suddenly, she howls. Lord, it's deafening, like a sound I heard once on a nature show. The bellows of a dying elephant.

My head is mushy like oatmeal. I can't get two brain cells to shake hands to save my life. My bearings are kaput. It's all flesh, pulsating and throbbing.

Christie is stripping off our clothes. I see a shirt fly into the air and parachute down to the floor. It's really beautiful. Socks zip like white doves. Christie's black jeans take flight like a spread-winged eagle.

Her skin feels like an extension of mine, a melding of flesh, and I grab the soft cheeks of her ass, two big handfuls, and I could be holding myself. She's thrusting her pelvis into mine, our pubes grinding fiercely.

She places her hands over mine on her ass and spreads her cheeks wide, then guides our fingers down to her asshole. Her index finger, dabbed with cum like melted butter, pushes up inside, and my finger, naturally, goes along for the ride.

I can see her jaw tighten, she clamps down on her teeth as she thrusts. Suddenly, I see something fall away from her face, like a layer of thick skin. Molly jumps up on the bed with us. I imagine in her dog brain, we look like we're having a blast, and she starts licking my face.

These noises come from Christie. Brand new ones, punching the air, and then a low-pitched moan shatters the sound barrier and poor Molly leaps off the bed and darts out of the room.

There is nothing hushed or whispered inside of Christie. I hold her ass tight, as she collapses in a sweaty pile, the particles of swirling sex are settling slowly like fallout from a bomb. Little aftershocks ripple from my finger, still lodged inside of her.

I feel strangely at peace, devoid of thought, completely drained of worry. I'm still unable to jump-start even the tiniest synapse. My brain cells are behaving like tired and sullen strangers on a bus.

I begin looking around us on the bed, searching for the part of Christie's face that fell off. I wonder if she'll want to slip it back on, or at least keep it, place it in a scrapbook or box of mementos.

She falls asleep on top of me. I remove my finger, and by gum, she's clean as a whistle. Christie has a pristine asshole. Molly comes back, this time with Sadie. They both jump up on the bed, licking me with their tireless tongues and boundless love.

It's barely morning when I wake. A dim light turns black to gray. Christie is gone. Next to me, propped on a pillow, is Cupcake, the teddy bear. Pinned to his furry belly is a note. My head and face are throbbing. My right eye will only half open.

I unpin the note and hold it close to my good eye:

"Maria: I don't know what happened between you and Cup," she writes, "but, I do know that the *greatest* thing Cup did was to get as far away from you as possible. And *that* is precisely what I'm doing! I'm reevaluating our friendship.

Please don't contact me. I make amends for hitting you."

"Hitting!?" I gaze at my witnesses, Molly and Sadie. "Belted, slugged, punched is more like it."

Christie conveniently forgot to mention the little matter of her cunt grinding my pseudo-groin, our fingers commingling up her ass, and the unparalleled orgasm she achieved.

Christie has doused her memory and her anus with a bottle of White Out.

I close my eyes and suddenly Sister Rose, Sister Ruth, and Mother Superior are standing on a stage that my brain cells have constructed overnight.

"*How do you solve a problem like Maria? How do you catch a cloud and pin it down? How do you solve a problem like Maria?*" They're dancing.

Sister Ruth: "*A flibbertigibbit.*"

Mother Superior: "*A will-o'-the wisp.*"

Sister Rose: "*A clown!*" she hisses wickedly.

When they finish the first number, I'm waiting for Mother Superior to call me up on stage. I want to kneel at her feet. Cling to the folds of her white habit. I want to see her thick old chin quiver as she sings to me: "*Climb every mountain, ford every stream, follow the goddamned rainbow to my dream.*"

I crawl to the kitchen. To the counter where my collection of painkillers and sleep agents are piled. I want relief. I clutch them in my hand and carry them to the bedroom. Sadie is at my heel, leaning into me as I walk.

God, Cup, what have I done to you? To me? To Christie? I deserved to be pummelled. If Christie ever knew what I did to you, Cup, I'm sure she'd plant my face on posters and pass them out to every lesbian on the planet.

When the phone rings, I have the pills strewn on the bed. Molly and Sadie have been conducting a very persuasive suicide intervention. Matthew's urn is perched up on the pillow next to Cupcake. I can use all the help I can get.

I grab the phone. "Peter?" I yelp.

"No, honey, it's your mom." It's six in the morning in L.A., which means trouble if she's calling.

"What is it?" I say.

"Fitz is in the hospital, he's been beaten pretty badly." I can tell she's crying, although trying to hide it.

"What happened?" I ask. A mushroom cloud expands inside of me.

"Oh, we're not sure." Her voice tremors with an aging sorrow.

"I'm coming home, Mom." I scoop the pills back into their bottles. Sadie sighs and licks my brow.

I grab Matthew, holding the urn close to my chest, and stroke it like a baby. I can hear his voice inside my head. *Let me come to be still in your silence.*

Molly and Sadie have nuzzled between my legs, a snout resting on each thigh, holding me down, keeping me safe. I keep stroking the urn, but there's no magic coming out, none of that warm burst of light in which Matthew glimmered. Ashes, ashes, we all fall down. I've got to catch Fitz.

I bend my knee, grab my foot and squeeze where Christie had. The pain is still there. So are the tears. I keep squeezing. I'm going home.

Part II

Fourteen

Where seldom is heard a discouraging word. It's not where my heart is, nor is it all that sweet. Families carry around wallet-sized photos of each other in their heads, and when you change, the photo they cling to, now worn and frayed at the edges, doesn't budge.

They expect you to look the same, act the same, be that person that they pull out of the pocket in their hearts, and they downright refuse to exchange that image for a new one. This is who you are, and who you'll remain, for all the days of your life. So help you, God.

I could come home bare-breasted, tit-pierced, tatooed, an asymmetrical design sliced into my skull, a dildo strapped between my legs, and my family would act as if nothing had changed. I'm still the smart one, the bookworm who takes a lot of baths, and does what she's told.

Case in point: When I emerged from the gate at the airport, my mom and dad were there, waiting. We hugged, in that quick way that keeps the huggers from letting their bodies divulge too much emotion. I was carrying Cupcake the teddy bear. I had sunglasses on, to cover up the black shiner Christie gave me. When I took them off, the black eye, like a neon sign, blinked trouble, trouble, trouble. My parents didn't say a word about my being a little too old for stuffed animals or the shiner. Maybe they think I whacked myself as a show of solidarity with Fitzy.

Once Molly and Sadie were unloaded from their crates, we packed into my dad's car. When we arrived at the house, and crossed the threshold, I was sure that I'd forgotten something back in L.A. Something essential. A whole suitcase crammed with chaos and sorrow like canned goods for a disaster. It's filled with the dead and the dying, a deck of cards, a cluster of medicine bottles, ashes, and a defective heart in need of a trained bystander. That's what I left behind. This is what familiarity breeds, not contempt, but the ability, the requirement that you stay hidden and out of sight.

Before dinner I take Molly and Sadie for a walk. Show them the landscape of my development. We cross the street to St. Gerard's. There's a new addition on the church grounds.

The Father Francis Memorial Garden. That's what the gold plaque says, along with, "A Friend to Us All." Carved below the statue are the words, "Donated by the Martino Family."

In the center of the garden is a statue of sour Father Francis, holding the hands of a little boy and a little girl. His eyes are lowered, smiling down at the gleaming faces of these uniformed kids. They are clutching his rotten spongy hands, carved in rock, forever bound to him in stone.

Molly and Sadie, as if reading my mind, jump over the string, tromp through the marigolds and carnations planted around the stone trio, and then they both take a dump right at his feet. I feel touched on the brow by the hand of God. "Bless me fucker, for I have sinned," I whisper.

We deposit our donation, tithe in our own personal way. The fucking Father Francis Memorial Garden. The only good part is the word "memorial." Father Francis is dead.

My mom prepared creamed tuna on toast, no peas, just the way I like it.

"Honey," my mom says, as she dumps another load of tuna on my plate, "we ran into Miss Cook last week."

"Oh," I reply, "how is she?" I can feel the tuna begin swimming in my stomach, heading upstream to my mouth.

"Well, Maria, she just went on and on about what a good student you were," my dad adds proudly.

"I bet," I mutter, choking down a gulp of milk. (Cunnilingus 101.)

"Maria," my dad says, "now that you're home, you can help me plant some shrubs on the hill at the side of the house."

"Sure, Dad," I say, "just can't get that grass to grow, can you?"

They still hadn't gone into detail about Fitz. I would have to be an expert can opener to pry any real information out of my parents. They've always lived by that great American family value that has now become an actual government mandate: Don't ask. Don't tell.

"I want to go see Fitz," I say. They both sagged in their chairs and averted their eyes. "What have you found out?" I press.

My dad began the ritual push away from the table. "There's nothing we can do for him," he says, as he walks into the living room to mainline the other kind of morphine—television.

123

Keeps all our aching, messed-up parts entertained.

My mother is about to serve me yet another helping of creamed tuna.

"No, Mom, I've had enough," I say. "I'm going to the hospital."

It takes me an hour to get out of my car. I sit outside in the parking lot doing this breathing exercise that Christie taught me. It's supposed to help ease anxiety. I've just gone into hospitals too many times and always with the knowledge that someone is dying.

Once, I practically killed myself driving frantically to Sherman Oaks Hospital because Peter called and said it didn't look good. We had taken Matthew in the week before for pneumocistis pneumonia. I had to drive from Hollywood way out to the valley. I stopped at Seven-Eleven and bought myself a Big Gulp because my throat was dry. I bought three Hostess cupcakes too. It worked for Beth, and I wasn't about to rub Mona in rush hour traffic.

When I walked into Matthew's room, Matthew was sitting up in bed without even an oxygen mask on. Peter was sitting next to him with a slice of pizza hanging out of his mouth.

"False alarm!" Peter hooted.

Immediately, this weird thought popped into my brain: *They're breasts, momma, breasts.* Then I realized that I was feeling like Sissy Spacek in the movie, *Carrie*, right after pig's blood has been dumped all over her pretty prom dress. At the very moment she sends all those stupid high school snots slamming into the gymnasium walls like basketballs.

Peter laughed. "Someone's on the rag."

"Don't go there, queen," I hissed, my finger pointed at him and cocked like a pistol.

Matthew repented, his eyes downtrodden. "I'm sorry, Maria, Peter thought we could have a party. Cup's here too, with her friend Mark. They're down the hall."

Then I heard it. The scraping on tile followed by the slow slide of slippers. Mark trudging into the room with the aid of a walker, and then you, Cup.

When I saw you, all the Sissy Spacek rage drained out of me and you held me close, feeling the terror coarsing through me. I was expecting death, not a party.

At last, my humor was restored. I turned to Matthew and said, "Girl, you look worse than Vanessa Redgrave in *Playing for Time*." Then I flung a greasy pepperoni at Peter's white linen shirt. Even the score.

When I walk into Fitzy's hospital room, the light is off. I turn the lamp on by his bed and I feel punched. He is so bruised, a peach that's been dropped and handled too many times. His eyes are swollen, ribs cracked, a broken arm. I think about Timothy Michael. The gay hairdresser from Maine who was bashed and left for dead. This is how he'd look if someone had intervened before the fatal blow, the toss into the river like a crumpled beer can.

Fitzy is asleep. An IV of nutrients seeps into his veins. He doesn't look like a little nimbus cloud anymore. He looks like something discarded, a torn-up sofa on the curb, stained and drooping. He's only twenty-three, but he looks aged and weary.

I lean down over him and begin to sing in a deep voice like Elvis. "*Love me tender. Love me true. Never let me go. . .*"

"Hey," Fitz says, his right eye opens just a slat, "where'd you get that shiner?"

The slow tears covering my eyes are like lenses. I run my fingers through a tussle of his dark hair. It isn't soft anymore, it's clumped over stitches on his scalp. "Hey, Fitzy," I whisper, "I'm so sorry."

He reaches his arm up and with his finger he circles my eye and the bruise staining my skin black-blue.

"You had to be there," I smile, and clasp my fingers around his, and press his palm to my face. His hand is the hand of a man, not a boy, rough and calloused, his skin dried from the elements. I want to crawl into the bed next to him, cradle his body to mine and watch *Captain Kangaroo*.

I wish I could arm wrestle with the hands of time, because when Fitz opened his eye, just a sliver, I could see that he didn't really want to be alive anymore. I know that look.

"I'm so tired, Mia," Fitz mumbles, and he closes his eyes and drifts away from me.

I sit with Fitz as he sleeps and trace my finger around the bruises on his arm. One of them is so bad it's dark black and I can hardly imagine a fist that could slam with such force. Did he fall when he was struck?

I stare at my own hand and curl it up into a ball. I have a

fist too. It was five, maybe six years ago, Cup, I've lost track of time, my marker is death. It was Christmas. No one was dead yet. We invited everyone over for dinner, some were positive, others didn't know, didn't want to know.

We were in the kitchen. I carried a plate of vegetables and dip out to the living room. Little symptoms were being tossed around like a beach ball at a stadium. James was losing sensation in his feet and hands. Mark had a weird rash. His lover Jorge's tongue was covered with thrush. Grunge between the toes. Fungus. Matthew had his first petite mal seizure. A strange buzzing in the brain. Nothing grand yet.

Was this our first Christmas? More symptoms slipped into the kitchen as you swung the door open to carry out the platter of feta cheese, salty olives, tomatoes in olive oil, and hot bread. *Diarrhea. Hair loss. Experimental drugs. Reagan is an asshole. Night sweats.*

I was shoving stuffing into the turkey, when you came back to the kitchen. We stood silent, and then you whispered, "They're all going to die."

I made a fist and splattered the walls and your blouse with stuffing. I punched you, Cup, the first time I've ever hit anyone. We were stunned.

I reached out to you and you reached back and held me close. "Sweet pea, it's okay," you whispered.

Peter blasted into the kitchen wanting more champagne. Then Matthew came in too.

"Look at the lovebirds," Peter said, as he rushed to the refrigerator.

Matthew caught my eye. He saw the stuffing strewn around the kitchen like confetti. "Let me help," he said, and he grabbed a wash cloth and started wiping the walls. His arms and legs were as thin as a bird's and each swipe of his hand took such effort.

In bed that night, Cup, you grabbed my ass hard, like you were digging furiously into soil, you spread my cheeks, opened me up and came inside, slowly at first, finger by finger, and then suddenly it felt like your whole hand was clenched into a fist pushing deep.

I exploded, a bomb detonating; a howl from my throat, from deep within my chest cavity, a burst of old groans and buried sobs. I was torn open. Then your hands played my clit like an instrument and I could feel your nipples hard against my back.

When we finished, you were lying on top of my back, and we were rocking in rhythm and your love spilled over me; your tears ran a dizzy path from your eyes, down my spine, rolling to my ass. "I'm sorry, Cup," I said.

"Me too," you whispered. "Me too."

I watched you as you fell into dreams and I saw the first trace of the bruise on your chest where I hit you. I wanted to peel it off like a strange rash, and I wanted to hit you again. I don't know why.

Fitzy's breathing is slow. Even in sleep he winces with each pull and release of oxygen. I wish I could reach inside and fuse his cracked ribs together; release him from so much pain.

The IV machine beats a steady rhythm, the nutrients seep in slowly like tear drops, one at a time. What invaded my little brother so long ago? I gave up on him; gave up trying to find out what forces were making him so miserable and here we both are—bruised and hopeless. I should have tried harder. I could have pinned Fitz to the ground and demanded to know why he wanted to be a threatening storm cloud.

I kiss Fitzy's brow. "Row, row, row, your boat," I sing, "Life is not a dream."

I leave the hospital and drive circles around town, hoping if I keep buzzing round and round, the mitten state will swat me away like a fly.

As I weave through the streets, I remember the one gay bar in town, way out, off the highway, where the buildings are spaced further and further and the traffic dissipates, just beyond the last gas station, before the farms spread. It's called the Square Peg. It's a hole-in-the-wall, hidden and out of sight. We're at home being hidden and out of sight. I need to sit with queers, catch my bearings, breathe a little deeper.

When I step out of my car, I can hear the faint sound of music coming from the bar. "*Someone left a cake out in the rain. I don't think that I can make it, cause it took so long to bake it, and I'll never have that recipe again!*" A handful of off-key male voices surge inside as I get closer to the door. I sigh.

I slip quickly onto an empty bar stool. It's dark inside with about a dozen men. Not a dyke in sight. The waiter approaches and eyes me suspiciously. Two older men to my right squirm.

"I'm an out-of-town friend of Dorothy's," I say. The bartender eases a bit and pours me a scotch. I grasp onto the glass and listen to the jukebox wailing that song about raining men, hallelujah. I feel drenched in an ugly hopelessness. The sudden realization that I've gone bad, belly-up, kaput. Useless. The same feeling I had with Matthew when he was dying. He couldn't eat. He couldn't move. He couldn't speak. When he tried to form words I would stare back at him bewildered and cursing myself for not being able to figure out what he was saying.

One day I was sitting next to his bed and he began grasping at his penis. It lay there like a small wounded animal and his fingers massaged and tugged as if trying to bring it to life. I laced my fingers through his and tried to help him. *Please, Lord, make him hard.* Together we rubbed his limp cock and then Matthew started to cry. I felt foolish and in that moment I wished I had been a man. Then maybe Matthew would cum.

The bartender puts another drink in front of me. "Compliments of these gentlemen," he says, pointing to the two men sitting next to me. They scooch their barstools closer.

My eyes finally catch up to the darkness and I turn to thank them for their hospitality. I almost pass out. I rub my eyes and squint.

"Matthew!?" I quiver, even though I know I'm addressing a dead person, but I swear it's him. "I'm sorry," I say, "you look like a friend, but he's dead."

"Maria? Is that you?" he says, leaning across the bar closer.

My chin has to be scraping the floor and then it hits me because I think about Jesus. "Brother John?!"

His companion laughs and begins singing, "*If there's a smile upon your face then the world's a happy place, won't you smile for us all Brother John.*"

It's a song from the *Singing Nun*, I recognize it right away as a quick-blip vision of Sister Mona on her scooter, whizzing past those grass-fat cows, zips across my brain.

"Brother John?!" I say again, shocked like I've been sideswiped.

"Maria!?" he replies, as if the very same car has struck him.

Fifteen

It feels so strange to be sitting across from him. After we recovered from our gay surprise, Brother John insisted on taking me out for a pizza. To catch up. I can hardly imagine it's the same man who scooped me up in his arms and carried me on his shoulders through the field of corn. Now, he's sitting across from me at Fabiano's, a red-checked tablecloth between us, a bulbous red candle dressed in mesh throwing light onto our faces, and a half-eaten large pizza with mushrooms and sausage waiting to be wrapped in a box.

We order another half-carafe of red wine. I keep having to restrain myself from toasting with, "The blood of Christ." I've been talking about Fitzy, secretly hoping to pry some priestly wisdom out of Brother John.

"Don't you remember when he was an altar boy?" I say. "He was so sweet, and then something changed."

Brother John squirms uncomfortably. "He was under Father Francis then," he answers. "I never really got to know Fitzgerald."

"That *fucker*," I spit. "Oh, I'm sorry, it's just that I hated Father Francis. He told my parents that Fitz was nothing but trouble. He was only twelve years old. He should have helped him!" I bark.

Brother John is fumbling with the check, his eyes glued to the candle's flame.

I heave a sigh onto the table. "I'm sorry, Brother, I mean, John," I say, "I just lost track of Fitz. I let him get away. I couldn't help him." Confessing to him feels so easy. I look to the flame too, then up at Brother John.

"I couldn't help him either," he says. Our eyes lock, his fingers now twirling the check rapidly.

"What do you mean?" I ask.

"Maria, you have to understand the church. It often makes decisions we cannot comprehend. I just think you should know that." He's not looking at me. I can see a buzzing behind his brow, as if trapped words are pushing to escape.

"Big news flash—and did you know, Martina is gay!" I sputter. "Most of the church is incomprehensible. What are you saying, what do you mean you couldn't help Fitz?" I press.

I want to open his skull like a box and dip my hand in fast. I can't believe I'm arguing with the man who picked me to say the words to "Bridge Over Troubled Water" when I was ten years old.

"I. . .left. . .the church," he says carefully, "not just because I was gay, I knew that long before I left. It was a confrontation with Father Francis." He looks over his shoulder as if we're swapping nuclear secrets. I look over mine too, suddenly feeling a surge of fear run up my spine.

"Confrontation?" I whisper, leaning forward. "What kind of confrontation?"

"Some of the boys." He stops. He drinks in a huge gulp of Christ's blood. "He was hurting them. I think your brother too. Maria, he molested them."

"Why do you think my brother too?!" My words like missiles. My face, inches from him.

His eyes are staring down at his hands. He has them folded, as if in prayer. He continues: "I remember Fitzgerald was punished for stealing a library book. . ."

"It was just a magazine!" I say abruptly.

"A magazine," he nods. "He had to clean the rectory. I knew something was going on. Father Francis had Fitz in his bedroom. I wasn't sure at the time. But then more boys—a few of them confessed to me." His praying hands, now clenched like mine. "I didn't know what to do. I tried to report it to the bishop. They did nothing but talk to him. I confronted Francis, but he denied it, said the boys were deeply disturbed. Then he asked me to leave. So I did."

The silence was eerie. Ghostly, like those still moments when funnel clouds inhale before releasing the tornado.

"You just left?" I whisper, low and coarse. I've stopped breathing. Dabs of light catch the wet drops falling down his face.

"*Godammit!*" I shout. Fabiano's comes to a halt. I stand above him and he sags in his chair. "Fuckers!" I slam my palm on the table. I hesitate, wanting to lash out at him. "I've got to go," I say, and leave the restaurant. I'm the iceberg hitting the *Titanic*. I'm a deluge of fire engulfing the *Zeppelin*. I'm an earthquake, a monsoon.

I drive fast, past the Square Peg, the farms and cows, out where woods spread and there are no lights signaling nearby humans. If I go home, I will want to hurt my parents. Pummel their aging sorrow.

There is only one thing for me to do. I spin the car around. I stop at the first gas station, race through the pages of the phone book, and dial.

"Miss Cook," I say, "it's Maria."

There is a long pause. "Oh my God," she says. "Maria, how are you?"

"Not so good. Not so good," I say. "I'd like to see you."

"Come right over," she answers. "I'd like to see you too."

The first thing I notice when I walk into Miss Cook's apartment is the poster. It's a seascape, a dove flying with a twig in its beak, and the message in fancy script: "God's peace to all who enter."

The next thing is that Miss Cook is not wearing any lipstick, or makeup. Gone is the scent of Jean Naté. No posters of Joan Baez or Judy Collins. She's wearing khaki slacks, a big sweater over a plain white blouse, and brown loafers. Her dark hair is cut in a short bob, and it's beginning to gray. The eyes, they're the same—sweet, brown, on the verge of tears.

One more thing. Miss Cook is wearing a little gold cross around her neck.

She offers me hot herbal tea, not wine, and I excuse myself to the bathroom. What am I doing here? In the bathroom, the walls are covered with little wood frames with more seascapes, mountains, waves of grain, and all adorned with sayings: "Keep Him in Your Heart;" "Love is Patient and Kind;" "His banner over me is Love." I look up at the ceiling, wondering if some Christian flag is waving above me.

I rummage through her cupboard. Baby powder and oil. Shampoo. Conditioner. Ivory soap. Towels. No Jean Naté, no makeup, no lipsticks to swipe.

I'm no detective, no Jessica Fletcher, but I can smell a born-again Christian a mile away. There is a little book on the back of the toilet called *Our Daily Bread*, and it's not filled with recipes. Bible verses and pleasant thoughts and instructions that make my saliva heat as I read. I collapse onto the toilet feeling defeated. What did I come here for? A kaboom between my legs in order to forget Fitz and this beast inside of me that wants to maul someone. My stomach boils. I sit on the toilet and start to sing, "*Romance finis, your chance, finis, the ants that have crawled up my pants. . .*"

"Maria," Miss Cook says, as she taps on the door, "are you okay?"

"I'll be right out," I answer.

"Do you need anything, sweetie?"

(Shit. Why did she go and call me sweetie!? Moan moan moan. Yes. I want you to pull your goddamned vagina out of the closet!!). "No, Pam, I'm coming out," I mumble.

She's sitting on the couch with her teacup and saucer balanced delicately on her lap. I sit next to her and an overstuffed awkwardness wedges between us like a pillow. Behind the couch is a stitched wall hanging of the Prayer of St. Francis. I glance at it, remembering the prayer by heart.

I want Miss Cook to help the ache that is is rooted in my belly to budge, just a bit. I stare at the wall hanging and let out a grunt when I get to the words: "Where there's despair, let me bring you hope." I'm no longer waiting for a gust of God. My hope is as puny as a fart.

"What are you thinking?" she asks.

"How about some music?" I say, as I stand and cross to her entertainment center. I flip through the albums and compact discs. Helen Reddy's *Greatest Hits*. Thank God. I place it on the turn table, and drop the needle. "You and Me Against the World" fills the emptiness in the room.

"I saw your parents," Miss Cook says. She's pouring us more tea. I think her hands are shaking.

"They told me," I respond, circling the room, staring at the Christianity that blankets the place like an avalanche of White Out. I stop in front of the poster of the dove with a twig in its beak. Signs of hope all over the goddamned place.

I point to it. "The twig represents evidence of land," I say. "The inhabitants of the Ark overjoyed with the promise of new life."

"Yes, that's right," Miss Cook answers, just as "*I am woman hear me roar*" begins to play. I lift the needle and start "You and Me". . .again.

"That's what I need, some bird to fly at me with a redwood in its beak," I whimper, then I laugh—a mean laugh.

A clumsy giggle flies out of her mouth like spit. "I was out in Los Angeles, four years ago," she says, "I meant to call you, but. . ."

"You didn't," I finish.

"No, well, I went with a church group," she says, "There wasn't time."

"Did you go to the Magic Kingdom? The happiest place on earth!" I sit down closer to her. The teacup and saucer on her lap are chattering because her legs are shaking.

"No. We went to the Crystal Cathedral." She's staring at her tea.

"The tackiest place on earth," I mutter and immediately regret my words. "I'm sorry. That was uncalled for." The loneliness lodged in my rib cage has the permanence of a vital organ. Next to it is a nimbus cloud, flaring like a cancer. I feel as if I'll bust open any second.

I stand again and begin pacing. Helen Reddy is irritating me beyond belief. I click off the record player just as the little girl repeats, "*Tell me again, Mommy.*" The song comes slowly to a halt, whining to a ghostly, low-pitched moan.

"You seemed upset when you called," she says. "Is there something wrong?" She's wringing her hands, wringing and wringing, wiping them briskly against her slacks.

My gaze finds a blank wall. No posters. Just white, and it calms me. "There's a poem I'm thinking of," I say. "A dead friend taught it to me. I've always remembered it because I think I want to *be* the poem. Do you understand?"

"I believe so," she whispers.

"*I like for you to be still. It is as though you were absent,*" I begin. In this moment it feels like Matthew is perched on my tongue. "*And you hear me from far away and my voice does not touch you.*" The wall in front of me is a skin and I see myself cross through the white white sheath as if entering an unspoiled place.

Suddenly, Miss Cook's hand is pulling at me because I guess I'm falling forward into the white wall and she wraps her arms around me just as my knees give out and she cradles and guides me, and together we fall to the floor. I dig my nails right through her sweater, so hard the blood seems to drain from my hands. A voice, my voice, strikes the air, hard like a bolt of lightning, and I lay myself on top of her, my face nuzzles into her neck, my mouth grips her skin, as weeping fills the room. Miss Cook is my wall—my wailing wall.

"It's okay, sweetie. Let it out. Let it go," she whispers.

I'm not sure how long we stay like this. Sorrow extends time, stretches it out, and seems to stop the sweeping second hand dead in its path. She's stroking my back, her hands feel so sturdy, and she dips them to my side, just barely grazing my breasts.

I begin sucking with my wet mouth, kissing her neck, breathing in her skin and the scent of clean Ivory soap. I can feel her nipples swell underneath my breasts.

"No, Maria," she says. Her hands ignore her words as they glide low and her hips press up into me. My hand is drawn like a magnet to the infinite ache between her legs. I pause and look in her eyes, now on the verge of longing and uncertainty, searching my face for a signal of absolution.

"Please," she says, and I don't move a muscle. I just lower my face closer. I can feel the rapid beat of her heart; the tightness in her body eases slowly, full of skin, muscle, and bone memory; a memory of holding a woman this close. It's indelible. Immersed in our bones, and not even Jesus himself can touch it.

Our hot breaths mingle and then her tongue, like a burning torch, is in my mouth. She's so thirsty, I can feel it. As if she's a desert-stranded drifter lapping blindly at a mirage of a bright blue lake.

I slide down her body, slipping her khakis off quickly, and surround her cunt with my lips, and for a few sacred moments, she is the twig in my mouth.

Where there's despair, let me bring you hope.

Miss Cook falls into a deep, full-body sleep. I'm wide awake worrying about Fitz. I've got to go back to the hospital. As I slip out of bed, Miss Cook grasps my thighs, her muscles and bones begging me to stay. Her face moves frantically toward my crotch and I push her away, by instinct, saving her from being swallowed up and lost forever, sucked into the black hole between my legs.

"Please Maria, let me." I slip off the mattress and reach for my blue jeans. I feel like a man who has hastily spent his sperm, leaving his lover empty as a pocket. I can't match her desire, her need as hopeless as distraught ivy on a brick wall about to be demolished.

Once in the bathroom, I bend over the sink and splash my face with cold water. Miss Cook hands me a towel. "Are you going?" she asks.

I bury my face into the soft cotton, then look into the mirror, meeting the reflection of her sad brown eyes pleading with me to stay.

"At least spend the night," she says. "Let me make love to you. It's been so long for me."

A horrible remorse grips my stomach. It's that damn infinite ache she's worked so hard to erase and now it's back, the awfulness of longing.

"I really have to go," I say, and I pick up the book, *Our Daily Bread.* I hand it to her. "What does it say for today?" I ask.

She's shivering from the cold bathroom tile and the fear of being left alone with her ache. She can't open the book. I can feel tiny twigs of shame growing inside of her, touching my own.

I guide her back to bed and tuck her under the blankets. I lie down and rub her brow, draw her eyes closed with my hand. I lean down and whisper in her ear over and over until her breathing slows and sleep embraces her. "I love you, Miss Cook."

Before I leave, I place the book on her chest, hoping when she wakes, she can still eat this food that sustains and eases her days. I wish I could tell her that she can have both of these; her daily bread and the indelible desire in her bones.

I'm sitting in the hospital's cafeteria having a big big bowl of oatmeal. It's 6:00 A.M. I'm telling myself it's too early to go up to Fitzy's room. My legs and arms are sore with that sweet, sweet ache of making love.

Cup, how many times have I felt that same sweet ache with you? When our sweat cooked and hissed and my body was pocked with marks from your mouth where I'd beg you to bite me, to sink your teeth deep in, as if I were an apple.

I'm holding my face over the steam from the hot oats, my pores soak it up. I'm so hungry, Cup. I wish you were here to help me with Fitz. I feel that same bewilderment sitting here in this hospital as I did when I went to see James and you couldn't come with me because Mark needed you. I had to go to San Francisco alone. I kept rubbing my arm, the sore place where a bruise was left over from your mouth and I wanted to peel it off and press it between the pages of a scrapbook.

When I entered James' hospital room, his sister was sitting by the window asleep. She came from Montreal to help Gaspar take care of him. I felt close with her, an ease in my marrow.

James had an oxygen mask clinging to his wet face. He was asleep too. I stood over him and in an instant my life with him ran through my brain. The first dandelion, the startling blue of his eyes, our innocent bodies groping one another like curious children, both of us dipping into dreams of a lover with a different body.

I didn't have the words then to describe how I felt with James. We were buoyed by the same spirit, like some wind picked us up, and I knew from my bones out—James and I were from the very same tree.

How he had dressed me for my high school reunion, coaxing this woman out who was frightened to see her own beauty. When I called James and told him that I had fallen in love with you, Cup, that we collided on the plane and landed in your apartment, your bed, and you gasped at my naked body, he cried.

"James, she said I was so beautiful!" I had exclaimed.

"Oh, Smudge, of course you are."

I stood at the end of his bed, rubbing his feet with rose oil. Christie gave it to me before I left. She told me it's for calming. He woke up, sat up in the bed, propped by pillows. His eyes were practically gone, those shimmering sapphires were layered with a white cloud. I still wanted to wrap them in a bandana and carry them around in my pocket like rare stones.

His lids and cheeks were all blown up with dark lesions, pus-oozing sores, ballooning his nose, mushrooming his ears, obliterating his eyes.

Where are you going, my beautiful friend? He gasped for air. His mouth was open wide as he took in tremendous, panicked breaths that went on and on until I could hardly believe he had the strength for them. For one more.

He lifted off the mask and begged for ice, his head darting across the room, scanning as if searching for a lost possession. I took a small cube and held it to his tongue. His sister and I murmered comfort. I let words spill out of me though I could not hear my voice. I didn't know anymore, what should be said, what should be kept in silence.

James raised his hands, like the conductor of a symphony

orchestra, and said two words. It was hard to hear, but I knew this language. "Quiet," he said. "Slowly." He was not talking to me or his sister. Some spirits were in the room, and he was directing them to be careful, to carry him off slowly.

James leaned his head back, dropped his arms to his lap, five more pulls of air from his belly, and he was gone. His search, over.

I breathed all five with him. The last came from a deeper place, from the center of his groin, and it was relief.

Then I lifted my rose-oiled palms to my face and groaned relief too, breathing in my friend.

I wanted to lift the bottle to his still lips, pour the oil into his mouth and let it slip over the tongue. I've lost a vital organ. I wanted the oil to stream down into James' lungs. Maybe then, I could hop in a boat and row gently down the stream, merrily, merrily, merrily, merrily, life is but a dream.

I'm frozen. Holding a spoonful of oatmeal midair. A gaggle of cackling nurses huddled around a table are staring at me suspiciously. Big soppy tears are falling fast down my cheeks. A doctor whisks by me, gasps at his watch, and grabs a banana and a bagel.

I drop my spoon and bolt for the stairs. I take two at a time and when I get to Fitzy's floor, I rush down the hallway towards his room, my steps quicken as I near. "Fitzy," I say, opening the door.

A woman is standing over Fitzy's bed. Removing the sheets. He's gone. "Sorry, sweetie, but he left here on his own about an hour ago."

I stare at her in disbelief.

"Can I help you?" she asks.

"I wish I knew how," I say, backing out of the room. I need a twig.

Sixteen

My dad is driving my mom and me to the farmers' market to buy those shrubs he wants to plant, some fresh summer fruit, and corn, if it looks good. I think they're worried. Besides my morning walk with Molly and Sadie for our dung deposit, I haven't left the house in three days. I'm waiting for Fitz.

We pass by long rows of corn—tall, waving in the breeze, bursting with ripe ears. I want to reach into the front seat and just touch my parents, but I can't. I can't bring myself to complete the gesture, the movement of my hands to their bodies. It's because I've got this huge lump in my throat, and I'm holding it captive, and if I touch them, it may burst so loudly that our station wagon could veer off the road. I haven't told them about my conversation with Brother John. I can't. I have to talk with Fitz.

"Have you heard from Cup, honey?" my mom asks. When she says your name, I swallow hard, hoping the lump will slam into my gut and I can feign car sickness.

"Just a postcard," I say. I fix my stare out the window, imagine myself running through the long rows of corn, becoming so lost, not even Brother John could find me.

A silence is looming in the car, a silence that is begging for more questions. (How is she? What did Cup say? Is she coming back to you?)

My parents are as ill-equipped to ask these questions as I am to answer. I can't string enough words together to explain what has happened, what my life looks like. Right now, I don't have the will to find a language.

My father tosses the silence out the window like a gum wrapper. "I can't wait to sink my teeth into a juicy ripe plum, how 'bout you?"

"I can't wait, Dad," I say.

"You got it all over us in the citrus department out there in California," he goes on, "but you can't beat Michigan apples!"

"No, you can't." Some things never change, like conversations with my dad. Weather. Food. Cars. He can talk for hours about these, yet pushes himself away from anything that is remotely emotional. Particularly Joseph's death and the trouble with Fitz. He disappears into himself and his absence amputates us from him as swiftly as skin is shucked from corn.

When my friends first started to die, I would call home and if Dad answered, we would whisk through weather, cars, food, the latest joke he'd heard, and then he would put Mom on. I could tell her about my dying friends, and she would listen, but not fully, I could tell. She's a mom, she wants to believe she can kiss a scraped knee and make it all better, but she's helpless when confronted with the big gashes and wide-open wounds of her children. They're too big. Too scary.

My mom is rummaging through her purse. "I have some old photos for you," she says. "You sent them to me years ago."

She hands me the small pile. Christmas, 1988. Cup's birthday party. I don't remember when, but Matthew and your friend, Mark, are still alive. I can't look at them. I roll the window down and let them fly, fly fast into the hot air, scatter along the road and end up like gum wrappers, strewn with dirt, oil, and other bits of life. Remnants carrying memory, as ordinary as a cigarette butt, as potent as a used condom, or as sad as a discarded gathering of mostly dead friends captured on film.

Both of my parents see me toss the photos, but like my black eye, it doesn't exist.

I lean forward and put my hands on the back of the front seat, steadying myself. My mom turns, places her hand over mine, and the lump in my throat bounces, but I'm able, anyway, to squeeze out a smile.

"It's good to be home," I say, as we push through the wind, bound for fruit, shrubs, and corn—if it looks good.

After my parents go to bed, I spend the night on the couch with Cupcake watching television. I watch old reruns. I've got fifty-two channels to choose from and it lulls me like morphine. After midnight, I watch three episodes of *M*A*S*H*, followed by two hours of *Murder, She Wrote*. I want to see Maine, where the show is located. I want to pretend I'm there with you, Cup. Mostly, I hope the detective slash mystery writer, Jessica Fletcher, will discover the bloated, fish-eaten carcass of a fat old has-been dyke identified by her dentures as Vagina Ham. She fell off a bridge into a river. Suicide? Hate crime? Murder?

Tonight I also saw my old boyfriend, Dave Martino. He's big as a house, and he's Greater Michigan's La-zy-Boy King. "C'mon down," he screams out of the TV, "and I'll practically give you a La-zy-Boy for free, factory direct!"

Oh, to turn back the hands of time. What if that ping ping ping between my legs had erupted when Dave kissed me behind the church, with his shoulder pads pinning me against the brick? What if by some fluke of nature, Mona cheered at the feel of his hard-on pressing into my thigh when we slow-danced at the high school reunion? Or worse yet, what if I were too terrified to follow the magnetic pull to Miss Cook, to her apartment, to her mentoring arms and lips.

If my terror outsized my hunger that night, I could now be as wide as Lake Superior, married to Greater Michigan's La-zy-Boy King. We'd have a bijillion fat kids, and I'd stuff a bijillion donuts down their thoats to keep the no-good brats quiet while I watched my soaps with my overblown ass stuffed into this really putrid powder blue Naugahyde chair that reclined, and I'd have my feet propped up on the footrest that popped out of this disgusting chair because the doctor said I had to keep my legs elevated to help the circulation and to reduce the flurry of varicose veins that run up and down my cottage cheese thighs like earthquake fault lines on a map of California, and I'd bark at my kids to bring me another Diet Pepsi and a bag of chips, and I'd stuff handfuls of those chips into vats of low-fat onion dip, then into my pudgy mouth with my pudgy fingers, and when the La-zy-Boy King came home, he'd stuff his lard ass into the matching tawny Naugahyde chair and bark at me to bring him a beer and the bag of chips, and I'd say, "Get off your fat ass and get it yourself," and secretly, sinisterly, I'd be laughing cuz I ate all the goddamned potato chips.

I'd hate my world as much as I hated myself, and only in nightmares or those sneaky blips of truth that pop out when you look in a mirror, I'd see it. I'd realize that I wanted to die, but the layers and folds of skin, the noise of the television, and the gnashing of my teeth, would have kept my heart from understanding why.

If I could, Cup, I'd turn time back, but only so far. Far enough to keep myself from hurting you. Further yet, to keep friends from dying. I can't erase any of it.

Around 4:00 A.M., I trudge down to the basement. It's that time when the day's identity hangs in oblivion, no longer night, not quite morning. The air seems uncertain as well, swirls of cool from the ground blend with the descending warm, wet, August air. I can smell rain.

It's a sad time, a time of contemplation for garbage collectors and mothers, whose nipples are aroused by a hungry baby. Or those like me, afflicted with a manic wakefulness in the dying evening. I'm rummaging through my father's tools in the storage room. My lips are parted wide, wrapped around the flashlight in my mouth. The same lips that danced with Miss Cook's clit. Her merciful moans and sighs covered us like an old soft blanket. I'm still savoring the memory of her taste, along with the acrid flavor of metal.

The shadow from the hammer in my hand fills the storage room wall and it looks like a spooky monster. I hold it firm, strike at the air, watching the monster descend on its imaginary prey.

Joseph's things are still in boxes, lined up against the wall. The flag is here too. I unfold it and wrap it around my shoulders. The blanket Beth and I shared. Fitzy was so little then. He held onto me for safety, for comfort. I looked out for him then, the way Joseph looked out for me.

I sweep the flashlight across the boxes and see one marked, "Joseph's books." It's got to still be there—*Portnoy's Complaint*. I blow off the layer of dust and open it up. There it is. A hardcover edition, copyright 1969. The pages are faded and yellowed. I never did ask Joseph what boffed meant, but I found out soon enough.

I perch myself on an old trunk, flashlight in mouth, the American flag keeping me warm, and I begin to flip rapidly through the pages. "Ahh, quit your whining," I snap.

The next thing I know, a huge shadow monster is swooping down on top of me from behind. I slam the book shut, leap and zip around fast, half expecting the ghost of Mr. Portnoy to whack me with a stick. I thrust out my flashlight and staring back at me is my dad, his broad belly is peering out from underneath his flannel robe.

"Maria," he says, "it's four in the morning. What are you doing down here?"

I feel like I've been caught playing with myself. He pulls a string, and the lone bulb hanging above my dad's workbench blinks on. His once-orderly tools are strewn in disarray.

"Dad, I'm sorry, did I wake you?"

He eyes his tools and then me. "No, I need some Pepto, my stomach's churning. Onions, I think." He palms his belly, disgruntled, and then looks at me suspiciously. "What are you looking for?"

"Oh, just browsing," I say. I slip the book onto a box behind me.

He surveys the storage room. "Gotta throw some of this stuff out," he says. "Oh well, turn off the light when you're done." He turns to go back upstairs.

"Dad!" I say loudly. For a split second I want to spill all that I know about Fitz.

"What?" he whispers back. "Keep it down, your mother's asleep."

"Yeah. Well, it's just that. . . I could use some Pepto too. My stomach is boiling too."

I click off the light and leave the tools I've selected in a pile. I sit with my dad at the kitchen table and we share a soup spoon, passing the bottle of Pepto back and forth.

"So, Maria, how was your visit with Miss Cook?"

"Memorable," I sputter.

My dad goes to the refrigerator and pulls out soda water, vanilla ice cream, and chocolate sauce. "How about an ice cream soda, that oughta settle our tummies."

We sit and slurp our sodas, scooping at the ice cream as the darkness outside turns a dim gray that seeps into the kitchen. The morning is filled with the promise of a storm and I welcome it.

"How do you like that rental car?" he asks.

"Pretty well, Dad, but it starts to shimmy at eighty." He smiles. My dad likes that I drive fast and that I notice the shimmy.

"Probably needs to be aligned, huh?" He rubs his face hard as if scrubbing his flesh with a course rag. "Y'know what? Why don't you keep that." He reaches over and grabs a corner of the flag that's still draped around my shoulders.

I wrap my hand around his finger. "Thanks, Dad, I'd like to have it." We linger for a small moment and then my dad stands.

"Let's clean up," he says.

I wash and my dad dries. When we finish, he wipes off the counter real slowly, as if to extend our time together. "Maria, I know you're worried about Fitz. Try the field, sometimes he sleeps out there. He's a crazy kid."

"It's a crazy world," I reply. "Dad, I need a favor."

"What?" he asks.

"I'm going to Maine and I'd like to leave Molly and Sadie here, if that's okay?"

"Sure," my dad says. "What's a couple of mouths to feed."

"I'm gonna leave now. Well, soon. Before Mom wakes up."

My dad is content to allow mystery to exist. He doesn't need to know all the details of his children's lives—keep it simple. At this moment, I need simplicity. He rummages through a drawer, an all-purpose drawer filled with expired coupons, warranties for discarded appliances, matchbooks, and a pile of maps.

"I think if you drive through Canada, you'll get there faster," he says, handing me the maps. We stand awkwardly and my dad lets out a big yawn. "Leave a note for your mother. I'm gonna get some shut-eye."

He begins to shuffle out. I want to hug him, put my arms around him and feel his broad belly press into mine.

"Maria," he says, turning slightly, "be careful. Pack yourself some sandwiches, there's plenty of good cold cuts in the fridge. Just take it easy, kid."

"I will." My anger is now at a safe distance, like the storm approaching. I've got a mission and I've got to find Fitz. I gather my tools, Cupcake, a bag of clothes, and kiss Molly and Sadie goodbye.

First, I park by the church and cross to the hill above the field. It is still too dark to see clearly. I begin to run, carefully avoiding any dips that could send me flipping onto the grass. I pass the spot where Fitz and I sucked our caramel suckers and drank Mountain Dew. The place where he pointed to the sky and told me he was a nimbus cloud. I run with all my might, my eyes scanning the expanse of land spread out before me. A thick wedge of wet haze layers the field.

"Fitzy!" I scream to the sky, to the field pocked with signs of sport and play. "Fitzy!!" I yell again. I taste the salt of my tears mixed with sweat in my mouth. My lungs wheeze a moan like the low notes of a harmonica.

"Maria!" I hear. "Maria, over here!" It's Fitzy. I can see the outline of him and my legs become rockets, pulling me rapidly and exactingly to his body.

I fall to my knees breathing like an old sprinter. I can't talk.

"Geez," he says. "You're in bad shape." He laughs. His face isn't so black and blue, it's just brown and a muckish yellow where the fist punched him.

My belly extends as I pull in a big heap of air. "Fitzy, why did you leave the hospital? What happened to you?"

He's sitting on his sleeping bag, lighting a cigarette. His hair is sticking out in several directions. His arm is still in a cast, dirt-strewn and almost black. "I didn't need to be there. I can take this off by myself," he says, lifting the cast to my face. He smells sour.

"Fitz, who beat you up?" I sit close to him, on his sleeping bag. On my jeans are two big wet marks where my knees hit the soppy grass.

"It was nothing. Some assholes. I'll get them." He sucks in a big drag, lifts his head and harshly exhales a plume to the sky like pollutants from a smokestack.

"Fitz, I have an idea. Why don't you come back to L.A. with me?" I rest my hand on his knee.

"What would I do out there?" he asks. A bit of longing slips into his voice.

"I'll get you a job," I say rapidly. "I have a friend who has a flower shop, she'll hire you." (Please, Lord, help Christie forgive me.)

Fitz leans back on his elbows. He scrunches his brow and I can see traces of the little boy—child cogitating.

"Fitz, I saw Brother John last night," I say, watching his fingers twirl the cigarette.

"He's a faggot," he grunts with amusement.

"Fitz, c'mon. He told me something about you." I can feel that same tense current running through me. I'm dismantling another bomb and I don't want to snip the wrong wire.

Fitz presses his cigarette into the ground and lights another.

"I know what happened to you Fitz," I say, and breathe in slowly—his smoke and the wet air fill my lungs.

"You don't know shit," he grunts. He slides away and stands up. I feel suddenly very small on the ground. My little brother is a big man.

"I know what Father Francis did to you," I say.

Fitz pulls at the sleeping bag. "Get off," he says, yanking it out from under me and leaving my ass to soak up more dew.

He rolls up the bag quickly, then stuffs it into his backpack and slings it over his shoulder. I stand. My face reaches his chin. (Why can't his feet dangle above the toilet?)

"Fitz, I love you. I want to help." I look him squarely in the eyes.

He's biting his upper lip. "Go back to your dead fag friends!"

I hear thunder, way way off, and I start to count in my head, measuring the distance between the storm and myself. I open my mouth. "Fitz," and then it happens. He shoves me with the might only a man can muster. My ass hits the ground like a boulder and Fitz runs fast toward the school. He turns back quickly. Maybe to see if I'm okay. Maybe not. Then he disappears into the wedge of haze.

"I'm not giving up!!" I scream.

Fuck. He doesn't want me to sing in a deep voice like Elvis. My butt aches and I think about Miss Cook scooping me up in her arms when I tumbled into the hot grass. I wish her big laugh was around so I could grab onto it like a balloon that would carry me off to the other side of space and time. Maybe I *should* go back and sleep with her, let her make love to me. Court and spark.

Is that it? Go back to the very beginning when the first tap of the clitoral tom-tom sounded under Miss Cook's twirling tongue. Mona, if I let Miss Cook make love to me then will your amnesia miraculously evaporate?

Mona will rise up out of her hospital bed, tears streaming down her labials. "I remember. I remember. My name is Mona. I want to go home," she wails.

The throng of doctors and nurses surrounding Mona are hugging, weeping, cheering. They have become so attached to the little lost *mons pubis* known only as Vagina Doe.

As Mona boards the Greyhound bus, headed back to me, she turns and waves her little Kotex panty liner in the air. The hospital staff yells, "Viva la Vulva!!"

The town's band plays a Sousa march as the bus pulls away. Swirling dust from the road coats the wet faces of the weeping well-wishers. The hospital's chief of staff turns to the crowd and says, "She may have discovered her name, but through knowing her, we have discovered the real meaning of life."

Cut to the bus rolling down the empty highway into a great ruddy sunset. Fade Out.

I start walking, not toward the church, but through the field to Tug's. I want a speckled gum ball. I want a whole fistful of speckled gumballs to shove in my mouth. Maybe Tug will spring for a box of Hostess donuts. My chest throbs right above my breasts where Fitz pounded.

As I round the corner, I hit a garbage can with Seven-Eleven printed on the side. Tug's is gone. My gumballs—gone. There's no turning back.

From far off I hear the churchbells ring 6:00 A.M. I've got to hurry before it's too late.

I peek inside and a handful of churchgoers begin mass. I carefully move my car to the Father Francis memorial garden. I've brought a chisel, a mallet, and some thick old rugs to mute the sound of each blow. I stare at him. "You fucker!" I spit.

I glide my hand across the little boy's cheek, and the little girl's. "Hang in there, I'm setting you free."

With each solid whack, I growl at him. I stare in his stone-cold eyes and pray he's in hell. I wallop him good and carefully release the hands of the children bound to his sour self. I've never felt so strong. The beaming kids seem to beam broader with each strike of the mallet. When I finish, he's at the center of the garden—alone. I had to completely whack off his hands, so now his eyes stare down at nothing but empty stumps.

I tromp through the carnations and marigolds, dragging each child through the flowers, and lift them into the trunk and drape the flag over them. Just as I finish, the heavy rain clouds burst open, claps of thunder ring out with no seconds to count in between.

Mission accomplished. My only concern now is crossing the border. What if the Canadian border patrol wants to search my car for perishables? How do I explain two cement kids wrapped in an American flag?

As it storms, Cupcake and I drive steadily east. I roll the window partway down, letting drops of rain splash my face, keeping me from the pull of fatigue. I rub my chest, feeling the remnants of Fitzy's fear under my skin. I push the car to eighty, then steady my foot, feeling the hum and shimmy of the car pass through me.

Cupcake is in the passenger seat. I rub my fingers through her soft fur. "You and me against world, kiddo," I say.

I can hear the cement kids vibrating in the trunk. I flip on the radio. It's Kasey Kasem's top forty. That ought to get me to the Canadian border. It's 8:30 in the morning. A new day. This is the only thing I'm certain of. And, I'm going to Maine to see Cup.

Seventeen

I was only going to rest my tired ass for a few hours. I was so relieved to be through with Canada. I stopped at Niagara Falls. It was past midnight and the park was closed, so I slipped over the fence and lay down on a bench.

The next thing I know is that I'm being poked with what feels like a stick. I incorporate the sensation into the dream I'm having. Christie is there. Peter. Fitz. And you, Cup. I'm lying in the backyard at our house, and everyone is jabbing me with their fists. Molly and Sadie are asleep in the dream, both snoring and farting.

When I wake, I'm sprawled on the park bench like a drunk, my mouth oozes saliva, my hair is matted, and my clothes are drenched from the steady stream of droplets from the waterfall.

I'm looking up at the face of a very stern fellow. It's daylight. There's so much gunk in my eyes I can hardly see him. I blink several times. His badge says "Norman" and he isn't welcoming me to Niagara Falls. He's poking me with his billy club.

"Lady, no loitering, it's against the law," he grumbles.

As my vision improves I see that I'm surrounded by a throng of freshfaced vacationing families all staring at me. The mothers are clutching their children and looking at me as if I am that child molester they saw on *America's Most Wanted*.

I want to say, "No need to worry folks, just your run-of-the-mill transient lesbian on holiday." I'm thinking that I should videotape the whole event because Norman is still poking me and I really believe I could convince a jury that this is unnecessary use of force. I'm telling my right hand to clench into a fist and aim and fire at his crotch, but my brain cells are all foamy, sloshing around as if they've been drinking beers in a hot tub all night.

"I'll need to ask you a few questions, ma'am," Norman says.

Now, my brain cells are playing a game of hide and seek, they scream at me, "You're it!" and all of them run off in a thousand directions before I even begin to count, one thousand one, etc. . . . I stare up at Norman quizzically. He has a round, mean face. Pinched lips. Squinty, tight-ass eyes.

"What is your name?" he asks, pulling out a pad and red

pencil. He's of the same species that Vagina Ham, Esther, and George Bush belong to—*anus Constrictus.*

I want to say, "My name is Vagina Doe." However, I don't think this crowd could appreciate the subtlety of the moment.

"I'll need to see some identification," he orders. This Norman needs a lesson in adequate response time. I'm a little stumped. I'm not sure if I pulled out my driver's license that I'd even recognize myself.

"Maria," I slur. "My name is Maria." The crowd doesn't hug, cheer, or weep. I fumble in my pockets to pull out my license, but because I never ever carry a wallet in my pocket, this gesture is not only useless, it makes me feel guilty-as-charged.

"My wallet is not here."

Norman and a few of the vacationers grimace. I feel the moment calls for a line, something like, "You who are without sin cast the first stone."

I decide to stand up, but not realizing that my legs have fallen asleep, I practically dive to the ground, but I catch myself by grabbing Norman's billy club. The crowd draws in a collective gasp of fear. Norman seizes my arm. Basically, I stand stock still in utter confusion. By the looks of things, you'd think I was brandishing a small handgun.

I can hear my brain cells mocking me: Some yell, "You have the right to remain silent." Others pound sticks and spoons, "Silence equals death!" The less aggressive ones are swaying, hand in hand, singing, "All we are saying, is give peace a chance."

I have to walk a straight line a bijillion times, do the finger-to-nose exercise, and take a breathalizer test. My blood alcohol level is zero. Norman is disappointed.

He searches my car for drugs and child pornography. When he opens the trunk, he almost reaches for his weapon when he spots my stone kids.

"They're statues," I bark, "I am an arteest!"

He finally lets me go but gives me an official Niagara Falls citation of warning. Asshole cop wannabe.

I drive out of there fast and I don't stop until I'm certain I'm not being followed. I pull into a truck stop for breakfast. I eat piles of french toast and down a dozen cups of coffee. Even the waitresses seem to be gossiping about me. Don't they know

I'm a hash-slinging sister? I go to the bathroom to splash water on my face and I see what all the hoopla's about. I look like hell. Like I've been rode hard and put away in a body bag. My clothes are soggy and dank, having been drenched in grass-dew, rain, and the waterfall.

I make two calls before I leave. One to Christie, and when she answers, I hang up. I just want to hear her voice. Then I call Peter and his machine picks up and the long beep tells me he's not answering phone calls. *Don't die, Peter.*

As I hit the freeway, my brain cells are high-fiving each other, triumphant in having successfully humiliated me. I need them to behave and get me safely to Maine.

The moment I see the sign, "Welcome to Maine," an old companion jumps into the car with me. I can feel my body filling up with those low blue notes, that deep sad song without words, just gloomy chords cascading through my veins. I wonder if you can hear me coming, Cup.

I drive past Ogunquit where Vagina's bed and breakfast is, and I keep going north for a few miles until I arrive at Old Orchard Beach. I like the name, old orchard, because right now, that's how I feel, like my body is an old piece of land that was once fruitful and abundant. What's left are twigs of shame, barren and twisted.

There's a string of one-room cottages and a vacancy sign that catches my eye. I drag my bitchy brain cells into the cottage with "manager" above the door. So far, so good. I smack the bell on the counter. The hum seems to go on and on and I hear a voice, muted and off in the distance.

"I'm back here, in the garden. C'mawn back!" the voice implores.

I wonder if I'm supposed to "c'mawn." I go around the cottages to the backyard and I can't see any signs of a breathing human being. It's an enormous garden with hundreds of flowers, huge and colorful, splashed with more shades than a box of crayons. I'm wide-eyed and openmouthed. It's startling, like opening the pages of a pop-up book filled with intricate and wondrous lands.

"Dog got your teeth?" the voice barks. My head darts toward the direction and still, no one in sight. Then I hear a raspy laugh. "Don't be shy, girl."

I wipe my forehead, check my temperature, then stick my

finger in my ear and twirl it a few times. What I really want is for someone to come along and scoop me up and take me to some really plush mental hospital slash spa where people from England go for bad nerves or sudden spells. A place where I can sit in a lounge chair overlooking a pond with ducks. I have a towel wrapped around my head, dark glasses on, and I obediently swallow the pills that are being handed to me by Inga, who looks like a mean old bulldagger on the outside, but really she's just as sweet as a teddy bear. Big, brawny, buxom, Swedish Inga, who picks me up in her solid arms and carries me back to my private room when the sun gets too hot and gives me a massage to die for.

"Shake a stick and hep me up." The voice strikes again. I scan the garden for a burning bush. I could use a talk with God.

I amble slowly through the garden, weaving toward the voice, and I finally see her. She's an old lady wearing a flowery housecoat that makes it appear as if she's been planted right in the ground. She has long, gray hair twirled in a bun and she's hunched over. Sweat drips down her round face and as I get closer, I can see she's thick-boned, bronzed by the sun, and handsome, like a man.

"That dawg's got your teeth and chords!" she hoots. She reaches her arms toward me and I grab them and pull her to her feet. She wipes her face with the back of her hand and leaves a trail of dirt across her cheeks, then staggers toward the cottages, balancing herself on my arm.

"My old bones get stuck from being bent for so long. Good thing I ain't one to believe that prayin' calls for kneeling. I always say, if God wants you on your knees, he woodna given us feet."

When we enter the manager's cottage she scooches her ample ass onto a stool behind the counter. "My name's Alma, Alma Lowell. Cottage will cost you fifty-five bucks a night, won't find cheaper this close to the ocean. I've been here for over fifty years, and we've always had the fairest rates. Old Orchard ain't exactly a town, but we're on the map. We're not fancy like Ogunquit and we ain't got the Bush's like Kennybunk, but who'd want 'em anyway? Am I right?"

"Sure," I say, hoping she'll hand me a little paper cup with pills in it.

"I'm from Chattnooga, 'riginally, but haven't left Maine

since I married Bud Lowell, a Yankee," she winks. "Want some iced tea?"

I begin to open my mouth but before I can respond, words shoot out of her like frantic bees from their hive.

"Lord, you look like you've chopped up your piano for firewood. Hmmm," she hums, staring at me as if I'm that last clue in a crossword puzzle. "You ever been to Chattnooga? I call it Tenne-*sissy* cause that's all that lives there, a bunch of scared old sissies can't accept change. Had I been there during Dr. King's time, I'd been pushing those stupid white folks off the bus entirely."

Alma slaps the counter and laughs, a big laugh that makes my spine jump. "I'm southern fried from Tenne-sissy, a state that's dull and full of prissies! I made that up. Bud would laugh his fool head off. He died laughing, doubled over and had a heart attack. We were blessed 'cause we laughed all the damned time. Didn't have no kids. Wanted 'em, but Bud's swimmers never left the diving board. Don't matter. Take what life offers. More or less."

She pauses. Her eyes are filled with so much zeal I feel as if I'm being punched.

"Yes," I say. I'm a slow drip of honey being zapped by a bee on a sugar binge.

"Yes what?" she yelps.

"Iced tea," I say, "I'd like that. And a room."

"Oh Lord, where are my manners? I'm so sorry. I'm ramblin' on and I don't even know your name. Just take my mouth and stick it in a moosaleum. Ain't that a tomb?"

"Yes. An ancient tomb," I reply.

"Well, if it's ancient, that's where I belong."

"My name is Maria," I say.

Her eyes light up. "Hmmm," she hums again. "Well, how do you solve a problem like that!?"

After six glasses of iced tea with mint leaves from Alma's garden, I finally make my way to cottage number six. I collapse on the bed and don't wake up until the next day. I wake to the sound of the waves crashing against rock. I wake to the smell of fog and fresh baked pie. Apple pie, I think. The sound and smell make me sad. Then I hear her voice, "Yoo hoo!" It's Alma in her garden, and a smile slips out across my face—a real grin. The first unforced smile I can remember.

Eighteen

I didn't realize I'd feel so wide-open, cut in two, my heart on full display. Something about this close proximity to Cup has caused my body to throb with grief. As if my cells, on the minutest molecular level, sense Cup, and are clamoring in anguish for a reunion with her atoms, their long lost mates. Along with the throb is a giddy panic, a shudder underneath my skin, a whizzing in my bones. As I walk along the jagged cliff above the Atlantic, I maintain a safe distance, afraid I could levitate right off the ground. I'm not sure my sorrow is hefty enough to keep my feet planted on the soil.

"How in the cat hair are you?!" Alma whoops as I round the corner to the backyard. "I hope you don't mind, but I snuck in your room just to make sure you were still breathing. I threw a blanket over you too. It's my job to intervene if I'm worried about a guest."

Alma's my woof woof woof with a cup of hot chocolate. My trained bystander. She motions for me to sit and join her at the picnic table.

On the table is the best spread I can imagine. Fresh peach pie. Vanilla ice cream and strong coffee. My eyes bulge and light up like sparklers. Happy happy happy.

"Hope you don't mind," Alma says, "but I think it's crazy to save dessert for supper. Why not begin the day with sweets, just in case you drop dead by noon."

I like her logic. I like her peach pie and coffee. I like her flowers. It makes me feel sad about Christie. She'd love it here. I can see her pushing a wheelbarrow full of dirt, the flex of her muscled arms and the way she'd scoop her hands into the soil.

After breakfast, I excuse myself and return to my cottage. It's just a simple room with a small bathroom attached. The walls are blank except for one painting of a Maine seascape. No words about God scrawled over it. There's no Bible in the drawer either. I like that. I won't let myself stare at the white walls for too long. I'm afraid I may try to slip through like I did at Miss Cook's and I can't be sure anyone will be there to catch me.

There's a bed, a dresser, one chair, one old woven rug, and

wood shutters on the windows. I sit at the edge of the bed and start to rehearse.

"Hey Cup," I say. "What's up, Cup?" "Cup, how are you?" Should I be more passionate: "Cup, I had to see you." A kiss with no greeting attached? An embrace? A tearful embrace *and* a passionate kiss?

I could say nothing. Stand stock still. Let her make the first move. What if that old dried-up slice of Ham is there? Ignore her? Extend my hand and say demurely, "Virginia Hamlin, how lovely to see you again. How is your adorable hirsute dog?"

Before I know it, the room is pitch black and the ocean roars; the moon-driven waves profess their union with the wind. The night has swallowed the busy frantic flow of human noise, the traffic on the highway is gone. I listen to the roar, knowing that the woman I love and lost is listening to the same sound a few miles away.

I clutch a pillow to my chest. In the black solitude of my cottage I pretend it is you, Cup, and I kiss you. My teeth leap out, hungry to bite your lips. Lips that are just a few miles away. Maybe, right at this moment, they are lingering on the edge of a wine glass, pausing like you will, to feel the rim, the cool crystal against warm flesh, and then the very tip of your tongue darts out to greet the wine first, like an anxious child breaking away from Mom's arms at the circus.

Is it red wine? What smooth gloss are you wearing? Revlon's Wine with Everything? When you see me, will you clasp on to my body like distraught ivy, twist around my limbs and stay?

In my cottage on Old Orchard Beach you occupy everything. Your cells tunnel through the barrier of dark matter between us and the gravitational pull is overwhelming. I can feel the room churning right down to the minutest frayed edge of the woven rug underneath my feet.

If you were here I'd spread my legs wide and you would kneel on the floor.

We were at the Russian River. Remember, Cup? It is you and me, James and Gaspar. We're at that bed and breakfast and this hairy dyke tells us there's nothing more powerful than squatting on mother earth and letting your menstrual blood drip onto her soil. "It's *really* powerful," she said.

The four of us, we're still whizzing from hashish. When

she told us to squat and drip, I thought our quartet would take a collective pee, we laughed so hard.

The river was slow and dreamy that night and the lazy current tugged at our dreams and they drifted out of us like slow prayers.

James and Gaspar were saving money to buy their own house by the river and James wanted to call it "Huckleberry Friends" for adventurers and misfits and queers on the fringes. He didn't think AIDS would kill him.

You talked about language, Cup, and wanting to learn all of them, study abroad, have enough time to read the classics from all parts of the world.

"What about you, Smudge?" James asked. I felt puny for a second and I slid into the river and submerged myself in the water. "This is my dream," I was saying to the current, to the fish.

That night I sat at the edge of our bed, just as I'm sitting now. And you pulled apart my legs and dove in. Then I pushed you down and I squatted on top of you. "*Really* powerful, sweetpea," you laughed. Your tongue licked and licked and I bucked your breasts. The next morning you said to the hairy dyke, "Squat on the heart, sister—that's powerful."

I'm squeezing the life out of the pillow in my arms. The roar from the waves seems to come from inside of me. Silence equals death. Fitz is carrying a roar inside of his belly and it's so earsplitting I'm afraid it will stop his heart. I think of my mother and I wonder if she also carries inside of her a scream and the scream is Joseph and the pain of a child missing from the fold. Has she forgotten that scream? Did she imagine heaving it at my father with a force so hard it would shear his skin and send it flying into the wind and he would be left exposed, all that is buried inside of him unleashed in an instant? Did my mother forgive my dad's silence? Should I have forgiven your silence, Cup?

My little one-room cottage seems as huge as an empty stadium. I go to the car and carry my stone kids into the room and put them in bed with me. I need to feel the bedsprings support more than just my flesh and your teddy bear, Cup. I need the company. I put one on either side of me and wrap my arms around them. They are still smiling like good little doobies.

I'm someone who's chopped up the piano for firewood. Hopeless. That's what Alma meant.

Nineteen

Action equals life. This is the mantra looping in my brain, but I'm a chicken shit. I've been here four days and I haven't gone further than my room and the garden. I practically wet myself yesterday when Alma asked me to go to Wal-Mart with her, an alarm ran up my spine and then fatigue like a backed-up sewer gushed out of my mouth. "I'm so tired, Alma," I said, as my head like a heavy bowling ball sank into my hands.

"You go lay down," Alma ordered, "I'm gonna get you some iron tablets."

I play a lot of solitaire with my stone kids and even taught them the game Go Fish. They weren't that interested and seem to beam the most when I toss the cards into the air. "Fifty-two pick-up!" I squeal, and I roll around on the bed with them as the cards descend and land on us like leaves.

My flesh is starting to sag a bit. These breakfasts are expanding my body—brownies, pie, cake, cookies. The only exercise I get is helping out in the garden. I like to find and pull the weeds. Weeds are unpleasant and tenacious, and as I release them from the ground, I feel as if I'm plucking the blight right out of my body.

August has closed up shop. I'm at the center of Alma's garden pulling these prickly weeds that pierce my skin and leave my palms pocked with tiny droplets of blood. The woods behind us are beginning to shed a few leaves. A red oak leaf collides with my shoulder and drops to the ground. I pick it up and run my finger up the spine of it. I crack it open and squeeze out the tiniest bit of water still swimming through the veins. I lick at the moisture and it tastes vaguely like wet dust and ash.

After James died, his sister gave me half of his ashes in a box. I knew where I had to take them and together, Cup, we climbed up Mt. Tamalpais. We pitched our tent at the top and in the morning a heavy cloud of water was perched above us. That cloud just sat there like a large stubborn woman dripping sweat. We found the highest rock and began releasing James to the earth. Gusts of wind whipped at us, as if our cloud woman was furiously shaking her skirt. The ash swirled and our queer lungs breathed him in, our mouths and noses layered with his remnants.

When we finished, our hair and clothes were drenched and cloaked with soppy soot. We looked like twin chimney sweeps caught in a downpour. Then we made love as that cloud woman boomed thunder and smacked her hands together. I knew she was cheering for us. I sucked your tongue and could taste James inside of you, clinging to your gums. *Wherever you're going I'm going your way.*

I'm on my knees and I jut my nose out like a dog and scent the air. I can smell fall coming and my body throbs for James. He's nudging me again, like he did at my high school reunion. "Okay, okay, I'll go," I mutter to the ground.

A shadow slides over me. It's Alma, carrying a pitcher of iced tea. "Hey," she says, "come plop your pork down, I've got lunch ready."

"Alma," I say, "can you smell it? Fall's coming."

She inhales deeply, her belly extends and her cheeks puff out. "You bet, darlin', she's almost here."

I park my car down the street from Vagina's bed and breakfast. I walk slowly down the road. One car passes, and as it does I have to restrain myself from jumping in front of its headlights. I'm wearing all black so the driver can rest assured he didn't see me coming.

I climb the long steep gravel driveway leading to the house. I feel sheepish and small. It's a huge, three-level white wood house with lots of windows framed by blue shutters. It's tucked up on a hill, set apart from the road, and surrounded by a dense forest.

Tonight it looks graceful and elegant, like a queen on her throne, resting on her laurels, full of a solid certitude as she overlooks her kingdom. I am a lowly peasant come to beg for food.

The windows glow from the light inside, a light so warm that you hope to be an invited guest. Which I'm not. I feel more like an intruder, a virus disturbing the peace. My stomach is churning and my eyes are pooling up with tears.

Action equals life. Action equals life. My mantra march as I head up the stairs leading to the lighted porch. My limbs are shaking and trembling like the first time you walk to the edge of a high dive. Right now the high dive feels more like a wood plank sticking out from a ship and someone's poking my back with the tip of a sword.

Instead of knocking on the door, I slip to the left, down the porch, and then suddenly I hit the floor on all fours and scamper like a dog to the darkest corner and duck behind a big wicker chair. Someone has opened the front door and now I overhear three woman discussing their plans for dinner.

One of them sits in the wicker chair. "I'm not moving until you two decide which restaurant we're going to. I'm not driving around in circles again while you two argue. I hate being the third wheel!" she whines.

One of the other dykes leaps onto her lap, slams the chair and me backwards, and my face is pressed flat against the house. My nose throbs and my lips, all prepared and rehearsed, are smashed against the filthy wood and I can feel the slightest trickle of blood or saliva dripping down my chin.

When the trio finally splits, I touch my lip and it stings. The front door is wide open. I crawl down the porch to the side of the house and climb up over the railing and onto a big storage box filled with chopped firewood. The box is surrounded by brush and I'm completely hidden.

I have a full view of the living room. In an overstuffed chair, illumined by an antique gold floor lamp, sits Vagina Ham. She's reading and lazily swirling a snifter of brandy. She looks staid and somber, has her legs crossed like a man, and I can hear the faintest sound of classical music. She's doing a great imitation of Alistair Cooke on *Masterpiece Theatre,* except he's a lot prettier.

I clutch a log in my hand and I want to hurl it through the window and knock her right off her demure ass. Antiques, expensive floor rugs, artwork clutter the place. Paintings by great artists with names I can hardly pronounce.

When I was here visiting with Cup years ago, Vagina was testing me, waiting for me to trip up. She pointed to a painting, "Of course, Maria, you must know this artist?" she said.

She was staring at me with a glimmer of sadism. "No," I answered, "I am most familiar with the works of Frida Kahlo." I felt like a brainless dwarf.

"Oh," Vagina grunted. "A minor artist with a crippling talent." She turned as you walked in to join us. "My dear," she swooned, "what kind of cultural experiences can you possibly encounter in Los Angeles?"

Where are you, Cup? I can't stand having the screen before

my eyes filled with Vagina. She pauses, seems to look right at me, then turns her head toward the back of the house, her lips flap, but I can't hear a word. She smiles and looks down again to read.

When the three dykes return from dinner, they stand in front of Vagina squawking. Everybody's having a gay old time. When the three leave the room, Vagina rolls her eyes, condescending, and closes her book. She clicks off the lamp and the room is black.

Above me, on the second floor, two lighted rooms go dark. The only sounds I hear are the distant crashing waves against rock, a chorus of crickets gossiping about my presence, and the low murmurs of the three dykes.

I close my eyes, willing my ears to locate your voice, the familiar beat of your heart, the faint low tone of your breathing as you sleep. I imagine gliding up the staircase, down the hall, into your room, and I slip between the cool sheets and press against your warm body.

My body shivers from the damp air. Shivers like Miss Cook. I climb off my perch and walk down the gravelly path back to my car. I really should have stayed with Miss Cook, at least through the night. Stayed and fallen asleep with her and the infinite ache that linked us indelibly.

Back in the cottage, Cupcake and my stone kids are fast asleep. I slide in and out of sleep. A frantic sleep, my head buzzing and circling the room like a disoriented fly. I pray for someone to swat me, slam and squash me to the bed and put me out of my misery.

Faces, like ghosts, fill the room. Vagina Ham hovering above me and pounding the *Dictionary of Cultural Literacy* on my head; Christie wrapping wilted day lilies in pages from *Ms.* magazine; Miss Cook pleading on her knees, pointing at me, "Get thee behind me, Satan!;" Esther and Norman piercing me with red pencils; and Cup with Mona zipping in an airplane heading into the Bermuda Triangle.

Then I have this dream about Peter and Lydia and they are riding on the back of a grass-fat cow and Lydia is feeding Peter bovine gunk and as he eats, the cow sprouts lesions, hundreds of them, until it becomes one huge spooky pus-oozing sore.

I wake up after the dream and sit on the floor, repeating the words over and over, "*Let me come to be still in your silence.*" But, it doesn't work. I can't get Matthew perched on my tongue. I can't feel him at all. The next thing I know a sharp ray of light is prodding my eyes open. I crawl out of my cottage and make my way to the garden.

Alma's in the center, making a clearing. She looks up at me, shading her eyes, and says, "I hate to be the one to break it to you, but your lips look like a swollen pig's ass!"

I slither onto a chair. I touch my lips and they are fat and puffy. The sun blasts my face like a furnace and my eyeballs seem to flap in the wind.

"Well, girl, you missed dessert, but there's a tomato sandwich for you, and iced tea. Hep yourself."

"What time is it?" I say.

"Past noon!" Alma says. "I'm glad to see you got yourself out last night." She's perched on her knees and struggling to rise. I go to her quickly and extend my hands to her.

"You look parched," I say, as she stands steading herself in my arms.

"Like a dried-up well," she says.

I pour us tea and I grab the sandwich and the tomato's juice stings my lip, but I suck on it anyway, the mayonnaise oozes out and comforts me.

"Your pig lips remind me of a story," Alma says, leaning back. Her eyes sparkle, as if she's reaching for an old photo album. "When I was a little girl, we had a big ole sow, we called Bitchy. She had hundreds of piglets and if you got near them, she'd try to kill you. One day, I was no bigger than a minute, my momma sent me down to the well for a bucket of water. She said, 'Be the quickness!' I skeedaddled, cause when Momma said, 'Be the quickness,' that meant she was ornery.

"So, I ran out to that well and I was so set on being the quickness that I ignored ole Bitchy's squeals. I drop that bucket down, and I see Momma way off on the porch and she's yellin' at me. But I can't hear a thing cause Bitchy is steady squealin', and I pull and pull on that bucket, thinkin', be the quickness, be the quickness!" Alma pauses, licks her dry lips, and gulps down the rest of her tea.

I'm wide-eyed like a child, no bigger than a minute, like Fitz when he watched *Captain Kangaroo*.

"Then Momma starts running toward me and she's got this

big stick in her hand and she's waving it in the air and my legs are trembling, thinking Momma's going to kill me. I'm pulling with all my might and then Momma lifts that big stick when she gets to me and *thwack!!*"

Alma slaps her hands together and doubles over laughing. I practically fall out of my chair.

"Next thing I know'd, my momma's yelling at my daddy, 'Hank, Hank, come on out here and gut this old sow!' Momma killed Bitchy. One of her piglets had gotten caught between the ground and a loose stone from the well and ole Bitchy was about to bite my leg off. It was the quickness of Momma that saved me."

Alma rubs her hands across her housecoat. I've got a big lump forming in my throat. "Bitchy died?" I say, a few tears slide down my cheeks.

"Now, now," Alma says, grabbing my hands, "my momma was just protectin' her youngin', like Bitchy, but Momma was stronger. My goodness, you're as sensitive as a horse tail swattin' flies."

I have to admit I feel silly for feeling so sad. A sow's love for its piglet just strikes me as so profound. In my present state, everything seems exaggerated. I feel pinned like that piglet, between the land and a huge rock, and there isn't anyone squealing on my behalf, being the quickness and pulling my ass to safety.

"Your mother intervened when you needed her," I say. "That's important." I'm thinking about Fitz and how nobody stepped in with a big stick to fight off the the monster that chewed up all the soft parts of him.

"Sometimes my momma still fusses over me. I call out to her in my thoughts and there she'll be," Alma says.

"Your mom is still alive?" I ask.

"Oh no, she passed a long time ago, but I can feel her. There are times when I'm missing Bud, usually at night when there's nothing alive to grab onto, and I'll find myself weeping and calling out for her like a baby."

"That's like corn," I say. "You have to plant it close so the leaves touch or they'll die. Maybe we're like that too."

"How does a city girl know about corn?" Alma laughs, and she reaches her arm across the table, holds her palm out and I glide my hand over her rough skin. "Be my corn stalk," she says.

161

We sit in silence until dusk watching the light sweep across the garden. I wake up, still perched in my chair with a blanket draped over me. I want to go and see Cup, but with my pig lips I decide to just slip on my perch at the side of the house and watch. There's no reason for me to be the quickness. When I drop my bucket down, the well might be full, but it could come back to me, dry as an emptied cup.

Twenty

Cup. My first look at you. Your back is to me and you are acting out the title of a movie. Playing charades with Vagina and the three dykes. They are stumped. I know the answer. Even with your back to me. I see your arms outstretched, then you run in place on the floor. *The Loneliness of the Long Distance Runner.* Your favorite movie. I almost blurt it out because I'm so caught up in the game, as if I'm an invited player.

When you finish, you sit down on the arm of Vagina's chair. Are you sad because no one guessed? Are you thinking of me? Vagina jumps up. It's her turn.

Her largeness blocks my view of you until she drops to her knees and starts barking like a dog. She's an exceptionally believable canine. Now you jump and scream, *"The Andalusian Dog!"* Vagina lunges at you and her arms and yours surround each other. Then the two of you, exalted, fall into her chair with you swinging on her lap.

Thwack!! I'm hit broadside. Never expected it. Wasn't prepared. Never saw it coming. My stomach like a fender is slammed up inside, my heart is whiplashed. I'll never move my limbs again. I'm waiting for a loud thud, like a box of books dropped to the floor. Will they hear my head strike this box when I pass out?

Now you pick up your wine glass and bring it to your lips. If only Jesus were here he could turn me into wine. Your white cheeks blush. I remember running my finger down them like a skier, jumping to your neck, winding round your breasts, "whoosh whoosh" I'd whisper and continue my shotgun run down your stomach, then tumble into the bushes of your curly black pubes. "The agony of defeat," I'd say.

Something about you has changed, but I can't put my finger on it. Your dark hair is framing that sweet damned face. Your thin lips are plum red and when you smile wide and free those lips seem to grow. You're wearing *our* blue work shirt loose over black jeans. It is unbuttoned and underneath a white T-shirt peeks out.

What is different about you? Suddenly the party is breaking up and everyone scatters and then you flip off the light and the room is black. It's as if the movie I've been watching ends too soon and the screen is dark. A wave of nausea hits.

I hear the front door open and I slide carefully off the storage box and peer around the corner of the house. Shit. It is you walking the hirsute dog. Alone. Oh, Christ.

I cover my heart with my hands because I'm sure it's beating so loud the neighbors will complain. All I have to do is say your name. Cup. That's all I have to do. I can see the barest outline of your legs and the dog and you are halfway down the driveway before my legs budge.

There are no gymnasts tumbling out of my mouth. My tongue feels like a wad of cotton, as if I've been tied up and gagged for too long without water. I move through the thick trees like a prowling cat, watching and listening. I step into something, not my foot, my whole body, into a sticky fresh spiderweb. The gooey string covers my face and I know there's a black widow crawling down my shirt. Fuck.

I've lost you in the black night. I can't hear the panting of the dog or the sound of your boots on stone. My fingers are frantically pulling off web, my spine tingling, my stomach churning and a surge of pressure slams my anus.

This is terrific. I'm going to have a bowel blast on the spot. I break out into a cold sweat. I need to be the quickness because my anus is not constrictus, it is bursting. I unzip my jeans, stick my butt out and shit. I grab some leaves from the ground and wipe my ass just as I hear the front door close and the porch light is snuffed out like a match.

When I get home there is blood between my legs. The intestinal bomb blast was just the preview of coming attractions. My stomach cramps and swells. I feel like a Macy's Thanksgiving balloon. Toss in my pig lips and the picture is complete.

Jessica Fletcher won't find Vagina Ham bloated in the river, it will be me, a nameless transient lesbian last spotted loitering at Niagara Falls with an unidentifiable lip condition.

My beaming friends are staring at me. "Wipe that smile off your face," I bark at them. I sit at the edge of the bed and touch their faces. "I'm sorry. Okay, this is a title to a song. Four words. First word." I point to my eye. "Fourth word." I point to my kids. They are stumped. "Give up?" I ask, "I Am a Rock."

"Look's like you got a visitor," Alma coos, and I jerk my head around, imagining Cup coming up the path.

"Who? Who's here?!" I say, my eyes like a bullfrog's.

Alma places a tray on the table and sits. "I mean your monthly visitor."

"How did you know?" I ask, my shoulders slump in defeat.

"I can always tell, you are glowing, plus the way your settin', like your intestines are banging at the back door."

She lifts the napkin off the tray. "This oughta please your tummy," she says. It's strawberry shortcake, piles of whipped cream, and coffee. Breakfast.

"Thanks, Alma." I mutter. I'm starting to depend on Alma. When I'm with her my loneliness eases a bit. It doesn't seem as permanent as a vital organ.

"Do you have family around?" I ask, dumping a dollop of cream into my coffee. It looks like a cloud. A puffy happy cloud.

"Oh, yes, they're scattered like stars, all over," she answers. She pops a ripe strawberry into her mouth, savors it with such pleasure, like something sacred. "Families are like that. Like stars spread out, and you look at them and each one shines bright in its own patch of dark sky. They seem close, some of them are connected and we have names for them."

"Like Orion," I say, "And the Seven Sisters, and. . ."

"The Southern Cross," Alma says. "Can't forget that one."

"I know this physicist," I say, "and she told me all about black holes and supernovas—the inexplicable brightness of a star."

"Ohhh," Alma hums, "I like the sound of that." She hands me another slice of shortbread. "Eat up, girl."

"So what about families and stars?" I ask. I pluck the green hat off a strawberry and hold it to my lips.

"Well, even though you're close to kin, blood relations, you're also scattered, sometime miles apart, not a damn thing in common," she says.

"Or light-years," I add, feeling sad.

"When you look up at the stars," she says, "you'll see, everybody's got a place."

Alma is holding a mug of coffee to her face. The steam of

it swirls around her and for a split second, her face looks like Mr. Quaker Oatmeal, and I want to tell her everything: How I love Cup; how I hurt her so; how my friends are dead and dying and I can't replace any of them; and I need someone to tell me I'm gonna be okay.

"You're good people, Maria, I have a sense about that," she sighs. "Bud would've liked you. He was regular folk too."

I wonder if Alma would think I was so regular if she saw me last night—stalking, panicked, shitting in the woods, and sleeping with statues.

"Did he make this garden with you?" I ask.

"Hell no. Bud didn't have a green thumb. I started this garden after he passed. It's a shrine for him."

"A shrine?" I think of the mess I left behind in Michigan. Sour old Father Francis and his stumps.

"Southern folk *love* shrines. My sister Lou will call me every so often and tell me that her crazy-ass neighbor, so and so, was sweeping the floor and suddenly the weeping face of Jesus appeared on her fridge door. Shrine it off! They call in an even crazier preacher and put flowers and candles up and before you know it the whole looney town is seeing Jesus, and Mary, and blessed Elvis himself."

Alma laughs deep and raspy and I find the same sound bouncing out of my belly.

"This is my shrine," she says, her voice dipping into sorrow. "My fingers were aching. No kids. None of Bud's bones to hold. I dug these hands into the ground and I can't stop. Bud's ashes are here too. Lord, I miss him."

Two lumps are forming. One in Alma's throat and one in mine. We're two horse tails swattin' flies.

"What are you gonna put in the center?" I ask, "In the clearing."

She sighs deeply like Sadie. "I'm not sure yet. I'm waiting for inspiration."

I can feel a squirming on my skin, like I have ants crawling up my pants. By lunchtime, I have an awful itch. I take off my underwear to inspect, and I have a rash the size of Texas all over my ass. I describe it to Alma and she gives me some sticky homemade goop that's supposed to clear up poison oak in a jiffy.

Alma didn't ask how I got poison oak on my hind end. I am

grateful for her Southern hospitality and good manners. I spend the afternoon lying naked in bed with white paste spread like butter on my pork. I borrow a file from Alma and I scrape away all traces of Father Francis from the hands of my stone kids. The itch subsides by nightfall, and I tuck them under the covers, press my puffy lips to their foreheads and say, "Night punkins."

Twenty-One

It is dark, dank, hidden off the road. A small bar called the Pine Cone Inn. The first thing I smell when I walk in is fish, then beer and tobacco chew. The tables are crowded with mostly men and a handful of women. One thing is clear, none of these fishermen are baiting their hooks for each other.

I gravitate toward the bar and pick a stool closest to where the bartender is hunched-over reading. I'm wishing I had asked Alma to join me, but when I left tonight I had no idea where I was going. I just drove until I didn't feel like going any further.

"What'll it be?" the bartender asks. I look down and see that he's reading a collection of essays, called *Broken Vessels*. He seems out of place here too, a migrant soul who could pitch his tent anywhere.

"I'd like a beer, and some chips," I answer. He sees me eyeing his book.

"Have you read this guy?" he asks, dipping a frosty glass and letting the brew flow.

"No," I reply, "but I like the title."

"You're not from around here, are you?" He pours a pile of chips into a wood bowl and slides it toward me.

I perch my elbows up and lean toward him. "Los Angeles," I whisper.

"Oh," he nods, "I'd keep that to myself if I were you." He slides his book toward me. "Take a look," he winks.

I finger through it, but I'm more interested in the buzz of bodies around me. One man, sitting alone at the opposite end of the bar, is murmuring into his bottle of beer, sucking cigarette after cigarette. He carefully circles his finger on the wet ring his bottle imprints on the wood, then slices the circle in half, then rejoins the droplets over and over. Does he have an orbit he belongs to?

Broken circles. The flowers on Joseph's grave; how I longed for glue to piece together my family, shattered like a dinner plate. We're stars, a constellation, distinct points of light, connected, yet separated by light-years.

I have another family too—queers; our atoms collide and there's unspoken kinship. It's about surviving the blows, the countless times people try to squash the love out of us. It's a love deep in our marrow and some queers don't survive. They kill themselves instead. Just how much a body can tolerate being hated, reviled, having that love chopped up like firewood, is a crapshoot.

My queer constellation is fading—too many dead stars in my sky, but sometimes their light still makes its way to the earth, to my body, in sudden bursts of memory.

I order another beer. A pack of boozed-up men creates a whooping blaze in the corner. They're young, like Fitz, a hissing current seems to flow inside of them. They pound their cans and bottles and it sounds like some primitive spooky ritual—they grunt and stomp, their heavy boots make the wood floor shudder beneath me.

"So, Los Angeles, how long you visiting?" the bartender asks.

I extend my hand. I need touch. "My name's Maria," I say.

He gives me a vigorous shake. "I'm Lloyd," and leans close. . . "I'm from Chicago," he whispers.

One of the buzzing circuits approaches the bar. He wants more fuel for the blaze. He is red-faced, meaty, and his arms are muscled and thick. My spine jumps. I can smell the flaring heat of him next to me and I'm seared—a spinach leaf shriveling. His elbow presses against my side, transmitting a clear message: I am an outsider. A woman alone. Suspect.

I slide nervously away from his arm and toss a submissive smile at him. I feel like giggling in that stupid way I did when Vinnie would pin me to the counter and press his cock into me. My belly wobbles.

"Lloyd, another round," he orders. He's holding an empty beer can and he crushes it like a sheet of paper, holds it so close to my face my nostrils smell aluminum and he tosses it into the trash behind Lloyd.

I can feel his eyes sniffing me. I'm staring straight ahead. My spine dials 911. I long to be anywhere but here.

The old guy sucking cigarettes grunts, "Leave her be."

Lloyd slides a trayful of beers in front of him. "Here you go." Lloyd says, and the guy slams a fistful of money down and returns to his corner.

I go to the restroom and walk a wide circle around the hiss, avoiding them like a downed electrical wire sparking and bouncing on the pavement.

Once safely inside the bathroom, I lock the door behind me and slump onto the toilet. I have to get out of here, back to Alma and my stone kids. I wish I could wriggle my nose and be on the boulevard back home, inside the Palms or perched on a stool at Matthew's old place.

Remember, Cup, when Clinton was elected, and you, Christie, Peter, and I were surrounded by happy queers filled with the promise of change. The boulevard was buzzing. Hisses and boos rose up in smoke-filled bars blaring election results instead of music. "Eat Bush! Eat Bush!" resounded like an anthem. Clinton and Gore filled the large-screen TVs, the gay boys were breathless, sighing and swooning like lovers at the sight of them hugging, their bellies pressing close. I was hooked with a hopeful bait, convinced we'd finally get protection, freedom, a cure, a voice.

My eyes swept over the clamoring queers. In that instant I felt like a bell in a city of bells being lifted and struck. Tolling the war is over. I didn't know then that the bait we so eagerly consumed would slice our lips off.

The floor underneath me still tremors. I've been nervously winding toilet paper round my hand like gauze for a bloody wound. The hissing boys begin singing and thumping the tables. It's a familiar song, but it sounds vulgar. I hoist myself up onto the sink and lean toward the vent above the door. Others join in the eerie hum, until the bar swells with song.

"Michael row your boat ashore, hallelujah, then we'll fuck you with an oar, hallelu-u-jah."

"You can beg and cry all night, hallelujah, sissies don't know how to fight, hallelu-u-jah."

"Swish your hips just like a girl, hallelujah, little faggot we did kill, hallelu-u-jah."

"Timothy Michael," I quiver. Crushed and crumpled faggot tossed into the river like a beer can. My heart pounds like a mallet striking stone.

I begin to flee out the back door, but some force stops me midscurry. I stand. A big dyke has invaded my body and she's mad as hell. My legs blaze like stealth bombers toward the klan of boozy men. I plant myself in front of the one that seared me at the bar. He looks up at me grinning. A wicked snarling grin. I curl my hand into a fist. WHAM! I strike his body and my hand explodes and so does the table. They explode in a roar of laughter—at me, and I turn with my head held high, my hand throbbing, and walk out of the bar.

The bulldagger within disappears the moment I hit the air because my knees start to shake and I run fast to my car, hop in, and speed away quickly through a thick wedge of fog.

I want to get to my cottage, crawl next to my stone kids and never move, stay until my flesh becomes cold, pale. Become bits of ash and bone in Alma's garden.

I pummel the dashboard with my other fist. The pain shoots up my arm. It doesn't work anymore. If only I could go fast enough I could leave the brute huffing and puffing behind me, but I can't outrun myself, Cup.

My eyes are like headlights blasting through the dark and all I can see is what I did to you.

I'm slugging you with demands, talk to me, talk to me. I'm sitting on top of you, then holding you down.

Your silence feels like a weapon swiping me with your wordless tongue. When you cut me off it's a form of mutilation. A murder of the soul.

We have to make love! I demand. Tie me up Cup. Bang me in the ass. Plant teeth in my skin.

Silence equals goddamed death! I scream as my fingers jab at the soft skin of your wrist. I can't pry you open, you've stopped licking back. I press my mouth to yours and push my teeth against your lip and a rivulet of blood spills. My hand is fierce and I press it between your legs, into your cunt and I won't stop. You try to shake loose. I don't care. I lock my thighs around your hips tight. I won't stop.

"No!" you yell. Your body goes slack and my sweat hisses at you like a snake.

After I pull out, release my thighs, you slap me hard in the face. The sting of your hand is the last time we touch. In the morning you are gone. Traces of your blood and cum stain the sheets.

I'm sorry, Cup. Tear me up into little bits and flush me. All of me.

I see the sign for Old Orchard. I rush out of the car and deep into Alma's garden. I drop onto a wet mattress of dead leaves. It is ghostly dark.

I clutch the damp leaves in my hands, pound my fist three times over my heart. Like an old nun at church. Forgive us our sins. Grant us peace. Mercy, Cup.

It's a hissing live wire inside of me and it spits and sneers. I don't know how to unplug myself from this beast.

I hear a sound and it seems to come from the wood, wailing through the garden. Finally! Its here! My tongue of flame, my burning bush. I sit up, cloaked in wet leaves, and listen to the voice whimper a tune way off-key.

"*Gone, love is never gone.*" God is tone deaf and singing from *A Chorus Line*?

"*Kiss today goodbye,*" the flat whine swells.

"*We did what we had to dooo!!*" When I stand up I can see a silhouette against the fog. It's Alma at the picnic table.

"*What I did for love!!*" she slurs loudly as I approach. Ice tinkles from her glass. The smell of whiskey punches my nose. A sliver of moonlight brushes her face and I can see her eyes are puffy with little bloody trails running across her pupils.

I sit down close. "Hey Alma, are you okay?"

"I cain't seem to get up, girl. My legs have quit." On the table a thick candle is burned down to the end, leaving a pancake of melted wax.

She squints her eyes at me. "You look like hell," she says.

"What are you doing out here?" I ask, pulling off my sweatshirt and wrapping it around her shoulders.

"Pissin' like a horse!" she garbles.

I look down at her slacks to see if she has peed on herself. Alma hands me the bottle of Jack Daniels. "Hep yourself," she says.

"What are you pissing at?" I ask, screwing the cap tightly back on.

"If that damned husband of mine talked more, then his heart wouldn't have given out. He clogged himself up and left me alone!" she spits.

I rub her back with my hand. "Some people are just like that," I say.

"Hrrumph," she spits again. "I cain't hold liquor." Her eyelids begin to droop like weary curtains and her head bobs up and down.

I scoop her up in my arms; she doesn't feel heavy, just fragile and worn down. Her face falls to my chest like a sleeping baby. As I carry her into her room she looks up at me. "You got more bugs pestering you than a lighted porch," she says, "just like that damned fool husband of mine." I ease her onto the bed, tuck her in, and peck her forehead. "Night, Bud," she mumbles.

When I get to my room I lie between my stone kids, with Cupcake pressed to my chest, and Alma's melancholy covers us like a blanket. As I dip into dreams, my bucket goes deep and I can feel a swarm of words inside of me. They *are* trapped, clogging my heart and just aching to be set free.

Twenty-Two

I rise with the sun and drive into Kennebunkport to buy Alma breakfast. I purchase an elegant German chocolate cake. I stop at Wal-Mart for supplies: construction paper, candles, and a package of colored markers. On my drive back I stop at a scenic lookout point and walk along the rugged cliff above the sea. My legs feel sturdy, less apt to levitate and pitch me over the side. It's a frosty fall day. From the north, a cluster of gauzy puffs spread and unroll high above the Atlantic.

Just as I finish arranging a bunch of flowers in a vase, Alma totters out to the backyard wearing my sweatshirt over her housecoat. She's holding a cold compress to her forehead.

"Ohh," she moans, "I feel like a toad sucker, girl."

"Park your pork," I say. "Breakfast is served."

Her eyes scan the table and she stretches her tongue across her lip. "Hmm, look at that cake just dripping with divine caramel and coconut."

"Here's your coffee," I say, extending the steamy mug to her.

I drape a napkin onto her lap. The gesture immediately invokes Matthew in his restaurant, as if his arm is in mine. A slight lifting, the dip of my wrist, the sway of the cloth as it lands.

"Oh, I was a foolish old woman last night," Alma says. "Once a year or so my thick noggin forgets I'm not one for spirits."

We sit quietly, surveying her garden. I watch as Alma's eyes travel over her creation, her shrine: a slow tender regard.

"Just listen to it," she whispers. "Once you learn to hear nature, you'll never forget what listening is after that."

I have slow tears falling, plop plop, into my coffee. My lips and chin tremble like Jell-O and Alma pulls a crumpled Kleenex from her sleeve and hands it to me without a word.

She scooches her chair closer, slips her arm around my back, and cups my neck with her hand. This makes me blubber like a baby. I blow my nose hard and soak in the feel of Alma's fingers digging into my neck as if I'm being kneaded like dough.

"I don't know what's what, darlin'," Alma whispers, "but if

I had to guess, I'd say you've been widowed too, like me."

I slump into Alma's lap and all my loves seem to pass through me. Cup. Joseph. Matthew. My sweet James. Fitz. And a seemingly endless procession of dead men. I am a widow.

After breakfast, Alma and I take a long walk together. I cherish the crunch crunch of our shoes in unison on the dried beach stone. We eat lunch at a coffee shop and splurge for ice cream. For the first time since I left Los Angeles, I feel like a real vacationer.

An ease is moving inside of me, in the particles of air swirling between Alma and me that I breathe in. An unfamiliar warmth is setting up residence in my ribcage, pushing some of my loneliness off to the side, shrinking the space where my beast roams. The neighborhood inside my body is changing, and I welcome it.

At nightfall, I go back to my cottage and stare at myself in the mirror. I light one of the candles in the bathroom and the shadow of my body fills the wall and it scares me. I feel so timid underneath it.

I know what I have to do, Cup.

Hamlin's habitat is locked up and dark, not a sign of life around. I keep wandering the perimeter of Vagina's house like the hands of a clock. I have my arms flapping and stretched out in front of me to avoid another spiderweb encounter. I slip up onto my perch and wait.

I stare up through the trees at the night sky, filled to the brim with silent stars, remote and distant. I'm thinking about Paulette and supernovas, the glow of a woman filled up with the pleasure of herself. Alma's like that. She flared like a new star in my dark patch of sky.

After Joseph died and my parents stopped intervening, we were covered over with a dark winter sky, like a death. We grew dim and dark, the light dissolved and the silence spread like snow. A form of mutilation. We ached to be cornstalks, but couldn't get our leaves to touch.

The light in the living room clicks on and you and Vagina collapse onto the couch and you slide your body up next to her. There's a chattering going on between you, both of you absorbed and interested. Rapt.

Look how you sink into her, Cup, like a gentle surrender. She makes you feel safe.

Virginia leaves the room and you're alone, looking right at me through the window, but you can't see me. I'm in the dark.

I gaze into the window at my own reflection staring back at me. I wait for a bitsy flicker of light, a sliver of recognition. I hadn't noticed the new lines on my face, hardening lines, clear evidence of anguish. The light from inside the house throws an amber haze around me and I feel as if I am an old insect that's been trapped in rock and crystallized.

Death has been our escort, Cup. I've been filled for so long with a silent shame and fear and it boiled like angry lava; the whole mixture spilled out of me. I've got too many buried words. Prayers for the dead stuffed inside.

Until you left, and Mona too, I didn't realize I had so much lava, that I had my own scream, like my mother, and I've gagged myself for so long, I'm afraid I'll shear my vocal chords.

I think I know what is different about you, Cup. There it is, in your eyes, the trouble is gone. That weary stunned look of disbelief. We've grown accustomed to seeing that look in the eyes of our dying friends, etched delicately onto the pupils: the helplessness of losing our kin, our kith. I couldn't erase it. You've left the landscape of our lives, pocked with lesions and ash. In your pockets, a bundle of posey.

From my perch, I watch as you ease your head back onto the cushion. Your eyes calm and drowsy like the moon hanging low in the night sky. Slowly they close and my only wish is that I could lick them, for an instant, feel the soft fur of your lashes against my tongue, taste the spice of your tears, and say, "Goodbye, my love."

I drop to the porch, place Cupcake carefully in the wicker chair so you'll find her. I kiss her furry cheek, and then head down the gravel driveway to my car. As I walk away, my shadow looms large just ahead of me like a phantom. Behind me the porch light is snuffed out and my shadow evaporates.

It takes me an hour to find the bridge. I park my car at the side of the road. There hasn't been a streetlight for miles. Cranked up choruses of crickets and cicadas surround me and the river-song of water rushing through and greeting stone. The crackle of animals scurrying in the thick wood comforts me, as if I'm not really so alone out here after all. My presence must be big, big news amongst the furry throng. I wish we spoke the same language because I am sure they know the truth about Timothy Michael.

It's a one-lane bridge of metal and wood. I stand at the center glaring down and it's too dark to see the water. A swarm of curious fireflies hovers above my head, then darts away fast like a team of sprinters carrying torches.

The air feels cool up here and a light mist or maybe beads of sweat cover my face. I climb up on the wood railing and balance myself. I trust my limbs. An owl calls.

I ready myself. Extend my stomach with air and a boom erupts from my gut and groin, a boom so loud it's sonic and the surrounding forest clamors with souls rushing for cover. My eardrums hum with the vibrations of my scream, long after my lips are closed.

A flurry of earthquakes runs through my body, rocking and carving new space in the caverns of my rib cage. I feel buoyed by the wind, like the swaying owl in the sky.

I climb down and retrieve the objects I've brought for my shrine. A large pink triangle made of construction paper with the words, *Silence Equals Death*, written in bold concise letters. I nail the triangle to the wood railing of the bridge. On either side I place a votive candle. I'm capturing the inexplicable, the mystery of the hateful brute, and I'm marking this place where the act occurred.

It's not the weeping face of Jesus on the fridge door. It's the infinite ache and the muddled trouble that comes from that ache, and right now that seems even more eternal than Jesus himself.

Jordan's river is chilly and cold. Hallelujah! On my knees I send my own muddled mess into the wind that streams through the air.

Chills the body but not the soul. Hallelujah! I think of my murdered queer brother, Timothy Michael, and as I pray, he seems so close, not at all distant and remote like the stars. So near it is as if he is perched on my tongue.

Sister help to trim the sails. Hallelujah! A great cold gust slaps my face and I know I'm pulling my sail close, setting the boat on its true course. I feel a wave of aliveness and I finally believe that I'm more immune from my deficiencies.

A gust of God. A tsunami of faith. My hope isn't puny. Whether we are praying, screaming, licking, or dying. Our queer tongues are all on fire and it's quite a blaze.
Michael row your boat ashore. Hallelu-u-jah!

Twenty-Three

I'm on my hands and knees pulling up the last few stubborn weeds I can find in Alma's garden. I woke early this morning to the smell of fog. I found myself stroking my stone kids, aching for Molly and Sadie. It's time to go home. To Christie. To Peter. And I've got to find a job, something more useful then scanning for errors, and stuffing dull words into my brain.

Alma comes up behind me. "Hot cocoa and rice crispy treats!" she hoots.

I wipe my hand across my sweaty brow and look up toward the sky. I'm listening to nature. Above me, a huge mass, a blossoming, spreading white mound whirls as several smaller clouds attach themselves to it, like so many arms grasping on. It's as if the heavens were forming a distinct new tribe. A mothercloud and her kith, twisting and spinning and running ahead of the wind.

As I sit, Alma slaps her hands together. "Inspiration!" she hollers. "Let's get those poor statues out of your bed and into the sun where they belong. Children are meant to be outdoors, watching life unfold."

"You know about my stone kids?" I say, embarrassed.

Alma's belly shakes with joy and I feel like a small boat being rocked by a ship. "Everybody needs company," she says.

We drag them out of my room and into the garden. We plant the kids in the center. Now they are really beaming.

I stand between them as Alma focuses her camera on us. "Now put your arms tight around those youngins," she says. She gazes at the three of us with a slow and tender regard.

"Sweetie," she says, "you look like you turned that glaring yellow bulb off and those bugs have flown away." She snaps the picture. It's a photo I'll never toss out the window. It's time to go home.

At the airport, Alma and I were two huge horse tails swatting flies. She hugged me close, held me firm, the way huggers do when they aren't afraid to let their bodies communicate.

"Alma," I whispered, pressing my lips to hers, "you're a superior mother."

"Ohhh," she hummed, "I like the sound of that!"

****

The flight attendant hands me what appears to be an omelette with two patties of brown swine flesh. I grab her arm. "Do you have any chocolate cake or peach pie hiding out somewhere?"

She winks at me and returns with a packaged brownie. "Now that's breakfast," I say, pleased. We hold eye contact for an extra sweet moment, silently murmuring, "Yes, I'm one too!" The brownie and the flight attendant are delicious.

I'm aching to see my dogs. My mom and dad are putting them on a flight to L.A. and they arrive an hour after me. I also arranged to have a plane ticket sent to my parents for Fitzy. No restrictions, just an open invitation from his big sister.

The airplane's roar shifts to a low hum. We're way, way up now, me and my fellow passengers. From down below, I imagine we're just a speck of swaying silver setting a course for home.

"Keep us safe," I whisper to the sky, to my dead brothers, to God. The next thing I know I hear the lowering of the plane's landing gear, the fragile sigh of my fellow travelers, indicating a safe return to earth.

Twenty-Four

Hospice (has'pis) n. a place of shelter for travelers.

****

A raspy pant like Sister Kizzie wheezing Jesus. Peter's lungs. This is the sound.

"I thought you forgot that you were my executor," Peter says to me over the phone. He pronounced it "ek'sikyoot-er," one who carries out the death penalty, not, "ig-zek'yat-er," one who carries out the provisions of a will. I didn't correct him, and I didn't forget my promise. I'd be there for him, in the end.

Peter was moved into a hospice a week ago. The bovine gunk caused a flourishing of lesions all over. One large Karposis Sarcoma mass is planted and feasting on his lungs. Others bloom like cauliflower on his chest, under his arms, behind his neck. CMV threatens to blind him. And every last one of his T-cells are gone. Flew the coop. Deserted. Packed up and left no forwarding address. So has Lydia. She's in Tibet to expand her higher self and commune with some guru. I hope she meditates her higher ass right off the fucking planet.

Peter's nurse, Leonard, is happy happy happy to see my face, the face of Peter's designated primary caregiver. Peter is refusing to eat and will barely drink enough water to keep a cactus alive. The staff at the hospice has resorted to puncturing his veins with needles, catering liquid food and beverages. He keeps pulling the needles out, causing infected blood to splatter the walls and the staff. He's considered "uncooperative."

When I walk into his room his bedside table is strewn with flowers and get-well cards. Christie's day lilies peer at me like friends. I haven't spoken to her but I put the word out with Sharon and Lynn that I'm back in town. I know my therapists slash friends will spill the beans.

"The strangest thing happened," Lynn said. "Right after you left, Christie dropped out of our lesbians loving lesbians workshop."

"Do you know why?" Sharon quizzed.

"Maybe she took up boxing instead," I answered. They looked at me as stumped as my stone kids playing charades.

I lock the door behind me. Peter's eyes are closed. I caress the day lilies, letting my fingers linger down the stems, like Christie's spine, a familiar and permanent part of my memory.

"Hey, Peter," I say, plopping down on the bed.

He smiles big and wide like a little boy.

"I see the Karen Carpenter diet is working like a charm," I chuckle as I stroke the length of his arm.

He surveys my body, pinches the pooch of my stomach. "Maintaining my girlish figure, which is more than I can say for you, cowgirl."

I rub my belly with pleasure like my father. "I've been snacking on sugar instead of women. Donuts do not break your heart."

"Mia, I was scared you forgot about me. I'm sorry I was such a fuck. I've missed you."

I unbutton his pajama top slowly. If I could, I'd connect all the lesions with a colored marker and wrestle the whole spooky mess to the ground.

"Peter, do you want to die?" I ask.

"Yeah, cowgirl," he answers.

"You've got quite a reputation around here as a big pain in the ass," I say. I lift his arm and slide my body next to his. "They are all afraid you are going to sue them because you're a lawyer."

Peter smiles slyly. He likes that he has a reputation and that the staff fears him. It seems this knowledge gives him a smidgen of power and when your body has been conquered, a pinch of authority helps.

"Look, Peter, I'll do what I can to hurry things up. But from now on, I'm in charge. Don't piss off this old bulldagger. I'm a lot stronger now."

"Fatter too," he hacks out a long laugh. His Adam's apple bounces. I keep caressing his chest, my palms slide over the lesions like bumps in a road. His eyes droop and he quickly falls asleep. Peter is going to die.

Men's Adam's apples seem to bounce like a ball when they suppress feeling. It's as if the fragile little lump of sadness is just too weak to get around that apple. I think it's why men clear their throats, hard, when they talk. Making sure that they can slam-dunk those annoying feelings back into the hoop of their guts.

My dad's Adam's apple has gotten bigger and bigger over the years. I don't know if this is just a natural part of a man's aging, like how their noses extend, taking up more room on the face, or how their ears seem to swell, and both sprout hairs like stubborn weeds. I think my dad has just been collecting layers and layers of gristle to keep his throat clogged. He doesn't know any better.

Peter's Adam's apple bounces as if being dribbled rapidly by a pro basketball player. I want to palm his throat with my hand and stop it, midbounce, hold on long enough for that sorrow-lump to push through to his mouth.

It's easier for women, we don't have such a large mass of cartilage in our throats, so the passage from our guts to our lips is much clearer. Maybe that passage is too clear, and that's why women seem to slam-dunk their feelings all over the place.

I lean down close and feel his sleepy breath on my cheek, and I sing to him, just a whisper, in a deep voice like Elvis: *"Oh baby let me be, your loving teddy bear, put a chain around my neck and lead me anywhere. Oh, let me be, your teddy bear."*

On my drive home, these lumps heave out of my gut like cannonballs and I have to pull over, park, and sob for awhile.

When I get home, I call the doctor assigned to Peter. Helena Carter. I have her paged.

"What are Peter's wishes?" she asks.

"His wishes," I reply, "well, he wants to make a bijillion dollars, have two houses, one on the ocean and one in the mountains, and a lover that worships his spit."

The line is dead. She isn't laughing.

"I'm sorry," she says, serious as a cop. "I meant, what provisions has he outlined in his will?"

"Oh," I say, "death wishes. Do not resuscitate. Do not plant a device, like a trained bystander, into his heart, and stop dripping chemicals into his blood."

Again she's silent. "Hello!?" I say.

"I'd like to have an oncologist begin chemotherapy and radiation," she says.

"Dr. Carter," I ask, "how long have you been treating patients with AIDS?" There's a long pause and I keep trying to think of that joke about Carter's liver pills. I'll have to call my dad.

"Start him on morphine and incrementally increase the dosage," I say.

"That will shut down his entire system," she answers.

"Bingo!" I sing. "Peter has more infected cells than Carter has little pills." That's the joke.

The next day I arrive early at the hospice. Leonard and another nurse, Angela, rush up to me and pull me to the backyard. I feel like an arbitrator between warring nations.

"I am fed up!" she moans. "He keeps pulling out his penis and masturbating. Every time I enter his room!"

Leonard is trying to swallow a laugh. "Maria," he asks, "do you think it's dementia? Maybe that's why he yanks out the IV?"

"I don't care about that!" Angela barks. "I can't sponge bathe him if he's gonna keep waving his thing!"

"The hospice is concerned," Leonard continues, "that we will get into legal trouble."

"You should move in," Angela relents. "Stay in his room with him, it's allowed."

I'm spinning. "Okay," I say bluntly, "I'll move in."

I fling open the door to Peter's room like a drill sergeant. "Peter, I'm gonna pickle your pecker if you don't start pawing in private! Get it?" I yell.

He has that look in his eyes, like a little boy, right at the moment the fat old teacher's butt hits the pointed tip of the tack.

"Hey, cowgirl. You sure do got your undies in a bunch."

"You're getting a roommate today," I say.

"I don't want anyone in here with me."

"It's not just anyone." I lean down and plant a big wet one on his lips. Then I whisper in his ear, "Peter, Peter, it's a pussy-eater."

His eyes bulge. "You're gonna stay here with me, Mia? Really?"

Suddenly, he grabs my neck, pulls me close to his mouth, and he whispers frantically, "You've got to stop them. They're trying to keep me alive. Help me stop them. Please."

I stare into his eyes and the little boy is still there, but there isn't any mischief left; it's a little boy trapped in a nightmare, a spooky monster hiding under his bed.

He breaks out into a sweat, begins shivering. His muscles twitch and his lips flap rapidly but I can't understand him. I sit dazed and watch as his Adam's apple bobs. That's why Peter keeps pulling the needles out of his veins. He's fighting for his death.

Sharon and Lynn agree to take care of Molly and Sadie while I stay with Peter. Their big, sad dog eyes practically fell out their sockets when I dropped them off and no matter how extensive my explanation, I know they feel discarded. I tossed them a dog bone before I left, and they didn't skip away happily, they stayed at my feet dripping saliva onto my jeans, and I felt sick.

Sharon and Lynn invite me to a dating slash therapy group for single lesbians. Dating. Singles. Having them articulate my reality in this way is disorienting, but not like a broadside accident, more like a fender bender. The kind where you're jolted a bit and maybe your legs shake when you step out to inspect the damage, but it's only a scrape, a little metal bent this way and that, no use reporting it.

After dropping the dogs off, I hurry back to the hospice for my meeting with Dr. Carter.

She has just finished examining Peter when I walk in. She's sitting in a chair next to him writing her clinical notes. Her hair is dark, straight, and pulled back in a pony tail that is flipped up with a barrette. No makeup. She looks like a bright, well-bred, well-balanced gal from the Midwest. Studied hard. Never dated. Considered an achiever. As she scribbles away, her left hand is in her lap and she's clicking her fingernails. Click click click.

"Hello, Dr. Carter, I'm Maria. We spoke last night." I extend my hand. She puts her pen down and shakes back energetically. The way a person does when they've attended a workshop on presentation skills. All the while, click click click is chirping from her lap. I sit down on Peter's bed. He's brooding.

Dr. Carter is wearing outdated glasses and, unlike my earlier assumption, she is wearing a hint of pink gloss. Peter's eyes are like lasers boring through her skin.

"Yes, Maria, please sit down," she says firmly. Workshop again—How to Convey a Sense of Authority.

"I am sitting, doctor."

She blushes and starts scanning through the pages like a speed-reader. I imagine her parents have lots of photos of Helena—smiling, smart, and sweet. I bet when she was five years old she wanted to grow up to be a doctor and help sick people like grammy.

"The MRI showed significant, irreversible atrophy in the brain," she says. "I believe we could begin with massive doses of an antiviral or combination drug therapy to bolster his immune system." She's talking as if Peter isn't in the room.

She continues: "Chemotherapy and radiation are indicated for the Kaposis lesions. We can reduce the size of the larger ones," she pauses. "So, how does that sound to you?" She doesn't look at me. Her hand seems to be circling anonymously around insignificant numbers.

"Like dropping another atomic bomb on Hiroshima," I say.

"Excuse me?" she replies, still circling, still clicking.

Peter slips his hand down his pajamas and pulls out his cock. Now Dr. Carter's eyes are glued to mine, her fingernails like a percussion ensemble. If I were really sadistic, I'd start tweaking my nipple. Instead, I lead her out of the room into the backyard.

Underneath her accomplished veneer, the white doctor's frock with her identity pinned to the lapel, I imagine there is a lonesome young woman who has never had an orgasm or a lover whisper into her ear that she is beautiful. Not only does Helena need a good fuck, she needs to know she's desirable to someone besides her mom and dad.

She has a face commonly referred to as one only a mother could love. It's plain. A face you would pass as easily as a bus stop, if you never rode the bus. Her figure is as nondescript. Neither thin nor fat. No curves. She has learned to hide any signs of gender underneath a white coat that erases sex.

Once outside, though, with the sun weaving through her ordinary dark hair and the shadow of the bougainvillea bouncing from her nose, to her cheeks, to her forehead, there is a lovely softness, a kindness that you want to kiss.

As she continues blabbering about Peter's prognosis, I try to imagine her masturbating, but I can't seem to conjure up even the tiniest fragment or image of her playing with that little nub of joy. I've always felt sad for people like that, and my compassion has quadrupled since I've joined the club. This draws me to Helena, not sexually, but spiritually.

"I know Peter is opposed to the anti-virals," she sputters, and I grab her clicking hand firmly.

"Dr. Carter, Peter is going to die. The important thing is that he isn't in physical pain and he doesn't suffer. That's what I want to discuss with you."

She slumps back in her chair. We have a long long talk and get real chummy when we discover that we are both from Michigan and that her parents live about two miles from mine and our fathers belong to the same Kiwanis club.

We swap Michigander stories, agreeing that we miss the change of seasons and especially the fall when you can drive to a cider mill, pick a bushel of apples, eat warm donuts, down endless amounts of sweet cider, and finish off with a gooey caramel apple that makes the dried autumn leaves stick to your hands.

Dr. Helena Carter is good people, regular folk, and Alma would like her. It's not that she lost her vagina, like I did Mona. Helena hasn't discovered hers yet. I'm not quite sure which one of us is worse off. By the end of our talk, she agrees to the morphine drip, no oncologist, and minimal use of medications, but only after another full blood work-up. Just to be sure.

By the end of our talk, Helena stops clicking.

Peter is asleep when I return. I unpack my clothes and survey my new quarters. Smaller than my room at Alma's. My side is empty. Peter's side is cluttered. The bed, the IV pole, the wheelchair, commode, oxygen tank, boxes of rubber gloves, needles, hundreds of bottles of medicines, bags of intravenous, milky nutrition in a small brown fridge, baby wipes, enemas, suppositories, thermometers, adult diapers, vitamin supplements, bedpans, a physical therapy contraption that seems more suited for a night of S & M, and penile catheter kits.

Tomorrow I'm going to go to his apartment and retrieve some of the photos on the wall. Remnants captured on film of life before the plague. I watch the morphine drip like slow tears into his vein.

Peter's too young to die. All of them are. Too young for this kind of fear and it's a fear too big for a lullaby. That's what I need, though, a song, a string of words, like a poem to lull Peter's fear, to calm and soothe. The morphine is like a tender lullaby for a body fretful and in distress. As if Morpheus, himself, enters through the veins, conjuring up dreams in the blood, into the marrow, floating from one troubled cell to another singing, *"Hush little baby don't you cry."*

On Peter's nightstand is a book about the AIDS quilt. I climb underneath the covers on my bed and page through it slowly and a fatigue permeates every pore. I fall asleep and have a dream about mother earth and she's so cold and tired that all of her children begin sewing a huge blanket for her from the bits and pieces of their lives. And I have my tiny swatch to offer, but I can't find any thread, so I keep searching and searching and finally realize that a string of white cotton is in my pocket. A single strand from Cup's shirt. So I carefully aim one end into the eye of the silver needle, tie a knot at the bottom, and begin to sew.

A heavy clump wakes me. The room is dark except for a beam of light coming in from the hallway. Someone is standing, arranging a vase of flowers at Peter's table. It's Christie.

"Hey slugger," I whisper. Her spine jumps and she turns, peering at me through the dark.

"Christie, it's me, Maria," I say. I sit up, lean toward her and extend my hand. She hurries out of the room. The band of light withers as the door closes behind her and I'm left in the dark. Peter's sleeping lungs groan low; the electric monitor whirs, regulating the drip from his IV, and a pang in my gut moans. We sound like a real sad song.

If my taste buds were a choir, they'd boom the Hallelujah Chorus. Helena and I have a new ritual. Every week she brings two caramel apples, crunchy, and dipped in chopped peanuts.

She and I are sitting in the backyard, silent as we hungrily lick and suck our afternoon treat under the unfortunate glare of late October's sun. It's a Santa Ana condition. A huge high-pressure system is sitting on top of Southern California. It is as if the powers above are holding the door of an enormous oven wide open and turned it up to broil. Little flash fires of brush erupt all over, off the highways, in the hills, and inside people too; on sidewalks, elevators, occupants of cars become match-sticks, threatening to ignite each other. It's comforting to live within the walls of the hospice. A place for travelers embarking on inexplicable journeys.

The caramel apples help Helena and me conjure up our own fall. The raking and rolling in colored leaves, the crunch of our apples like the sound of boots over a thin frost.

When we finish, I turn on the garden hose and both of us gulp down streams of cool water. We continue to increase the morphine. Peter's liver is departing as well, swollen up with lesions. Dementia is moving into the neighborhood of his brain.

When Helena talks medicine her voice is as confident as a handsome quarterback. Even when she discusses death, it is like the final call in a playoff game. I figure she learned how to do this from a textbook. Otherwise, she's as shy as a fluttering petal on a discarded wallflower. She has no social life to speak of, except for one monthly meeting of Los Angeles alumni from the University of Michigan. We're becoming friends.

"Hey cowgirl, bring me a man," Peter moans, as I rub his spine with massage oil. The bedsores are like adolescent acne—keeps returning no matter how much goo you put on your face. I do this every night before bedtime.

"What kind of man do you want?" I ask, noodling my fingers the way Christie did when she massaged my feet.

"A breathing one," he answers.

Peter's much thinner. The skin on him hangs loose, as if detaching from his skeleton.

"What do you want him to look like?" I ask, lifting his left leg. The bone is like a thin tree branch wrapped in flimsy bread dough.

"Father is dead," he grumbles.

Here it is. A defective brain cell has jumped to another circuit. It's tricky keeping up.

"Where is your father?" I ask. His eyes are swarming, as if chasing an answer that runs fast ahead. He doesn't reply. I've been getting to know Peter's father. At night he comes. He is an unwelcome guest in the frantic twilight.

Matthew had told me a story about Peter's family. His father was a wealthy and powerful San Francisco litigator. Peter told Matthew that he ran away from home when he was fourteen. His father had beaten him after he found Peter with his cousin Tucker playing with each other's cocks in the garage. According to Matthew, Peter said that years later he saw his father in a sex club, bent over on all fours while a greasy, fat leather queen fist-fucked him. His father was whimpering like a baby and he whimpered even more loudly when Peter's hot piss shot at him like acid. I've always wondered if this story is true, but I've never had the courage to ask.

I hate Peter's father. I don't know if he is alive or dead, but he blazes out of Peter's hallucinations at night like a ferocious genie and his ghost fills the room. I do the best I can to wrestle him to the ground.

My bones cheer when they see Helena. She's sitting on a chaise lounge in the backyard.

"Hey doc," I say, plopping down next to her. She's clicking her nails. "What's wrong?" I ask, sliding my hand over hers.

"Now Peter has lymphoma," Helena says. Her chin quivers.

"Lets get out of here, go to dinner. What do you say?" I ask, slipping my hand around her back. Her forehead scrunches and her shoulders begin to bounce. I pull her to her feet and we walk out without saying a word.

I order a bottle of wine and Helena slowly relaxes; with each glass her shyness seems to dissipate.

"How is Peter doing at night?" she asks.

"Not so good," I say. "He's having some awful hallucinations. Except for last night. He was talking with Matthew. His old lover. It was so nice to have Matthew in the room."

"He was visiting?" she asks.

"Well, Matthew died. But he was there, Helena," I say. "I could feel him. Peter was talking to him. From what I could gather, they were speaking the secret language of lovers."

Helena is silent. I can see her expanding every day. New shapes and words and sensations are filling her up and there's no turning back.

"Helena, have you ever been involved with anyone?"

She gulps her red wine. "No, not really. The last boyfriend I had was in junior high." Click click click.

"Me too," I say.

A chuckle bubbles out of her. "Well, you've been with women, Maria, I've always been so focused on school and now work."

"Yeah, and look at you, you're a superior doctor," I say, lifting my glass to toast.

"Thanks," she mutters.

My heart sank. In her twenty-seven years she's never had a tongue down her throat. It's as if she were telling me that her entire family was wiped out in a freak accident while she ran to the store for milk. It's a natural disaster. A mudslide of need. Not enough trees exist to print a newspaper so thick that it could chronicle the daily disaster of every lonesome soul dreaming of a lover.

I'm feeling grateful. Blessed by the soft sweet whispered orgasms with Christie. Stirred and awakened by the frenzied, sometimes death-driven nights with Cup. I've been told I was beautiful and when those words entered my body my shame lifted for one compassionate moment of belief.

After dinner we walk back to the hospice under a heavy yellow moon. Breezy Santa Anas bristle through the palm trees; the air is pungent and sweet. I look up to the sky, and just a few stars pierce through L.A.'s ceiling. I think of Alma and I'm filled with a tenderness and I put my hand in the crook of Helena's arm and we're like cornstalks, touching.

As we round the corner to the hospice, an ambulance is parked in front. Our steps quicken in unison. Inside my mind I'm seventeen again, rushing home, pulled by the sound of a harsh sob. My mom and dad curled up on the floor surrounded by weeping children.

I hit the porch and gathered in the front room are staff members, volunteers, a few patients. I don't see Peter. That's when I hear it. The familiar grating noise of a thick zipper being pulled. A body bag. The sound hurts my ears. It should be quiet. An envelope being sealed or a good book closed.

It's Roberto. Across the hall from Peter's room. I step in as his mother begins to murmur the rosary with her priest. I stand as they carry Roberto out, his body zipped up. Helena links her fingers through mine and like a gesture as ordinary as licking my lips, an old prayer forms in my head: May his soul and all the souls of the faithful departed, through the mercy of God, rest in peace.

Leonard looks at me, brushes a hurried tear from his cheek, and begins to remove Roberto's linens. Another traveller will be arriving soon.

I sit outside alone for a long while. The priest who said the rosary didn't look sour but I kept my distance anyway. I keep thinking about Fitz and Father Francis and imagine this awful rotten man hurting my little brother. Holding him down. Pulling at his little boy clothes. His spongy sick hands wearing away all the child inside of Fitz. Leaving him stained. What did he make Fitz do? Touch his cock? Suck him off? I want to kill Father Francis even though he is dead; I want to kill him all over again.

Peter and I have a bad night. The arms of Morpheus began to weaken from the weight of Peter's body and the demons returned. Peter is like my infant, because I woke up and I was at his bedside even before my dreams had lifted from my pillow.

I could hear Leonard frantically moving in and out of other rooms. Calling for his aide to bring fresh linens. Wrestling with a stubborn fever by carrying a patient into the bathtub. Unclogging terrified air passages by vacuuming up phlegm.

I felt like David and the spirit of Peter's father was Goliath. It was as if I were witnessing a child being beaten and bloodied and I was standing by just watching. My attempts to soothe couldn't penetrate the hallucination, the blows of a phantom fist. I wanted to amputate his father. I caressed Peter's brow, his cheek. "You're safe, sweetie, you're safe," I said, over and over.

I was boxing and the shadow was winning. An atrophied brain gone awry. The match went on forever, it seemed, until I emptied a bottle of liquid Valium into his arm, and let a few drops land on my tongue. Goliath finally fell. I snuck a quick peek under Peter's bed just to make sure the spooky monster was gone.

Leonard came in at 5:00 a.m. to check on us. He walked up behind me silently and began massaging my back, pushing his thumbs firm into the hard marbles of tension in my neck. I was leaning over Peter. He was calm and cooing, fondling my breasts, pawing at them like a well-fed baby. I kept wiping streams of saliva that dribbled from his mouth as he cooed.

Little shudders of release ran down my body from where Leonard pressed and I felt a strange comfort in the strength of his muscled arms loosening my flesh. Peter clutched my tit and pulled it toward his mouth and began suckling through my T-shirt.

I looked at Leonard. I didn't want to do anything that might rouse Peter, and in this moment, he was my child.

Leonard whispered, "We all want mama in the end."

I let Peter suckle. Besides, it felt good and my breasts seemed to swell with phantom milk.

I wish I could capture this moment on film, the familial ease of kindred spirits. We were a perfect trio of queers, so at home on the landscape of the body, the dialect of stroke and suck. A language that crosses borders easily.

Mcrning has broken. Like being walloped on the head with a skillet. I open my eyes slowly and look over to Peter. He is staring at me with a big wide smile. He looks like a sunflower.

"I want a man," he whines.

It's ironic that the kindness of an atrophied brain is forgetting.

A glimmering horny look is in Peter's eyes and I climb into bed with him and we're like schoolgirls passing secret notes in class. Angela storms in and Peter grabs my tit quickly and starts to moan. She turns on a dime and zips out of the room. We don't have to behave; we killed Goliath last night.

Twenty-Five

I'm circling and circling Santa Monica Boulevard. I keep passing by Christie's shop but I'm too chicken to go in. She hasn't returned to the hospice. Every two days she sends a new batch of flowers and this morning they were day lilies wrapped in pages from the Lesbian News. Mercy. I think Christie is beginning to forgive me, but I'll leave it up to her to decide when it's time to meet.

When I see him, I pull over, just a block away from her shop. He's tan, chiseled, thick-chested, and except for the dirt under his nails, he could be on the cover of GQ. His blue jeans are bleach-stained with precise frayed holes revealing snatches of skin and bulge. They hang loose around his taut waist and butt, and I imagine that without effort or thought he could step right out of them.

His chest is perfect, as if carved carefully by a master sculptor, hard and smooth. One lonesome silver ring pierces his right nipple. Wisps of shiny black hair escape from the bandanna wrapped around his head. In his face is a rabid hunger, not for flesh, but for food, a panicked salivation across the lips, and the tense stare of a gnarling appetite.

I inch my car up closer and roll the passenger window down. He doesn't approach. His eyes keep darting back and forth, surveying the boulevard like the referee of a tennis match.

"Excuse me?" I yell, aiming my voice like a precise arrow, hoping the scruffy drunk lumped on the sidewalk behind him won't stir. He ambles slowly toward me with a snotty attitude. His thick hand gropes his cocky bulge and he bends down and says, "I don't do girls."

I'm prepared. I emptied my savings account. I pull a thick wad of bills out of my glove compartment. "Get in," I sputter, holding the cash out.

He looks at me suspiciously, palms his cock again, and hops in.

Mr. "I don't do girls" is called Tony on the streets, but his legal name is Chester. He's twenty-two. He told me that he remembered Peter, and wondered why he hadn't heard from him.

I take him to lunch at the French Marketplace. He orders a double cheeseburger, French fries, a dinner salad, a chocolate shake, and coffee. I order a dinner salad. Although I find cowgirl, Peter's new nickname for me, endearing, I prefer sweetpea.

Tony doesn't know his HIV status and isn't interested in finding out. He's tricking on the boulevard hoping to save up money to record an album.

"What kind of songs do you sing?" I ask.

"Ballads," he answers. "Sad ones, romantic ones, the old stuff mostly."

My eyes light up. "Oh, like, romance finis, your chance finis, the ants that have crawled down my pants finis?" I sing.

Tony eyes me like I have just dribbled food down my chin.

"No," he snaps, "old, like Barbra, you know, memories, may be beautiful and yet."

"Oh, that old," I groan.

The waiter asks if we'd like dessert. I go ahead and order peach pie with vanilla ice cream. What the hell, I could drop dead any moment.

As Tony chews the last bite of pecan pie, he stretches and yawns and rubs his belly. The silver ring around his nipple jiggles when he moves and it's hard for me not to stare at it. He agrees to come by at midnight. I drop him back off at his corner and before I pull away, he bends down and says, "Peter, the lawyer, right?"

Once back at the hospice, I borrow Leonard's manicure and shaving kit and spend the rest of the evening preparing Peter for his date. I sponge-bathe him with a mixture of water, rose oil, and aloe vera gel. I clip his nails carefully and have to skip his left foot because the build-up of grunge and fungus is permanent around the nails and between the toes.

I trim his sideburns and leave his face scruffy with stubble the way Peter did when he'd go on the hunt for a man. As I run the washcloth behind his neck, I feel the bulge of lymphoma; it's like his body created a new bone as big as a lemon. I'm struck with how flexible skin is, stretching to accommodate abnormal growths from inside.

I carefully wipe his penis and he lifts his balls for me as I run a stream of warm water around them.

"I can't feel a thing, cowgirl," he whispers.

"I know what you mean, Peter. Just use your imagination."

"Comb my hair again," he says as he surveys himself in the mirror.

I run the comb through his hair and massage his skull with my fingertips. I can feel the heat of him, blood-warm, his veins still pulsing, beating a rhythm of time. How many beats are left before Peter disappears from this house—from this warm skull that I hold in my hands?

We're listening to an old tape that Matthew made of classic Motown and every so often I can see Peter's foot tap to the rhythm, trying to dance.

Leonard comes in to help me slip Peter's faded black jeans over what is left of his legs and hips. He wants to wear his blue button-down silk shirt. We unhook his IV in order to get his arm into the sleeve. Then we push his feet into his lizard skin cowboy boots. He instructs us on how to cross his legs and pose him so he has the appearance of a self-assured man.

When we finish, Leonard kisses Peter and says, "Girl, if only I were single."

I set up some candles around the room and Leonard brings in a bottle of champagne.

Now we wait.

"Are you sure Tony wants to see me?" Peter asks. It's 11:45. Almost midnight.

"I'm sure, Peter. I'm totally sure!" Inside I'm chanting. Please show up. Please show up. Please show up.

Leonard opens the door like a staid butler and announces the arrival of Peter's guest. "May I show him in, sir?"

Peter nods, then beams like my stone kids with their infinite smile. Tony has on the same jeans with a neatly pressed white dress shirt and spit-shined black boots. His hair is slicked back and his skin is lightly spiced with the scent of patchouli oil. He is carrying a single red rose delicately between his thumb and forefinger. He cleaned his nails. I want to hug him, even though I can tell the red rose came from the bush in front of the hospice.

As I leave the room, Tony bends down and kisses Peter fully on the lips. Peter's foot is dancing as Aretha Franklin sings, "Answer my prayer, say you love me too." I close the door.

I'm floating just above sleep, sitting in a lawn chair lulled by the sounds of traffic and the hovering police helicopters patrolling the night sky. I think of Maine, the chorus of crickets and cicadas, the rush of water against stone, the mild surprise of a breeze ruffling through Alma's garden.

I realize how noisy my own voice had become over the years, bouncing frantically against the ceiling in my brain, so noisy that I had almost forgotten how to hear the infinite rhythm of life echoing off the remote ceiling above. Now, I know how to listen, and I'll never forget.

A finger is nudging me. It's Tony.

"He wants to talk to you," Tony says. I follow him into the room.

That look is in Peter's eyes, and I lean down and whisper, "There's no monster under the bed."

He pulls at my collar. "I want you here. Don't leave, okay?"

Maybe Peter wants me to stay so I can sew this last swatch of his life into my memory and keep him alive.

I look at Tony and he just shrugs his shoulders, like no big wup, and so I stay. I sit on my bed and hug my legs close to my chest, resting my chin on my knees.

A single candle flickers on Peter's bedside table. The vase of day lilies casts a shadow onto the wall and it looks like the arms of worshipers in a church, stretched toward heaven, making a joyful noise unto the Lord.

Tony kicks off his boots and unzips his jeans. They fall to the floor as easily as a silk slip. He flexes his buns like biceps, his ass is so unlike a woman's. There isn't one extra pooch or tuft of skin on him, nothing to press, to feel the shape of flesh change and dip under the weight of your body.

He begins gliding his hands on Peter's chest with sure and certain brush strokes, easing right over the hard lesions as if they were just minor bumps in the road. He pinches Peter's nipples, then bends to lick and bite and then kisses Peter, teasing with his tongue, over and over like playing hide and seek.

Tony fingers the top silver button on Peter's jeans and Peter clenches his wrist and stops him. He is staring at Tony's cock, willing it hard under his gaze, he reaches toward it, gropes and clutches as if trying to grab a rope extended toward a falling man. Tony's cock is a leash that yanks at Peter's desire, jerks it out of him like a pulled tooth.

I see a fury in Peter's eyes. He musters up enough energy

to move to the very edge of the bed. Peter bows his head, as if in prayer. Maybe he is begging God for a gust of strength. Suddenly, he flings his body forward in abandon, then thrusts his head toward Tony's erection.

I close my eyes, bury my head into my pillow and just listen to the slippery sound of saliva and sucking and I hear Peter groan. The deep harsh sound of a man heaving the discus.

A long time passes and I fall asleep cradling my legs like a lover. When I look up, Tony is lying silently on top of Peter. I watch them with a slow and tender regard.

The shadow on the wall dissolves to a solitary, lone worshiper. The tiny tongue of flame sputters from the candle and the light evaporates. A single thin blue line of smoke rises to the ceiling and I imagine grabbing on and flying up, way up, dreaming and flying, like Joseph told me to do so long ago.

In this moment I don't know what else to do. I'm yearning for a simple evening kiss before slumber. The kind of kiss that graces a child's forehead or woos lovers, assuring safe passage through the night.

Tony and I are back at the French Marketplace, this time eating piles of pancakes with fresh strawberries and mounds of whipped cream. We clasp legs under the table like high school sweethearts. His white shirt is wide open and loose and he lazily circles his pierced nipple with his finger as he lights a cigarette.

The place is packed, the tables filled with boozed-up bar queers tossing tired old queen jokes back and forth like a beach ball at a stadium. Tony and I don't talk to each other, we just laugh along with the crowd, and then Tony looks out to the boulevard and says he has to get back to work.

I pull out the wad of money and he shakes his head "no." He refuses payment. I pay for breakfast, slip twenty bucks and my phone number into his pocket when I hug him.

"Consider it my contribution to the arts," I say, holding him tight. *Don't die Tony.*

I sit at our table and watch as he strips off his white shirt and ties it around his waist. He leans up against a telephone pole, palms his cock, and immediately, a burgundy Jaguar pulls over and Tony disappears.

I relax in my seat and just listen to the clamor of queers speaking the language of survival, just like the shadow of worshipers on the wall, making a joyful noise unto each other.

198

Twenty-Six

I'm lying in bed as Molly and Sadie pounce and jump and trounce me with their paws. All is forgiven. My extended absence, forgotten. We're making up for lost time. Big mushy wet tonguefuls of loose love drip from their mouths.

I'm filthy. I've been scouring the house. Vacuuming up all the dustballs, spiderwebs, and layers of smog-soot that have infiltrated the place. I even followed Sharon's and Lynn's advice and mopped the floors with eucalyptus oil and water. Brush away the losses; erase all the relics that swirl in the air; the discarded layers of derma from Cup and from me.

I emptied the den and converted it into a spare bedroom. For Fitz. My little nimbus is coming. He cashed in the airline ticket I bought and is hitchhiking his way to California.

"What made you decide to come?" I asked him when he called.

"Watching you trash that statue," he answered. "I was hiding behind the school. You're pretty strong—for a girl."

"I love you, kiddo," I said.

"Me too," he answered. "Me too."

Peter's been dead for two weeks. I picked up his ashes yesterday in a nondescript cardboard box. I had to sign for them like a package at the post office. When I had asked Peter where he wanted his remains, all he said was, "You keep me, cowgirl."

I'm balancing my artwork on top of Peter's box. Repairing the stolen figurine, gluing Little Bo Peep back together. I found all the pieces except for the top of her head. I couldn't find it, so I took a butt plug, cut it in half, painted it to match the porcelain, and glued it on. Necessity is the mother of invention. Now she looks like Little Bo Conehead Peep.

"C'mawn in!" I shout when the doorbell rings. It must be a friend because Molly and Sadie don't budge and their tails are wagging with anticipation. It's Christie.

She stands at my bedroom door, lingers as the dogs rush to her, their hind ends sashaying wildly. Christie kneels to greet them, digging her face into their hide. I miss her so. I brush my wet cheek, leaving a trail of Bo Peep pink mixed with salty tears.

We both sigh simultaneously, then giggle self-consciously.

I extend my hand and she sits on the edge of the bed. Sadie plants her snout on Christie's lap, looks at me and I know what she's thinking. Apologize.

"Christie," I mutter, "I'm sorry. I'm really sorry." I hold my breath. She reaches her hand toward my face and I flinch.

"You've got pink paint on you," Christie says. "I'm sorry too." She holds her hand steady, cupping my cheek tenderly.

She points to Bo Peep on the box.

"What's that?" Christie asks.

"Bo Peep, deconstructed," I reply.

"No, not that, what's in the box?"

"It's Peter."

Christie's whole body withers and I wrap my arms around her tightly, feeling the swelling and sinking of her chest. My own lungs are weary from a week of endless filling and emptying, responding to the broken call of the heart's mourning. I feel strong in this moment, able to surround the grief in my arms. I take in slow, deliberate, deep puffs of air. Christie's sobs ease and we inhale and exhale together. A rhythm of hard sorrow.

"Have you heard from Cup?" she asks. The moment she says Cup, Molly and Sadie lift their heads in an instant, recognizing her name.

A sliver of sadness passes through me. "No, I haven't," I say. "Not a word. But I have good news. I found a job."

"Where are you working?" she asks.

"Being Alive. I'm the new editor for their newsletter."

The backyard gate clinks open and the dogs bolt toward the kitchen doggy door.

"Maria! I'm back and I have the manure!" It's Helena. She's helping me with my garden.

"Who's that?" Christie asks. Her body tenses up in my arms.

"Peter's doctor. Helena Carter. You'll really like her," I say. I hop out of bed and go to the bedroom window. "I'll be right out!"

"I better go," Christie says, starting toward the door. "Congratulations on your job."

I rush up to her. "Don't leave," I say, grabbing her shoulders. "I really miss you, and I need your help, Christie. I'm going to plant a garden." I turn her toward me. "Look, I'm not snacking on the doctor, either. She's more your type."

She scans my face suspiciously.

"Cross my heart and hope to die," I say. "Now come out with me."

I drag her by the arm into the backyard.

The three of us spend the entire afternoon shoveling manure and soil and by sunset we gather the remains. Matthew's urn and Peter's box. Silently we dig our hands in and scoop out the coarse ash and bits of bone. We cover the whole garden in dust and memories. Peter and Matthew are coupled once again.

I set up the barbeque and light the coals. Christie and Helena are in the kitchen making a salad. I watch them stand beneath the light over the sink, standing so close their shoulders are touching. I'll write the Christian Coalition and let them know we've recruited another one.

"Court and spark," I whisper and a huge grin covers my face. Methinks a lesbian maybe inching toward the birth canal.

I wonder if Christie will be the first lover to slip her tongue into Helena's bashful mouth. To whisper a soft hushed orgasm with her lips. I feel like a proud mother. My Christie, marrying a doctor, God willing.

By the end of dinner, all three of us are slack and loose and filled up with the pleasure of hard work and good food. Tomorrow they return for the planting. I walk them to the front yard.

"Since you are both coming back in the morning," I say, "why don't you drive together." I'm nudging Christie with my elbow.

Helena's eyes hit the pavement.

"Besides," I say, "Christie's had a couple of glasses of wine and I couldn't live with myself if anything happened." I kick Christie's shin.

"Oh, sure, I'll drive you home," Helena sputters. Click click click.

I hug them both hard. I want to hold on to those extra moments. Even though I know I'll see them tomorrow, I start to cry. I am remembering the sad long embrace with Peter, the very moment his body sighed and whispered goodbye.

I spread out Joseph's flag in the center of my garden, my little patch of land. I gaze up at the night sky and try to catch a twinkle. Molly and Sadie are fast asleep on either side of me.

Sadie is snoring. Molly's punctuating farts are slicing the air. Helicopters whir way off and the ghostly omnipresent hum from the tangle of freeways surrounds. This is as close to silence as it gets.

The day's work has left a sweet soreness in my muscles. If memory serves, it's the kind of body ache that people experience when they have sex. A tender pain that renders lovers giddy over croissants.

I loosen the tie around my sweats and sneak a peek at my crotch. I slide my sweats down to my ankles and stare at the alien mound. I feel like a curious kid who has happened upon a furry lump in the woods, picks up a stick—pokes and pokes. Is it sleeping or dead?

A hushed breeze ripples and the trees shimmy. It feels as if hundreds of fingers are running up and down my body, as light as feathers. Maybe, the angel hands of all my dead brothers coaxing me.

My palm with a mixture of trepidation and courage eases on down the road of my belly and stops just a hair or two shy of my pubes. I close my eyes and listen. Hum. Whir. Snore. Fart.

My brain cells like gymnasts begin to spin and twirl in my mind, bouncing from one tiny trampoline of memory to another. A bedpost floats by. A squawking *Portnoy's Complaint* flaps away like a bird. A bathtub filled with Pond's warm cream sloshes by. A river of lipsticks flows out like many-colored kayaks. Then a waterfall of Jean Naté and deep Bordeaux collide with Mandy's Bedroom Rouge Velour. A day lily bursts radiant. A sweet little escargot calculates the laws of gravity. A band of Cup's Wine with Everything streaks across the stratosphere like a Merlot meteor. Boing! Boing! The brain cells boomerang. I'm dizzy and I gulp in air.

Mona whizzes by on a scooter. She's wearing khakis and singing, "Domineeca, neeca, neeca." A dingo is in hot pursuit.

"Be careful Mona!" I cry. I'm perched on a mountain of wood, chopped up pianos.

Mona turns, sees the dingo. "Yikes!" she screams. A throng of people trail the dingo, cheering for Mona: "Viva la Vulva! Viva la Vulva!"

I can't reach her. I'm paralyzed. My legs won't budge. I try to dial 911, but a bitchy voice tells me that the number I have dialed has been disconnected. Please hang up! Then I hear it! A crash! Kaboom! A plume of smoke rises. With all my might I begin to run down the mountain of piano wood. My legs like warheads. I pass Sisyphus on my way down. He's wearing Camille Paglia, the studded dildo, and muttering about the rock, the push, the struggle, the meaninglessness. "Get a life, Sisy," I say.

I slam through the crowd ferociously. When I get to the scene, Mona is lying on the ground. Her little scooter is crumpled like a beer can. She wasn't wearing a helmet.

I am the trained bystander! I fall to my knees and pump Mona's chest. Everyone is breathless. I keep pumping. I throw my mouth over Mona's labials and blow. Pump. Blow. Pump. Blow. The crowd begins to swell with a chant: "Beat the meat! Beat the meat!"

Suddenly, Mona's eyes flutter. She gasps. Ping. Ping. Ping. She's beating. A gust of God. She's alive. Mona's alive! We're rushed to emergency. Oprah and a camera crew pursue us.

I am lying in a hospital bed. A single bed. The room is white. The walls. The curtains. A big poofy down comforter levitates off my body like a cloud, leaving me naked.

A half-dozen nurses enter the room. Real beauties. They surround me. Inga is there. They begin wrapping white gauze around my entire body as if I am one huge pulsating wound.

One nurse monitors my rapid pulse. Another delicately holds a thermometer between my lips. Inga is performing your standard breast exam. Another does the Pap. Suddenly, Inga plants her mouth right over my nipple. She licks and plucks with such conviction it brings tears to my eyes.

Then the head nurse's tongue storms down my throat and she sucks as if determined to get to the chocolate center of a cherry lollipop. I'm a screen door flung wide open by a torrential wind. Sister, help to trim the sail. Hallelujah!

A wet finger dips in my ear. Another circles my clit like the sweeping second hand of a clock. A teasing tap tap at the back door of my anus.

My personal team of health care providers whispers lovingly from their precious pampering lips.

Inga straddles my thighs. The rest finger me like a string quartet. My heart skips as if caught in the center of a jump rope. Boom boom boom boom between my legs.

No doubt Cal Tech registered a sudden burst of seismic activity at approximately midnight. "We believe this temblor indicates the existence of a brand new fault."

Atta girl, Mona! A bang, not a whimper.

When I open my eyes, Molly and Sadie are staring down at me, their gaze enlarged with bewilderment. I stare back as baffled as they are.

I'm lying in a heap, my legs spread wide. I'm lying on top of dirt, manure, ash, bits of bone, and the American flag.

I'm no longer beyond recognition. I am beneath a constellation of stars. I cannot see them from here, but I have faith. A big faith, not puny. I can hear them—all my brothers surrounding me.

"Hey, Smudge," James sings. "Wherever you're going, I'm going your way."

"Giddy-up, Cowgirl," Peter hoots.

"I'm here, Maria," Matthew hums, "to be still in your silence."

"Action equals life, sister," another murmurs.

"Who are you?" I ask, gazing up at the dark sky. The dogs look up too. "Who are you?" I repeat.

"Timothy Michael," the voice answers. "We met on the bridge."

"Milk and honey on the other side," I sing, "Hallelujah!"

Molly and Sadie howl at my song. We're a perfect trio, singing a language of survival, and making a joyful noise unto each other. Shrine it off.

"Thanks, guys," I whisper to my brothers.

"For what?" They're listening.

"Being alive," I cry. "Just being alive."